Not Quite Dating

Also by Catherine Bybee

Contemporary Romance
Weekday Bride Series
Wife by Wednesday
Married by Monday

Paranormal Romance
MacCoinnich Time Travels
Binding Vows
Silent Vows
Redeeming Vows
Highland Shifter

The Ritter Werewolves Series
Before the Moon Rises
Embracing the Wolf

Novellas
Soul Mate
Possessive

Erotica
Kilt Worthy
Kilt-A-Licious

CATHERINE BYBEE

Not Quite Dating

Montlake
Romance

Text copyright © 2012 Catherine Bybee

Published by Montlake Romance
P.O. Box 400818
Las Vegas, NV 89140

ISBN-13: 9781612187143
ISBN-10: 1612187145

For my Nana

Shamrock Bybee

The world is a little dimmer

with your passing.

Chapter One

"This one's for the ball," Mike said, slurping down his tequila shot. "And this one's for the chain." He chased it with his beer. "Your turn."

Jack sat back as Mike pushed Dean to another round. Dean, the bachelor of the weekend, was well beyond three sheets but kept drinking anyway.

"W-what time is it?" Dean asked.

"You're not allowed to ask until Sunday," Tom reminded him.

"It's not Sunday?" Dean's gaze followed a cocktail waitress wearing a skintight miniskirt.

Jack, Tom, and Mike busted out laughing. "Damn, Moore, we might need to stay in your fine establishment for an entire week to work the bachelor out of this groom."

Jack Morrison's friends always called him Moore: more money, more women, and more time to do whatever he wanted due to his family's portfolio. His buddies at the table had known him since high school. If they ever wanted to stay at the Morrison Hotel and Casino on the Vegas strip for a week or a month or however long, for that matter, Jack would make it happen. They all held executive positions or owned their own businesses, making it nearly impossible for them to get together as it was. The weekend bachelor party would have to do.

Jack had insisted they drive instead of jet over the California desert. With Dean walking the plank—or aisle, as it were—they wouldn't have this golden opportunity again. Dean was the first of the four of them to get married, making this their last trip together as single men. The last time one of them didn't need to rush home to a wife or kids. The last time they could all get pissing drunk and not *have* to explain themselves to a woman. One last bash, complete with Vegas and a road trip…what could be better? Once Dean said "I do," it was all going to change. Deep inside Jack knew this…was ready for it. Life was a series of chapters, and this one would end in style if he had any say in the matter.

"Oh man, is that Heather?" Tom nudged Jack's arm and nodded toward the casino floor.

Jack followed Tom's gaze as it landed on the back of a woman he knew all too well. She had her platinum blonde hair piled high on her head; her shoulders were bare except for the spaghetti straps of the slim-fitting dress that hugged every surgically enhanced curve of her body. Just when Jack thought he could turn away without her noticing him, she shifted a glance over her shoulder and offered a painted-on smile.

"Well, hell, how did she know we'd be here?" If there was one woman Jack never wished to see again, it was probably Heather. As she swayed her hips while walking in his direction, Jack knew he wasn't going to get his wish.

"She probably heard through the grapevine it was Dean's bachelor party. And you do own the hotel, so where else would the party be," Tom reminded him.

"Jack, sweetheart, what a surprise finding you here." Heather's wispy tone was born of practice and not sincerity.

Unable to avoid her, Jack stood as she approached. She leaned in and kissed his cheek. He quickly stood back and motioned toward his friends. "You remember Tom, Mike, and Dean?"

"Of course." She offered them the fakest of smiles, her eyes narrowing on Dean momentarily before moving back to Jack.

"What brings you to Vegas?" Jack asked, as if he didn't know.

"You told me this was one of your nicer hotels. I thought it was past time for me to spend time in it."

"My father owns the casinos, Heather, not me." All Heather saw was money. Didn't matter where it came from so long as she could access it.

She waved a hand in the air. "You're splitting straws again, Jack."

"Hairs. Splitting hairs."

She placed her fingers on his arm and squeezed. "You know how I dislike being corrected," she reminded him.

You know how I hated you always showing up where I didn't want you. And that was when they were dating. Jack had broken up with her midsummer.

It was now November.

She leaned in and whispered in his ear. "Can we find a moment alone?"

He loosened his tie and tilted his Stetson back on his head. "We're in the middle of a bachelor party, Heather."

Dean tossed back another tequila and sucked on a lime.

"Won't take but a minute, darling."

It hurts to smile when you're gritting your teeth. Jack forced his jaw to unclench at her syrupy endearments. He remembered the day he put a halt to their brief affair. They were attending a fundraiser at the club in Houston and Jack noticed a beautiful brunette across the room eyeing him. Heather had scolded him with her breathy voice. *"Jack, dear, please try and keep your eyes on me when we're together. I don't care what you do or who you might play with once we're married, but to be so obvious when we're standing next to each other, it's simply boorish, don't you think, darling?"*

Where Heather cooked up the idea she would ever be Mrs. Jack Morrison, he'd never know, but it was then Jack realized how superficial his arm candy was. In a way, he felt sorry for her.

"Well?" Heather pulled him into the present with her question.

Jack knew exactly how to get rid of her, for the last time.

He nodded toward Tom. "Out front in ten?"

Tom grinned. "We'll walk this one around, sober him up a little."

Mike helped Dean to his feet while Jack motioned Heather toward the door.

The two of them wiggled around the people hovering at the slot machines. Someone at a craps table yelled out and the crowd around him cheered. An older woman leaned back in her chair as Heather walked by and brushed against her. Heather scowled and muttered something ugly under her breath.

"Excuse me, miss."

Heather tilted her jaw higher, said nothing, and walked away.

The older woman looked genuinely sorry but at a loss for words.

Embarrassed, Jack took Heather by her arm and led her outside under the bright lights of the valet parking lot. The valet noticed him and snapped to attention. Before the valet moved a foot, Jack waved him off.

"So what are you *really* doing here, Heather?"

She angled her head to the side and painted on a smile. "I don't like where we've been lately, Jack. I miss you."

Jack held his ground when she moved forward. "There isn't a *we* any longer. I thought I made myself clear."

"I've given you a break. Now I want the break to be over." She slid her hand over his chest.

He stopped her by holding on to her wrist.

"I didn't ask for a break. I said we were over. We don't want the same things." He didn't want a trophy wife, and that was all Heather could offer.

The edges of her lips fell into a pout. "We know the same people, play in the same circles. We're perfect for each other."

"No, we're not. I want someone to be with me for more than my wallet. We both know that woman isn't you." Jack noticed the diamond-studded bracelet hanging off her wrist. They had been dating during her last birthday and Jack had given it to her. He regretted the gift now.

Heather's fake pout faded and a spark of anger flashed in her eyes. "Every woman with you is going to be there for the money, Jack. I just happened to be honest about it."

Her words stung, probably because they held some truth. It was hard to look past his father's billions and Jack's own millions. Still, the blonde in front of him had just made it clear she didn't care about him at all. Jack drew the line there.

He waved to the senior valet, who quickly ran over.

"Yes, Mr. Morrison?"

"Can you bring my car around?"

The valet glanced at Heather, then back at Jack. "A hotel car, sir?"

"No, my car. The one I arrived in."

"Yes, sir. Right away, sir."

Heather smiled up at him, probably assuming she'd won something.

"Is there somewhere I can have my driver take you?" Jack asked. "Or are you staying here?"

"I have a suite at the Bellagio. But I don't mind a move." Another sickening smile lifted her lips.

Jack's friends made their way out of the casino through the heavy glass doors.

"The Bellagio is perfect for you. I suggest you enjoy your time there."

Her facade fell and anger straightened her jaw. "You'll regret this someday, Jack. You're going to marry some woman thinking she loves you and in the end be brokenhearted because she wants your trust fund."

Out of the corner of his eye, he noticed his ride pull up. He walked to his twin cab, a well-past-its-prime pickup, dirty from the long drive, and opened the door.

"What is that?" she barked and stepped away as if the truck was a snake about to strike.

Finally, a real smile lifted Jack's lips. The look of absolute horror on Heather's face was worth her annoying presence. "It's your ride to the Bellagio."

"I'm not getting in that thing. What did you do, drive it from Texas?"

Actually, he'd had it shipped to California for his latest business venture, and that's when he and the boys had decided to drive it to Vegas. "Something like that. C'mon, get in."

"I will do no such thing."

"Suit yourself." Jack opened the door wide and waved his friends in. "C'mon, boys. We have a bachelor to send off." Jack turned to the kid who had jockeyed the truck around. "What's your name, buddy?"

"Russell, sir. I'm new here." The kid was maybe twenty-four.

"You know your way around Vegas, right?"

"Lived here all my life."

Jack patted him on the back while Mike helped Dean into the backseat. Tom loaded in behind them. "Well, Russell, my friends and I need a driver tonight. We have some serious drinking to do and could use someone sober with us. You game?"

"I'm working."

"And I'm paying you." Jack waved the head valet over. "It's Carrington, right?" he asked the senior valet.

"Yes, sir."

"Carrington, Russell is going to help us out for a few hours. I hope that's OK."

"Of course, Mr. Morrison. Whatever you want."

Jack winked at the man and turned toward the truck. When he lifted his foot into the cab, Heather called out.

"What about me?"

Jack spared her a glance. "I offered you my ride, darlin'. Maybe a Vegas cabbie would suit you better. Carrington, would you mind finding Miss Heather a ride?"

Carrington shifted his eyes from Heather to Jack a few times and then lifted his hand for one of the many cabs waiting in line to take guests to their next destination.

Heather lifted her arms over her shoulders. "Jack!" she yelled as he shut the door.

He tilted his hat as a good-bye while Russell shifted the truck in gear.

"Jack Morrison!" Jack could still hear her screaming as they pulled away.

"Ho boy, that is one ticked-off woman," Tom said, looking over his shoulder. "I don't know what you ever saw in her."

"She was a mistake." A huge one. Jack was thankful his heart never got involved.

"Jack Morrison. Hey, you wouldn't happen to be related to Gaylord Morrison, the owner of the hotel, would you?" Russell asked as he pulled out onto the strip.

Dean, Mike, and Tom started laughing.

"Did I say something funny?"

Jack buckled his belt and sat back. "That would be my dad."

"Overdue...overdue...oh great, a shut-off notice." Jessica Mann placed the highlighted water bill on the top of her pile with a grunt. Looking around the tiny break room of the twenty-four-hour diner she worked in proved just as bleak a view as her future. She really did need to make some changes in her life, and soon.

Leanne, the other graveyard shift waitress who worked with her, poked her head through the door and said, "You're up. A party of four just sat on twelve."

Jessie glanced at her watch and saw that it was twenty minutes past two in the morning. The after-bar crowd would soon start strolling in for black coffee and a place to sober up before their trek back home. Like clockwork, Sunday mornings were the worst. The truly stupid actually thought they could grab a cup of joe and still manage to make it to work on time. After tucking her bills into her purse, Jessie stepped out of the break room, through the short hall separating the kitchens from the service counter, and proceeded to table twelve. With any luck, one of the four people in the party would be sober enough to remember to tip her before they left.

Hearty male laughter met her ears before she rounded the corner to greet her customers.

Two faces peeked over open menus while the other two caught her gaze as she approached.

"Whew, hey, darlin'. Are you our waitress tonight?" a dishwater blond sitting on the end of the booth asked. With his question, the other men at the table lowered their menus to look at her.

A quick assessment told Jessie that the yahoos at the table were definitely coming off a night of drinking. Maybe even a couple nights from the state of their five o'clock shadows.

Dishwater flashed his white teeth and a little-boy smile. The man to his left elbowed him in his side. "Pay no attention to Dean. He hasn't been sober for three days."

"You're one to talk, Mikey." These words came from a robust man wearing a baseball cap and at least two days of stubble on his chin.

"Jack is the only one remotely sober," Mikey said.

Yep, definitely a party crowd.

The one they called Jack took his time lowering his menu before acknowledging Jessie. His dark brown hair, topped with a Stetson, tilted as he moved his head. The stubble on his chin held the perfect amount of sexy. The slow, steady soaking in of his stare settled on her from the most unusual gray eyes Jessie had ever seen. Those smoky eyes took their ever-lovin' time as his gaze slid over her hair, her face. After looking his fill, he caught her eyes again and held them. As if calculated for effect, Jack allowed a slow and delicious smile, complete with dimples, to spread over his face. A smile meant only for her.

Smiles like that should come with a warning label. His staunch attention did a number on her belly and raised gooseflesh on her bare arms. She swallowed hard, and her skin tingled as if he'd caressed her.

Jessie blinked a few times, broke eye contact, and asked, "How about some coffee?"

"That would be great," Jack replied with an accent that matched his cowboy hat.

The Texan accent pulled a warm and fuzzy blanket over her insides. Southern California natives didn't have any discernible accent at all, so when she heard one, she remembered it.

Pivoting, Jessie shoved her notepad into her apron and walked to the coffeepot.

"Isn't she something to look at?" one of the party boys said.

Jessie knew she wasn't ugly, but she didn't see all that much when she looked into the mirror. Her light brown hair sat twisted into a knot at the base of her neck; her dull hazel eyes had dark smudges beneath them indicating a lack of sleep, and it was hard to be fat when all her money went to bills and care for her son, Danny.

The four men…no, make that boys…at table twelve probably didn't have one decent responsibility to scrape together if they combined them. They were all wearing jeans and T-shirts, and two of them smelled like beer.

Frat boys who never grew up. Heck, maybe they were all still in school. Jessie guessed their ages to all be about the same, around twenty-eight or so.

Returning to the table, Jessie set down coffee cups and filled them. "Thank you…Jessica," Jack with the mysterious gray eyes said after a quick glance at her name tag.

"Jessie, actually. Where are you boys coming from?" she asked, making conversation.

"Weekend in Vegas," the one named Mikey told her.

She should have guessed.

"Our buddy Dean here is tying the knot in a few weeks, so we decided to send him off in style."

"Vegas can be a dangerous place to have a bachelor party," she said.

"See, that's what I said," the man sitting next to Jack told them. "But does anyone listen to Tom? Heck no. You think everything went great and next thing you know your drunk ass is dancing naked on YouTube with some chick you don't even remember."

"I didn't dance naked with some chick…did I?" Dean rubbed the back of his neck and frowned.

Jack shot a dimpled grin at his friend. "You were pretty wasted."

"I still don't remember any naked dancing."

"Oh, chill," Mikey told him. "No one was *taping* you dancing naked."

Jessie had to smile. The boys were giving their friend a hard time, and it was fun to watch. From the look on Dean's face, he wasn't entirely sure he hadn't danced in the buff.

"You guys know what you want, or should I give you a few more minutes to decide?" Jessie asked.

"I know what I want," Tom said, setting his menu on the table.

The others chimed in the same. After taking their orders, Jessie left.

Leanne smiled her way once Jessie gave the cook the order. "Looks like a handful over there. Cute times four," she sighed with a smile.

"Two of 'em have accents, too."

"Lookie you, checking them out."

"I'm not checking anyone out. The last thing I need is another playboy messing up my life."

Jessie turned around and refilled the coffee cup of one of her night-owl customers sitting at the counter. "How are the pancakes, Mr. Richman?"

"Fine, just fine," he replied.

When Jessie turned back to Leanne, the other waitress continued talking. "Who's to say they're a bunch of playboys?"

"Frat boys who never grew up, most likely."

"Playboys, frat boys, whatever. One of 'em could be the rich guy of your dreams."

Jessie raised an eyebrow. "Right." Grabbing Leanne's hand, Jessie led her to a far window overlooking the parking lot. "Take a look, sister. See any crazy-expensive cars out there?" Actually, the only cars in the lot belonged to the employees and Mr. Richman. Except for one lone pickup that was new sometime in the mid-1990s. That seemed about the right speed for the cowboys at table twelve.

"That doesn't mean nothing." Leanne pulled away and frowned. "Besides, dating means free meals and a movie. Nothing wrong with that."

"Dinner and a movie in my world consist of McDonald's and *SpongeBob* on TV. Dating and Danny don't mix."

"Your sister will watch him for you."

"Yeah, but why waste my time on someone dreaming of the future instead of living it? You know my mom isn't the wisest woman in the bunch, but she told me once that it is just as easy to fall in love with a rich man as it is to fall in love with a poor one."

"Yeah, so?"

"So don't date poor men."

Across the restaurant, Jack with the gray eyes and the Stetson was watching her over his coffee cup. When he caught her gaze, his lips pulled into a grin, dimples and all. Then, without any provocation, he winked.

"Oh boy." Jessie lowered her eyes and tried to ignore the flirting frat playboy and the way his attention made her insides squirm.

"Mr. Cowboy is sexy." Leanna giggled when she spoke.

"I'll bet Mr. Cowboy mooches off one of his friends for the bill."

"Oh, come on, he can't be that bad."

"He's flirting with a waitress at Denny's, Leanne. His ambitions can't be all that high."

"Dissed!" Mike laughed, punching Jack in the arm. "Doesn't look like the waitress is taking a liking to you."

"Might have something to do with the way you're dressed, Moore."

"There's nothing wrong with the way I'm dressed." In fact, he liked the fact that Jessie, the sexy waitress wearing a god-awful brown skirt, had no idea who he was. Jack stayed out of the spotlight as often as he could. Here in California, people didn't know him by sight. In Houston, the story was entirely different. The thought of charming the waitress without waving his wallet felt like the right thing to do, especially after his recent encounter with Heather.

Jack removed his wallet and quickly handed Tom a twenty.

"What's this for?"

"Breakfast."

"Why are you giving it to me now?"

"Just hold on to it. If it comes up, I'm just a shit-kicker coming off a long binge of a weekend." Jack followed Jessie's movements until she disappeared around the corner.

Hell, he'd be in Ontario, California, for several weeks, overseeing the construction plans of a new hotel off the convention center. He might as well hook up with someone while he was there. He would love to burn the image of every Heather he ever knew out of his mind once and for all. Plastic *What can you do for me baby* women who flirted with his wallet more than him. There were times this kind of woman didn't bother him at all, but lately he'd been searching for someone he could talk to, someone to share his ideas and dreams with, maybe a down-to-earth waitress who wasn't ashamed to get her hands dirty and work for a living. Or ride in an old pickup truck.

Jack wasn't afraid of hard labor on the ranch or pushing papers at a desk. Ever since he'd finished college and his father put him in acquisitions and mergers, he'd gone out of his way to excel at his job. Unlike his sister, Katie, who probably did lunch with Paris Hilton, Jack actually wanted to work for a living. Living off his father's money didn't sit well with him. When the day came for Jack to take over for his father, no one could accuse him of being a slacker who was handed the job without any knowledge of how to do it.

"Hookay, I see what you're doing," Tom said.

"Do you?" Jack asked.

"Yeah, I do. I saw you this weekend, dodging the women at the hotel. For a while there I was wondering who was getting married next month, you or Dean," Mike said. "Tired of all the gold diggers, aren't you?"

"Tired of all the liars."

"That would suck," Tom agreed.

"My Maggie is the best th-thing that's ever happened to me," Dean told them.

"Lordy, now he's gonna go and get all emotional on us." Tom pushed Dean's coffee cup closer to him. "Drink up. Maggie, the fair maiden, isn't going to like it if you come home smelling like a bar."

Dean propped his elbows on the table and held his head up with his hands. "She's the best. And the sex."

"We've heard it, Dean."

"All friggin' weekend," Tom chimed in.

"You guys are just jealous."

Jack sipped his coffee and kept his mouth closed. He was happy for his friend, but not so sure Maggie was the right choice. Dean loved to play: motorcycles, camping, boating trips on the river. He wasn't afraid of hard work to pay his way, either. But ever since Maggie walked into his life, Dean gave up a little bit of himself daily.

"Maggie's worried that I'll get in an accident on the motorcycle."

"Maggie doesn't enjoy the river; boating makes her nauseous."

"Maggie would rather stay at one of your hotels instead of an RV."

Maggie might make Dean smile, but how long would it be before he blew his lid being molded into what she wanted him to be?

Jessie strolled around the corner with her arms stacked with plates. With choreographed ease, full breakfasts slid over the table and condiments emerged from the pockets of her dull, stiff uniform.

"It smells great, Jessie," Jack told her before she walked away.

"I'll let the cook know you're pleased."

Tom and Dean shoveled food into their greedy mouths.

Jessie disappeared long enough to grab a pot of coffee to refill their cups. "Are we missing anything?" she asked.

"I think we're good." Jack tried to capture her eyes, but she avoided them.

"Let me know if you need anything. You can see we're just swamped tonight."

Jack noted the one lone customer at the counter. "I'll bet you could tell some stories about working the graveyard shift at Denny's," Jack said, trying hard as hell to get her to reveal a thing or two about herself.

"It's hard to stay awake most nights. We start to pick up around four thirty."

"That's an ungodly hour," Tom said between bites.

"You'd be surprised at the number of suits that come in for a bite before heading into LA to work. They start early to avoid traffic."

"I'd heard that LA traffic was bad, but *that* bad?" Jack asked.

"The worst. You must not live here if you have to ask."

"I'm from Texas, mostly. My most recent job brought me here, near the airport." Ontario International Airport took some of the burden off LAX and Burbank, but the land around those airports was built out, without any ability to grow. Ontario provided plenty of room for new hotels.

Mike nudged him in the arm. "Bums off my place when he wants a decent night's sleep."

Which wasn't exactly a lie, Jack thought. Mike lived over in Claremont, and Jack sometimes stopped by to crash when he wanted a break from the hotel. The Morrison was a five-star luxury hotel filled with champagne and caviar. Sometimes Jack just wanted pizza, beer, and a ball game on the tube with a friend.

Jessie seemed to mull over the information a bit too long. She shrugged her shoulders with a flash of disappointment. "Well, enjoy your food." With that, she turned and walked away.

Dean laughed. "Not so easy, is it?"

"I'm not done yet," Jack told him as he picked up his fork. *Not by a long shot.*

By three, most of the food was gone and a few new customers had shown up at the counter, pulling Jessie away from their table.

An older man in his seventies turned in his chair to leave the counter and Jessie rushed to his side. "I told you to let me help you, Mr. Richman."

"I can do it," the older man said. But as he rose to his feet, he swayed against Jessie.

"It's the moisture in the air. Swells up my old bones," he explained.

Jessie wrapped her arm around his waist and helped him to the door, where he'd left his walker. Even then, she didn't turn away.

"I can make it from here," he told her.

"I'm sure you can, but I could use some air. All this bacon grease is getting to me. Walk me outside?" she asked him.

Mr. Richman offered a small smile as she opened the door and helped him to his car.

A couple minutes later, she walked back in with a contented grin on her lips.

"Hey, Jessie," the other waitress called from the cash register. "Yeah?"

"Your buddy didn't leave enough money again."

Jack watched Jessie's eyes travel to the door. She shrugged and reached into her skirt pocket and pulled out her tips. "I've got it, Leanne."

Leanne shook her head. "I don't know why you cover him all the time."

"It's pancakes, Leanne. And he doesn't have anyone. Give the guy some slack."

Jessie covered the rest of the man's bill and walked away from the register.

Something inside Jack clicked into place. He absolutely needed to know more about Jessie.

Each time she returned to refill the coffee, Jack tried to engage her in some kind of conversation. She didn't bite. Jack started to think that maybe she wasn't interested, but the fact that she wouldn't look him in the eye, and how her cheeks took on an adorable rosy color when he paid her a compliment, proved she wasn't unaffected by his charms.

Jessie cleared their table and placed the bill in the middle. "I'll take this whenever you're ready," she told them.

For a minute Jack was tempted to toss his credit card on the table and cover the meal to see if Jessie would look him in the eye then. Tom saved him the trouble.

"Guess you want me to cover this one, too, huh, Jack?"

"Hey, I drove," he said.

"And we paid for gas." Which actually was the arrangement; staying at the Morrison Hotel and Casino in Vegas was on Jack.

Tom, Dean, and Mikey tossed bills on the table and handed them to Jessie. "Keep the change," Tom told her.

After Jessie walked away, Mike said, "Looks like you struck out with this one."

"Man, I can't believe my head is still spinning," Dean said.

Jack dug into his pocket for the keys to the truck. "Here, Mike. Why don't you see Tom off at the airport? Dean and I will stay for another cup of coffee."

"You know, that's a great idea. Getting in a car right now probably wouldn't sit well with my stomach." Dean looked a little green.

"When does your flight leave again?"

"Six," Tom said.

"We best get you there. Airport security takes forever to get through these days."

They all stood and shook hands.

"See you back home next month," Jack told his friend.

A strong pat on the back and Tom said, "Good luck, Moore."

Jack sat back down after Tom and Mike left. Dean laid his arms on the table and rested his head in them. "Why did you guys let me drink so damn much? Maggie hates it when I drink too much."

"We'll get you sober before we drag your sorry ass home."

Jessie did a double take when she noticed only two of their party leaving. Jack waved her over to the table.

"Your friends leaving without you?"

"Tom's flying back to Texas, and Dean is in need of more black coffee before we release him to his fiancée."

"Fair enough." Holding a pot in her hand, Jessie poured another splash for both of them.

Before she could walk away, Jack flashed his winning smile. "So, Jessie, could I interest you in a night out?"

She cocked her head to one side. "Was that a pickup line?"

Miffed, Jack shook his head. "If you have to ask, I must be losing my touch."

Dean laughed but kept his trap shut.

"I'm flattered, Jack. It is Jack, right?"

He nodded. "Why do I feel a *but* coming on?" Jack asked.

Jessie placed a free hand on the table and leveled her eyes with his. "*But* I'm a very busy woman. So unless you have a checkbook as big as your ego—and my guess is, since your friends spotted you for your meal and gas, you're probably broke—I'm not interested."

Dean blew out a whistle.

Jack was nearly too stunned to answer.

Jessie just kept on staring at him until he uttered, "Well, I'll be damned. I think that's the first time anyone has ever said that to me."

Jessie straightened her shoulders and lifted her eyebrows. "Well, at least I'm honest. You're cute, cowboy, I'll give you that. But cute doesn't buy you a cup of coffee in this town. Now maybe in Texas it does. You might try a waitress back home."

"I'm not in Texas. Besides, it's you I want to take out."

"Again, I'm flattered, but no thanks."

"You think I'm cute," he said, which wasn't the highest compliment he'd been given in recent years, but he'd work with it.

A smirk played on Jessie's face. "You don't give up, do you?"

"No. Not easily."

"OK then, how about this...I wait tables in this dive at night so I can spend more time with my five-year-old son at home."

Jack's gaze flicked to her left hand. No ring. "If you're married, why don't you just say so?"

She shook her head and rolled it back. "Married, as if. Honey, I don't even get child support. Not that any of this is your business."

Not married, raising a son on her own, and having to work graveyard to do it. No wonder she was looking for a wallet and not love. Heather's words hovered in his mind. *Every woman is going to be with you for your money, Jack.* But this woman, Jessie, didn't have a clue about his wallet. And if she was so money hungry, why did she routinely foot the bill for her customers' pancakes? There was more to this beautiful woman than she was letting on. Suddenly the challenge of winning her over besieged him.

Jessie started to turn away.

He stopped her. "Kids love me."

Jessie's jaw dropped. "Does he ever give up?" she asked Dean.

"Nope."

"Do all the women fall for him?"

"Yep."

She mumbled something as she walked away.

"Dude, you're barking up the wrong skirt," Dean said after she left. "She's just not into you."

"No, she doesn't *want* to be into me."

"She has a kid, Jack. She's smart to not wanna date men who are posing as losers."

The gentle sway of her hips kept his attention as she walked away. In that moment he realized how long it had been since he had to pursue a woman. "*Posing* being the key word." Jack scratched the stubble on his jaw and smiled beneath his hand. *Posing as a loser.*

Chapter Two

Jessie tossed her keys on the kitchen counter and hung her purse off the back of a chair. The water was running in the bathroom, indicating that her sister, Monica, was getting ready for her day. At twenty-one years old, Monica was more grown-up than most. Her last year at the community college nursing program had started in September. Jessie had vowed to help her out as much as she could. Monica stayed with Danny at night while Jessie worked, and Monica lived in the apartment rent-free.

Monica worked about eighteen hours a week as a nurse's aide at the local community hospital to help with food, but for the most part, Jessie took care of the bills. The two of them had made a pact years ago. Monica would go through school first, with Jessie's help, and then when she was finished, Jessie would do the same.

In the beginning, Jessie thought maybe nursing was something she'd enjoy doing. Lord knew the profession paid well, but the thought of working with the sick and injured all the time didn't sound appealing.

Jessie actually liked the service industry. Not that she wanted to become a career waitress or anything, but maybe some type of manager position in a fancy establishment. Maybe catering events, or organizing big parties. The thought of being a wedding planner had a nice, clean feel about it. Not like nursing, with all the blood and body fluids.

Jessie did manage to take one class each semester online to help her out once she started back full-time. She had a year to figure out what she wanted to do for a living.

Of course, dating a rich guy couldn't hurt.

Jessie considered the overnight crowd at the diner, especially him...Jack. The guy with the sexy, cute smile and never-give-up attitude. He hadn't left the restaurant until after five in the morning. When he did, he climbed into the worn-out truck in the parking lot and sputtered on down the road. Before he left, he promised to return.

Jessie hadn't encouraged him, didn't even reveal her schedule when he asked. By the end of the evening, she and Jack's conversation had been reduced to snarky comments and witty comebacks.

If she were being honest with herself, she'd have to admit her shift had flown by and left her with a smile on her lips. It didn't suck to know someone actually acknowledged her as a woman and not just a mother.

The soft patter of feet tapped down the hallway of the apartment. Danny sported his race-car pajamas and hair that stuck up in several places. He rubbed sleep from his eyes when he said, "Good morning, Mommy."

"Morning, buddy. How'd you sleep?" Jessie knelt down and pulled her son into her arms for a hug.

Danny gave up one arm to join her hug, but continued to scratch his eyes with the other. "Good," he said with a big yawn. "Auntie made us sundaes last night after you went to work."

"Did she? Were they good?"

"We didn't have any nuts to sprinkle on the top, but they tasted good anyway."

Danny pulled away and climbed up onto the stool at the kitchen counter.

Jessie removed bowls from the cupboard and brought a box of cereal off the top of the refrigerator. "I'll buy some nuts before we do our Christmas baking. Next time you can have nuts on your sundae," she told him.

He yawned again. "OK."

While Danny took a few minutes to wake up with his bowl of cereal, Jessie stepped to her bedroom to slip into a nightgown.

The bed was tousled since Monica slept in it on the nights Jessie worked. Otherwise, she took the sleeper sofa bed in the living room. They really could use a three-bedroom apartment, but that was a luxury they couldn't afford. It was hard enough rubbing her tips together to pay for what they had.

Monica slipped into the bedroom, wearing her student nurse uniform. The stark white outfit would hang on most people, but not Monica. Her slim build and naturally blonde hair accented the clothes. "Oh, good, you're home," she said as she sailed around the room picking up her clothes from the night before.

"Day shift showed up on time for once," Jessie told her.

"That's good. I need to be at the hospital at eight thirty sharp."

Jessie glanced at her watch. "Can you still take Danny to school?"

"Yeah, that's not a problem."

Good. Danny had started kindergarten a couple of months prior, which afforded Jessie a few hours of uninterrupted sleep. Sleep was heaven. Only on her days off did she manage more than about five hours.

"You work again tonight, right?" Monica asked.

"Right. Off tomorrow."

"What about Thanksgiving?"

"I couldn't give up the shift, Mo. Time-and-a-half pay is needed this month if I'm going to give Danny any Christmas at all." Jessie would have to work graveyard on both Wednesday and Thursday nights, leaving a small window of time to sleep and enjoy the holiday.

Monica leaned against the dresser. "You know Mom is expecting us at her place at two."

Jessie rolled her eyes. "Yes, I know. Has Pat come back, or are we taking him off our Christmas card list?" Pat was her mother's latest boyfriend.

Renee Effinger, Jessie and Monica's mother, three-time divorcee, no longer married the many men in her life. Instead, she dated them, let them move in for a few months, and then kicked them out when she tired of their crap. Pat had actually left her around Halloween. Renee hadn't seen it coming, and ever since his departure, she moped around her singlewide mobile home playing the jilted woman. Too bad the woman didn't follow her own advice and marry a rich man. No, Renee Bradly-Mann-Smith-Effinger fell in love three times in her life, all with losers, dreamers, or wannabe men.

William Mann, Jessie and Monica's real father, married her mother after she found out she was pregnant. The marriage lasted through Monica's first birthday. Jessie was three the last time she saw her dad. She held no memories of the man. Only a few scattered pictures shed any light on the person who fathered her.

Damn if Jessie hadn't fallen into the same path as her mother. As much as she hated to admit it, Renee and she were a lot alike.

Jessie's high school boyfriend, Rory, stuck around long enough to take her to her senior prom. When Jessie confirmed she was pregnant, she actually wanted Rory to step up and take responsibility.

What a waste of a dream that turned out to be. Rory bolted the day after he earned his high school diploma and never looked back. Some days Jessie hated him for it; others, she was glad he didn't stick around to screw up Danny's life. A part-time dad who didn't care was worse than none at all. A couple years after Danny was born, Jessie met loser number two. Jessie's last boyfriend, Mathew, had convinced her to let him move in with her to "help out" with the expenses and then left with her full month's rent in his pocket after two months. Jessie swore then she'd only date guys who had their shit together.

"Pat's gone for good," Monica told her while she put on a pair of stud earrings.

"How can you be sure?"

"Mom said his friend came over to her house and took all his things. I'm guessing that means he's not coming back."

Jessie toed off her shoes and sat on the edge of the bed. "That's too bad. I actually liked this one."

"I did, too. Oh well. You know Mom; she'll have another guy by Christmas…New Year's at the latest."

"No doubt she will. Listen, Danny asked if he would see Grandpa Pat on Thanksgiving."

"Oh no."

"Yeah. I told him that Pat wasn't his grandpa but just a friend of Grandma's and that Pat was visiting some of his family for the holidays." Monica was sharp.

"I knew this would eventually happen with all the men Mom has in her life. I guess I need to be more careful with who I allow her to bring into his life." Jessie hated to have to avoid seeing her mother when she had a new man in her life, but in order to save Danny's long-term feelings, Jessie didn't have a choice.

Once Danny had started school, he'd asked about dads and grandfathers. Neither of which he had.

"Mom?" Danny called from the kitchen.

Dragging her tired limbs off the bed, Jessie walked into the other room to see what Danny needed.

"What's up?"

"Do you remember about the party at school tomorrow?"

Jessie laughed. There were two flyers littered with pilgrims and pumpkins hung on her refrigerator about the party. Danny was superexcited about it. "Of course I do."

"Good. The teacher asked if some of the moms could bring treats. Can you make those pumpkin cookies again like you did for Halloween?"

Jessie ruffled her son's light brown hair with a smile. "Of course I can." She'd just have to cut an hour out of her sleep and make it to the store to gather the ingredients and make said cookies before her next shift.

She would also have to skip sleeping on the day of the school party until after Danny returned home from school. With one day off between then and Thanksgiving, Jessie figured she'd manage only a handful of hours of sleep combined.

"Let's get you dressed so Auntie can take you to school."

More awake, Danny skipped to his bedroom and started pulling clothes from his dresser. Within ten minutes, the two of them had left and Jessie fell into bed.

"Oh boy, what is *he* doing here...again?" Jessie asked Leanne the minute the bell on the door leading into the diner rang and Jack sauntered in from the cold. He caught her eyes, smiled, and tipped his hat in greeting.

"I told him you were working," Leanne said.

"Why did you go and do that? Don't encourage him."

"I think he's cute. And so do you, don't even try and deny it." Leanne pulled a hot plate from the window and left Jessie's side.

"Hey, darlin'," Jack said while sliding into the swiveling seat at the counter.

"What are you doing here, Jack?" Jessie folded her arms over her chest and ignored the beat of her rising pulse.

"Checking on you."

"I thought I made myself clear last night. Not interested."

Not offended in the least, Jack grinned and offered a glimpse of the dimples that framed his lips. "Why, I'd love some coffee, Miss Jessie, thanks for offering."

Jessie grumbled while twisting to retrieve a cup and the coffee.

She served him quickly before rushing off to take care of an order. The diner was busy this early in the evening with the late dinner crowd. Hopefully she could ignore the cowboy at the counter enough so he'd just go away.

Didn't happen. Even after she ignored him for nearly an hour, Jack just smiled and waited until she couldn't disregard him any longer. "I would love a piece of pecan pie to go with this coffee."

"Do you want that à la mode?"

"Now you're talking my language."

Jessie went about preparing his pie, feeling the weight of his stare on her back the entire time.

When she set it in front of him, he rubbed his hands like a kid. "I love pecan pie, don't you?"

"At two thousand calories a slice, I don't indulge very often."

He shoved a forkful in his mouth and spoke around his food. "You don't look like you need to worry about your figure." His gaze raked up and down her frame. Not exactly the desired response she wanted.

"Every woman worries about her figure."

"Oh, I don't know about that. I've been told many times that skinny women don't think about it much at all."

"They're lying."

His brows turned up. "Really?"

"Really. Every woman would love to eat all the steak and pecan pie there is out there, but they know if they do they'll be fighting the flab by the time they're thirty."

"Makes me wanna tempt you with my aunt Bea's homemade pecan pie even more. It's the best. This isn't bad, but it has nothing on Aunt Bea's pie."

Jessie smiled despite herself. "And where is this Aunt Bea of yours?"

"Texas."

"Does that mean you'll be driving home for the long weekend?"

"You mean for Thanksgiving?"

"Yeah." She poured him more coffee.

"Nope, not this time. Maybe for Christmas."

"Do you go home often?"

He took his time answering. "Sometimes."

Vague answer. Not that she should care.

Jack finished his pie while Jessie wrapped up two of her tables. Only a sprinkling of customers littered the restaurant when Jack suggested that Jessie sit and take a short break.

Instead, Jessie leaned against the counter and folded her arms over her chest. "Jack, listen, I'm flattered."

"You said that last night."

"And you obviously didn't listen. I'm flattered, but I'm not going to go out with you."

He nodded. "Yeah, I know."

Her hands fell to her hips. "If you know, then why are you here?"

"I'm so glad you asked," he said. He patted the seat next to him. "Sit, let me explain."

Something in the way his eyes followed her around told her he wasn't completely dispelled from the thoughts of dating her. If sitting would hurry him along, then she might as well get it over with. Jack distracting her all night would end with fewer tips than she needed.

When Jessie slid into the chair beside him, the scent of his cologne washed over her. Musk and spice, very masculine and very Jack.

Ignoring the fluttering in her stomach at sitting beside him, she said, "OK, explain."

Tilting his hat back, Jack shifted in his seat to give his complete attention to her. "I've decided to help you."

"Help me what?" She hadn't asked for any help.

"Help you find the rich man of your dreams."

Jessie's jaw dropped. "What?"

"You said you only want to date rich men. Well, I know where you can find men like that, and I'm going to help you hook up with one."

She'd never heard anything more ridiculous in her life. She didn't even want to honor his words with a response. Jessie started to leave her seat when Jack stopped her by holding on to her arm. "I'm serious."

"You're ridiculous," she snapped, doing her level best to ignore the heat of his touch.

"Just sit a minute and hear me out."

Begrudgingly, Jessie sat back down and shook out of his hold.

"I realize you don't want to date me. Which is a crying shame, since I think we'd get along great, but if I can't convince you to go out with me, I can at least be a friend. Nothing wrong with having friends."

"You and me…friends?"

"Friends. You have those, right?"

"Of course I have friends." She wasn't a complete loser. Yet when she thought about it, outside of her sister and a few waitresses at the diner, she didn't know whom she'd call a friend. Most of her school friends had all gone off to college or somewhere new mothers didn't. Sadly, Jessie's friendship pool was rather shallow.

"Great. Friends help friends."

"And you want to help me?"

"Yep. Do you know where The Morrison is, over by the airport?"

"The hotel?"

"Yeah."

"Yeah, I know where it is."

"Well, this Saturday night there's a big Christmas cocktail party taking place. I happen to know plenty of deep pockets are going to be attending."

She shook her head. "What are you suggesting?"

"I'll get you in and point out the men who fit your wish list."

The Morrison was a top-notch hotel that Jessie had never had the pleasure of visiting. She'd be lucky to afford a Motel 6. "Wait a minute. Let's say you could get me in—not that I'd have anything to wear to a cocktail party at some fancy hotel, but let's say you could. Why would a guy who admits to wanting to date me hand me over to a different guy?"

"I told you…I'm deeply wounded you don't want to date me, but I get it."

Deeply wounded. Talk about overkill.

"I'm not your type," he continued. "The least I can do is determine if there's someone I can help hook you up with to make *you* happy."

That all sounded well and good, but something wasn't right about the proposition. "How exactly are you going to 'get me in'?"

"I'm serving that night. I can slip you an invitation."

So he waited on people for a living, too. "Won't that jeopardize your job?"

He shrugged. "I'm not worried. It's a temporary thing anyway."

Still, something felt wrong. Jessie stood and said, "Well, thanks anyway, but I don't have anything to wear."

"What if I can get you something?"

She cocked her head to the side, baffled. "How?"

"You wouldn't believe the things people leave behind in high-end hotels. I found this watch once, cost about two thousand dollars. Some guy just left it on the counter in the bathroom."

"Didn't you try and get it back to him?"

"It was in the lobby bathroom. We left it in the lost and found for months, but no one claimed it."

"So you took it."

"No, I wore it a couple of times, then I put it back."

He borrowed it. "Are you saying women leave evening gowns at the hotel?"

"All the time." His boyish smile was growing on her. It wasn't as if she'd find a rich husband, or boyfriend for that manner, waiting tables at Denny's.

"I don't know..."

Jack stood and stepped close to her. He was a good four inches taller than she was, and Jessie wasn't exactly short.

"What are you, a size eight, ten?"

"Eight, not that it's any of your—"

"Business," he finished for her. "I know." His white teeth flashed in a grin. "Shoe size?"

She was still stuck on giving out her dress size to a stranger. At nearly five eight, being a size eight was perfect. Still, saying it aloud left a bad taste behind her tongue.

"Well?"

"What was the question?"

"Shoe size?"

"They leave shoes, too?"

"Sometimes."

"Seven. I wear a seven in shoes." That was easier to say.

"We're good then."

"I don't know."

"Come on, Jessie. What do you have to lose? A fancy night out, plenty of champagne, wine, shrimp cocktail, fruit, cheese, the works. All free."

"I don't know."

"You're not working, Leanne already told me."

Jessie shot Leanne a dirty look from across the restaurant. "Traitor," she mumbled.

Jack nudged her with his elbow. "I'll bring the dress Thursday morning."

"Geez, did Leanne tell you my whole schedule?"

"Pretty much. I'll bring the dress and the invitation. All you have to do is show up."

"I won't know anyone."

"You'll know me." He winked at her and her stomach did a small roll in return. What did she have to lose? She could show up, have a glass of wine, and leave if it felt wrong being there.

"Oh, all right. I'll go."

"That's my girl." Jack pulled out his wallet and placed a ten on the counter.

"I'm not your girl."

Jack chuckled. "Right. See ya on Thanksgiving, Jessie."

Chapter Three

Samuel Fields, the Ontario Morrison Hotel manager, sat behind the desk from Jack with his back rod-straight and his lips forced into a tight smile. His three-piece suit fit perfectly around his shoulders, his tie impeccably neat. He'd been the manager of the Ontario hotel for over ten years, since its inception. Unless the man wanted a different view, he'd be there for the next ten. "It feels strange with you on the other side of this desk, Mr. Morrison."

"Not sure why that would bother you, Sam. This is your office, not mine."

"Yes, I guess it is."

"I'm really not one who lords over things. My stay in Ontario will keep me here throughout the holidays. Once the initial construction is set in motion for 'More for Less,' I'll be returning to Texas."

"It's been some time since anyone in your family has used the penthouse suite. I hope it meets your needs."

The penthouse *family* suite took up nearly half the west tower's top floor. Like in all the Morrison hotels, the family suite was just that: a suite the family could use to either sleep in during an overnight stay or as a perk for the many dignitaries that Jack and his father, Gaylord, associated with throughout the world. The Morrisons informed the hotels when the suites would be used and allowed the hotels to book them on the other days of the year. The suite had three bedrooms, three bathrooms, a full gourmet chef's kitchen, dining room, and living quarters. The veranda and patios overlooked the airport and the flickering lights of the Inland Empire. The space could easily accommodate a house party of a hundred people, not that Jack was planning such an event. Deep mahogany hardwood floors covered the living and dining rooms. Plush sofas sat across from each other while occasional chairs and heavily wooded wrought-iron tables filled out the space. Live plants filled corners, and fresh flowers sat in vases by the front door and in the kitchen. At night, when the floor-to-ceiling windows that covered two walls couldn't let light in, up lighting, down lighting, and recessed lighting could be used to set any mood.

Unlike any other room at the hotel, this one felt like home.

In Houston, his home took the entire top-floor penthouse, nearly double the size of the one he was in now. Living in a hotel wasn't something he'd planned. In reality, he lived in the hotel only half the year. The other half was spent at his father's or in hotels like the one he was in now.

His father's estate sat on over five hundred acres; the sprawling ranch house screamed Texas in every way. He loved being there. Yet something about being a grown man living with his father never settled comfortably inside of Jack.

One day, Jack wanted to set down roots of his own. Roots he would plant firmly on the ground floor. He loved the open plains of Texas and hoped whomever he chose to be by his side would love the land as much as he did. Then he could find his own oasis to return to instead of the never-ending hotel suites.

"I've sent out the invitations as you requested," Sam told him.

"Did you open up access for the employees to rent appropriate attire?"

"Yes." Sam nodded. "The local tux rental and women's boutique in the shop downstairs was told to allow any employee with a badge to rent an outfit for free over this weekend."

Good. "Actually, Sam, let's keep that invitation open throughout the holidays." Jack thought of Jessie. "I'd like the employees to use the service, and if they can't make it to the benefit party this Saturday, they might be able to make it to another over the next month."

Sam's face clouded over. "Are you sure, sir? I mean, what if the clothes are ruined? It could cost the hotel quite a bit of money."

Jack huffed. "Have some faith. Most people care for other people's property better than their own. We'll deal with individual issues as they come up."

"If you say so, sir."

"Please, call me Jack. That reminds me. On Saturday, I'll be taking part in the employee/employer swap as well. I'll need a uniform."

Sam's eyes grew wide. "Oh, Mr. Morrison, I mean Jack, are you sure?"

"It's good for morale. Every staff person who usually wears a suit and tie is going to be wearing waiters' uniforms, and the cleaning staff will be in evening gowns. The only paid guests are those we've invited, all of whom know the staff and management have swapped roles for the night. My name tag will say Jack, so please don't call me Mr. Morrison. It will be fun, you'll see. You might even learn a thing or two about your employees and yourself before the night is over. When was the last time you served food from the kitchen?"

"I've never had the pleasure." From the twisted expression on the man's face, it wasn't a pleasant thought.

"Well then, you'll be shocked at the pressure your waiters are under." Jack ignored Sam's scowl. Jack had held a similar party the previous year in the hotel he lived in full time. The next day, the staff returned to their normal jobs appreciating their colleagues' titles a little more.

It was the perfect setup to bring Jessie to. She would think he was a cocktail waiter, a transient one at that, and he could wait on her for a change. He thought of the single men on the guest list, the ones he planned to point out to her. Admittedly, Jack didn't think any of them were her type, but maybe after seeing her options, she'd consider dating him.

Of course, someone could blow the whole thing by calling him out, but Jack hoped he could keep his identity a secret long enough to get to know the real Jessie. She might be hard on the outside, but he was betting on her insides being all soft and comfortable. All he had to do was needle under her skin until she couldn't stand it anymore.

Jack stood and offered his hand to Sam.

Sam shook it. "We'll be decorating the hotel on Friday. Would you like us to supply a tree for your suite?"

"That would be nice. Nothing too fancy. Traditional red and green would be great."

"I'll see to it, sir."

Jack detoured past the bank of elevators to the women's boutique. *Time to shop for Jessie.* Only he wasn't sure what to pick out.

Behind the counter was an older woman, about sixty, he guessed, with graying hair and glasses perched on her nose. She saw him walking in and offered a kind smile. "Can I help you?"

Jack shrugged out of his suit jacket and laid it over a chair in the middle of the showroom. "I'll bet you can," he told her. "I'm looking for an evening gown."

She lifted the glasses off her nose and placed them behind the counter. "We have plenty of those. Anything in particular?"

"Something classy, nothing too fussy."

"Will this be to rent, or will you be buying this for your lady friend?"

Jack glanced over to a rack of long dresses. "Buying."

"OK, then. My name's Sharon, by the way."

"Jack," he told her, leaving his last name out on purpose.

"What size is the woman we are dressing?"

"She's a size eight. She's comes up to about yea high." He lifted his hand to his nose. "Light brown hair and hazel eyes. Shoe size is seven."

"OK, since she's not here, might I give a suggestion?"

"Of course, Sharon, that's why I asked you."

She smiled. "Floor-length formals really do have to fall all the way to the floor, with the lady's shoes on. Since she isn't here for a fitting, I'd suggest something just as elegant, only at a three-quarter length."

"You mean so the dress will show off her legs?" Jessie had amazing legs—what he could see of them from under the hideous Denny's uniform.

"Right."

"Sounds good to me."

"Why don't you have a seat, Jack, and I'll pull a few things from the rack. Is there a budget we're trying to stay within?"

Jack sat in the chair. "You just show me what you have, don't worry about price."

Sharon smiled, lifted her eyebrows, and then disappeared behind the drapes separating the store from the small storage room. When she returned, she brought a rolling pole and proceeded to show him half a dozen dresses.

"Hazel eyes spark with a little color," she told him. She displayed an emerald green off-the-shoulder dress with sequins down the neck.

"Not that one." It reminded him of a Christmas tree without a star.

The next one had only one shoulder sleeve, leaving the second shoulder bare. He liked the red silk, and the slit up the thigh had him imagining the possibilities. "Maybe," he said.

Sharon placed it on a separate rack than the green one.

A cream skintight number with an open *V* at the top would be nice, but he knew from his own experience that most women stayed away from white. A silver sequin would be perfect for a New Year's Eve party, but not right for Jessie on Saturday.

"What about this?" Sharon saved the best for last. "Women love wearing black and this one has the one-shoulder look you liked in the red. A simple slit up the back will keep the woman wearing it dancing throughout the night. I even have a wrap the lady can wear over her shoulders should she get cold."

Perfect. Not too daring or suggestive. Elegant and slightly understated, but with Jessie's figure, it would pop once she stepped in it. "You have shoes to match?"

"Of course. I even have a nice pair of jeweled earrings that will dangle from your lady's ears. I don't think a necklace will work with this neckline. If you're against costume jewelry, Mitch over in fine jewelry has the real thing. He's just down the hall."

The image of Jessie walking toward him in the dress danced in his head. He could hardly wait. "I'll take it."

"And the earrings?"

"I'll have to think about that," he told her. If he were to show up with diamond earrings, Jessie would likely think ill of him. The last thing he needed was for Jessie to think he was a thief. She'd be a lot more comfortable in costume jewelry anyway, he told himself. Still, he didn't really care for the sound of fake anything associated with Jessie.

Jack stood and reached for his wallet. From the front of the boutique, Sam walked in with a phone in his hand. "There you are, Mr. Morrison. Sorry to interrupt."

Hearing his name, Sharon's gaze narrowed before shooting up in surprise.

"No problem, Sam."

"Mr. Morrison is on the phone, said he needed to talk to you."

Jack reached for the phone Sam held. "Would you mind putting all this on here?" he asked Sharon, handing her his credit card.

She glanced at the card, then back to him. "Of course."

"Hello, Dad," Jack said as he placed the receiver to his ear. He turned away from the clerk and braced himself for his father's outburst.

"Jack, what's this I hear about you not coming home for Thanksgiving?" Gaylord's gruff voice filled the earpiece of the phone, causing Jack to pull it away from his ear.

"I have a lot to do here. Getting away isn't smart right now."

"Horseshit, son. No one works on Thanksgiving."

"Lots of people work over the holiday," he corrected. "The hotels don't close."

"Still doesn't mean you have to be there. The hotels run themselves."

"I'll try and get home for Christmas," Jack offered.

"Try? Trying isn't good enough. Aunt Bea won't know what to do with herself if you aren't here to cook for."

Jack smiled, thinking of his aunt's easy smile and quiet disposition. How she and his father were both children of the same parents and yet turned out so differently had always been a mystery. "Is Katie home?"

"Barely; she's here but gone most of the time." Disappointment laced Gaylord Morrison's words. Neither Katie nor Jack spent as much time at the ranch as their father would have liked.

"I'll give her a call and see if I can reel her in. I should have a break midmonth. I'll come home for a few days then. Tell Aunt Bea to save some pie for me."

His father grumbled a little more, but finally relented and hung up.

Strange how things had changed over the years. Gaylord had been an absentee father most of Jack's childhood, building the hotel chain and taking over other, weaker chains, all of which took time and years. With Gaylord's advancing age came the realization of what he had missed. Now he wanted it back. At least that's what Jack thought. Had Jack told him the real reason he wasn't returning to Texas for the holiday, Gaylord would be having his pilot fire up his jet so he could meet Jack's lady friend.

Jack didn't need that.

"All set to go, Mr. Morrison," Sharon told him while she handed back his card and the box. "I went ahead and put in the earrings, no charge. Although it seems crazy charging you for anything at all...considering."

"It's all good, Sharon. It's been a pleasure." Jack tucked the box under his arm and left the boutique with a smug smile.

Unlike any other time he'd bought something for a woman he was attracted to, this time he'd done it for the sole purpose of making her happy. He wasn't doing it to find a lover...not completely, anyway. In reality, he hadn't taken a lover since Heather. Not because Heather broke something inside of him, but because he couldn't see past the plastic facade the women he'd met wore.

And plastic no longer held any appeal.

Jessie stirred something inside of him that pushed meaningless sex from his mind.

He pressed the elevator button and fished a pass key out of his pocket. He needed to change into his Jack Moore clothes so he could make a certain waitress's day...or night, as it was. He couldn't wait to see Jessie wearing the dress that weekend, to see her eyes light up when she saw it for the first time.

He couldn't wait.

Jessie wiped her hands on a towel before she led Jack into the break room in the back of the restaurant. "I don't know about this," she told him, staring at the huge box he held in his hands.

"What's to worry about? I'm telling you, the guy bought the dress for someone and then never picked the thing up."

"Why would anyone buy a dress and leave it at the store?" That was crazy. Just staring at the box brought on little waves of anticipation. How long had it been since she'd worn a nice dress? Forever!

"I don't know, maybe the girlfriend dumped him."

"Then why wouldn't he ask for his money back?"

Jack shrugged. "Maybe he was embarrassed. Rich people spend money as if it grows on trees. Don't shoot your own foot." Jack's constant use of clichés made her smile. It must be a Texas thing. "Aren't you even curious about what's in the box?"

Curious? Heck, her palms were all sweaty.

Jack waved the box under her nose and said in a singsong voice, "Come on, Jessie...open the box."

"Oh, give that to me." She grasped the package out of his hands and sat it on the table in the middle of the room. She tugged on the lid until it pulled free, and gasped.

There, in the delicate gold tissue paper, sat a beautiful black dress that must have cost a fortune. "Oh. My. God. I can't wear this. It's too much." Even as the words left her mouth, her greedy fingers grasped the dress as she lifted it for a better look.

The material slid in her hands. Silk, she mused. Only nothing like anything she owned or had ever worn. Her heart skipped in her chest with the thought of slipping it over her body.

"It's beautiful, Jack. Why would anyone leave this at the store?"

"You like it?"

"Like it? I love it." She pushed past him to look in the full-length mirror that hung outside the door to the employee lockers.

She pictured her hair up, or maybe down...a little more shadow on her eyes. This wasn't *a* little black dress, this was *the* little black dress that every woman wanted but seldom had. The dress would require a strapless bra, but she had one of those. What was she thinking? She couldn't wear a dress meant for someone else.

Or could she?

She couldn't stop smiling at her reflection...at the dress. "Are you sure you're not going to get into any trouble with this?"

He leaned one shoulder against the frame of the doorway and offered her a sexy grin. "I'm sure."

Like he'd say otherwise. She watched him through the mirror and questioned him with her stare.

"Did you see the shoes?" He nodded toward the box.

Jessie glanced over her shoulder and saw two strappy heels with tiny rhinestones adorning the edges, perfect for the dress.

"Are they my size?"

"You said seven, right?"

"Yeah."

She moved back over to the box and gently laid the dress inside. "I don't know, Jack. This is pricey stuff. I'd hate for you to get caught borrowing it and find yourself canned all on my account."

"I'm telling you, no one will be the wiser. This dress has been sitting there for months. I'm surprised it hasn't collected dust. Seems a shame to let it sit in the box instead of being worn by a beautiful lady."

Jessie passed him a frown. "You're incorrigible."

"Been called worse."

"Still."

Jack helped her put the lid back on the box. "The party starts at eight this Saturday night." He fished out a piece of paper from his pocket. "Here's your ticket."

She glanced at the embossed paper with the time, date, and place stamped on it. A tiny bit of holly took up a corner. Elegant.

Pam, another of the night servers, poked her head through the break room door. "Getting busy out here," she said.

"I'll leave you so you can get to work," Jack said. "I'll see you Saturday."

"As long as you're sure you won't get in any trouble."

Jack rolled his eyes. "I won't. Promise."

Jessie slid the box on the top of the lockers and turned for the door.

"Hey, Jack," she called out to him before he could leave.

He turned and gave her his signature smile, dimples and all. "Yeah."

"Thanks."

"Eight o'clock," he said with a wink.

"Got it."

He gave her a little salute with the brim of his hat and sauntered his Levi's-clad butt right out the door.

"Who was that?" Pam asked.

"A-A friend."

"Right. Is that what we're calling them these days?"

Jessie turned away from her. "Oh, stop. Not you, too."

"If he needs more *friends*, you can give him my number."

"You have a boyfriend," Jessie reminded her.

"Ha! Exactly." Pam shuffled around her and mumbled to herself. "Friend…yeah, right."

Chapter Four

"You're stalling," Monica said with laughter in her voice.

"Am not."

"Are too."

Jessie wrinkled her nose at her sister and turned to the mirror one last time. The dress fit perfectly. The cut of the dress accentuated her slim waist and the shoes showed off her calves.

Her hair sat piled on her head with plenty of whimsy strips falling to her shoulders. Jack had even tucked a pair of earrings into the box. Or maybe the man who originally bought the dress had tossed them in and Jack had no idea they were in there.

"You look gorgeous." Monica was sprawled on the bed, gazing at Jessie while tossing popcorn in her mouth.

Jessie ran her hands over her nervous stomach and turned to the side. "It's not bad, huh?"

"So tell me more about this guy...Jack."

Maybe it is time to get going? "I've already told you. He's just a guy I met at the restaurant who wants to help me find a nice, well-off man who can help dig me out of this hole I'm in. And then I can finish my degree, too."

"Is he cute?"

"Who, Jack?"

Monica rolled her eyes. "No, the well-off guy you haven't met yet! Of course I mean Jack."

Answering Monica's question honestly would result in constant harassment. "He's all right, I guess." *If you want your men sexy, gorgeous, and confident beyond reason.* Jessie pictured his dimpled grin and couldn't stop the smile from spreading on her own face.

"He's from Texas?"

"Yep."

"Accent?"

"One that matches the cowboy hat he's always wearing."

"When are we going to meet him?"

Jessie turned to her sister and placed her hands on her waist. "It isn't what you're thinking, Mo. Jack is a friend. That's it. I've told him no to him and me dating."

"So he is into you!"

"A lot of good that does. He's a waiter at the hotel. From the sound of it, he doesn't stay put for any real length of time, and he mooches off his friends when he needs a place to stay. I need a guy to actually help around here, not want it for free."

Monica pursed her lips together in thought. "Is he a bum?"

"No," Jessie burst out, and then answered more honestly, "I don't know. I think he does OK for himself. Listen, I need to go."

Her sister scrambled off the bed and handed her the wrap that came with the dress.

"I've got everything here, so don't worry about rushing home. You deserve a fun night out."

"Thanks." Jessie hugged her sister and exited her bedroom.

Danny was curled up on the couch with his own bowl of popcorn. "You look pretty, Mommy."

"Thanks, sweetheart. You be good for Aunt Monica." Danny was always good for her sister.

"We're going to watch a DVD," he told her.

"OK, but I want you in bed by nine."

"I know."

Jessie grabbed her purse and headed for the door. "Thanks again, Mo. I owe you."

"Go. Have a great time."

Jack checked his watch for the third time in fifteen minutes. People were still filing in, but he'd yet to spot the one woman he'd been searching for.

Maybe she changed her mind.

He turned to offer one of the guests walking by one of the miniquiches he carried on a plate, acting the role of waiter. With a few exceptions, many of the people at the party had no idea who he was. Most of the staff at the hotel who did know were also dressed as waiters, adding to the disguise.

Several members of the room service staff were standing in a circle talking. Two of the men held beverages in their hands, while the women kept glancing around the party looking nervous. Jack saw Sam hovering by the bar, staring at the tray of champagne-filled glasses. Jack walked to his side. "Hey, Sam."

"Hello, Mr.—"

"Jack," he quickly interrupted. Those kinds of slips would blow his cover should Jessie actually show up.

"Hello, Jack."

He motioned toward the fidgety women. "Isn't that Louisa and Shelley from housekeeping?"

Sam nodded. "Yes, it is."

"They look thirsty. You might help break the ice by offering them an adult beverage."

Sam tried not to scowl, but he failed. He removed several glasses from the tray before attempting to pick it up. Jack noted the skinny black tie and vest covering the white linen shirt, the same uniform Jack was wearing, and thought, *You can make him look like a waiter, but you can't expect him to perform like one.*

Sam's tray tilted when he lifted it. When he walked over to his staff, he did so at such a slow pace, Jack thought it would be an hour before he crossed the room. Even if he managed to make it, half the liquid would be spilled out of the glasses, if they didn't fall over altogether.

He chuckled.

Then he felt her.

Jack swiveled toward the entrance, caught sight of Jessie, and blew out a breath. His entire body kicked into gear. His heart pounded hard in his chest, his eyes felt hot, and the swelling in his pants reminded him of how long he'd been without a woman.

There wasn't a singular word to describe the fresh beauty he saw when he looked at her. Her bashful smile danced behind her eyes as she scanned the room. The dress caressed her curves like a lover's skillful hands. Her long legs peeked beneath the material and lifted enough in the heels to make him want to touch the spot behind her calves. Jessie was rainbows and unicorns and Jack knew he absolutely had to have her.

Jessie must have felt the weight of his stare because her gaze slid to his and an instant smile spread over her face. She sent a timid wave.

Jack tried not to act too rushed as he walked to her side. He stopped by one group of people, offered the appetizer, and then met up with Jessie.

"You're stunning," he told her.

Her cheeks grew pink, her teeth flashed in a smile. "You don't look half bad yourself, Jack. I hardly recognized you without your hat." When she spoke, she straightened his tie and gave it a tiny pat before lowering her hand.

"The hat doesn't match the uniform."

"It would set you apart from the rest."

Sam took that moment to walk up to the two of them. Jack held his breath, hoping the man wouldn't say anything to tip Jessie off. "Holding this tray is easier when you don't have so much on it," Sam said.

"I told you you'd get the hang of it." Jack removed the last glass from the tray and handed it to Jessie. "Sam, this is Jessie, a friend of mine."

"A pleasure to meet you, Jessie."

Jack nodded to Sam. "You might want to fill that tray before the new boss thinks you're slacking," he told him.

"Good thing this is only temporary," Sam told him. "I don't think I could do it full-time."

"Builds character," Jack said.

Sam agreed before turning toward the kitchen and marching away.

"Temporary?" Jessie asked.

"The hotel beefs up the staff for the holidays. Sam is new at his job." *Very new!*

Jessie tilted the sparkling wine to her full lips and took a sip. "It's nice of you to look out for him."

Watching her tongue chase a drop of champagne on her lip caused his stomach to warm. Lord, he had it bad. Jack forced his gaze to her eyes. "Sam's a good sport. Come on over here." He led her toward a far wall so they could scout the entire room. "Perfect people-watching position, don't you think?"

"It is. This place is beautiful. The decorations are amazing, elegant."

Jack glanced around the huge hall completely decked out with holiday lights, poinsettias, garland, Christmas trees with sparkling ornaments. "The decorating staff does a great job. You'd never know this place screamed Thanksgiving two days ago."

"The hotel has a decorating staff?"

"Yep."

"I'll bet that's a fun job."

"The coordinator drives them hard, but the same people come back year after year."

"My sister, Monica, is finishing up school this year. Next year I plan to go back. Take a design class or two."

Jack noted the distant gaze in her eyes. Her words were his first glimpse into her dreams. "What do you want to do?"

"Anything but what I'm doing. I'd like to be an event coordinator, maybe even a wedding planner. I want a job I don't have to wash off at the end of the day."

"Emily is the coordinator here, she works plenty hard."

Jessie huffed. "I'll bet she doesn't go home smelling like french-fry grease and sticky syrup."

Jack shook his head. "Probably not."

She tipped the glass back, and Jack noticed her tongue peek out to lick the rim. The movement wasn't meant to be sexy, but he had a hard time tearing his eyes away.

"So, where are all those eligible bachelors?" she asked.

Snapping out of his daze, Jack turned to scan the room. "I don't see too many here yet."

"Really?"

No, but he didn't want to point out anyone she might actually consider dating. "Wait here, I need to pass this around and appease my boss. I'll be back in a flash. Here, take a couple." He offered her the bite-sized egg puffs on his tray.

"Quiche?"

"Yeah."

"Do cowboys eat quiche?"

He laughed and then popped one in his mouth. "Not bad."

Jessie glanced behind him and swatted his arm. "Better watch it. Those are for the guests."

He winked at her concern and placed a couple of quiches on a napkin before handing it to her.

"I'll be right back."

Jessie was on her second glass of champagne, and Jack had stuffed more than her share of appetizers onto her napkin. She insisted on moving around the room so he wouldn't get in trouble with his boss for hovering around her the whole night.

For a brief while, she was certain he wasn't going to point out anyone to zero in on for a date. Passive proof that he wanted her for himself and joining the party was a ploy for his hidden agenda. She could have easily been irritated if Jack wasn't so damn cute as he passed out food and laughed with his customers. And how long had it been since she'd had an adult night out? Forever! That's how long.

She'd just about given up on Jack finding an eligible man when he pointed to a lone man sitting at the bar.

"Which one?" she asked, peeking over Jack's shoulder. There were a few men at the bar; two were sitting next to women, another sipped something from a martini glass, another could pose as her father.

"Don't stare." Jack scooted in front of her eyes, blocking her view. "Joe Richard, he's been married before. Divorced now, kids stay with his wife."

Hmm, she wasn't sure about having more to deal with. Then again, who was she to talk? "Which one is he?"

Jack turned slightly. "He's the one with the thinning hair."

Of course, the father figure. "Isn't he a little old for me?"

"So he needs to be young and rich?"

"It would help if I didn't look the part of a gold digger."

Jack leaned against the wall. "Do you feel like a gold digger?"

"Hook me up with a rich guy, and I'll tell ya in about a week." Jessie continued to glance around the room. "Tall guy, by the clock." She pointed out a man in his thirties who was laughing at something the man next to him had said.

Jack frowned. "Married."

"Really, I don't see a ring."

"Which is part of his problem. He's a player."

Jessie diverted her gaze. "I don't need that."

"Third table down from the buffet table. Dark hair, a little thick around the middle." Jack moved to the side so she could see whom he was talking about.

Thick? "At least he couldn't be my dad, but please, Jack. He looks like a gangster." Boy did he, short, calorically challenged, and with too much flashy jewelry.

"He probably is. He has what we call 'family money.' I don't think he's worked a day in his life."

"A bum with deep pockets," Jessie said.

"Right."

"No bums, rich or not. A man has to make his own living. I don't want someone who will drown if the stock market drops. The guy has to be able to dig himself back out." Jessie glanced over the heads again.

"So let me get this straight. Rich, not too fat, self-made, young…did I leave anything out?"

"He's gotta like kids."

Jack blew out a long breath. "That's a tall order, darlin'. You sure that kind of guy is out there?"

It was a lofty list. "I'm not sure of anything, Jack. This was your idea." Her tone was short.

"OK, all right, don't get all defensive. The night's still young."

She glanced at her watch. Actually, it was past eleven already. And no one new was walking in the door.

"Gray suit, just stepped up to the bar," Jack pointed out.

The man in question had his back to her, and Jessie waited for him to turn around. When he did, she skirted her gaze away. "That nose. Lord, what a shame."

Jack laughed and so did she. "That's a honker."

"How can he see past it?" she asked.

"Not sure he can."

One of the female guests walked up to Jack and picked up a piece of shrimp he had on his tray. "These are divine," she cooed as she plucked it into her mouth.

"Glad you like 'em, ma'am."

"Ma'am. Goodness, that makes me sound so old."

Jessie figured the woman was in her forties. The sequined dress she wore sparkled when she walked. Her fingers dripped with diamonds. When her eyes traveled up one length of Jack and down the other, it was all Jessie could do to keep her eyes from rolling in disgust. *Could she be more obvious?*

"I was brought up to be respectful," Jack told the woman as his gaze passed over her without as much as a hint of interest.

"Oh, and a cute accent, too. How delightful."

Jessie wanted to laugh. *Next thing you know the cougar will be slipping her room key into Jack's pocket.*

"Do you want another one?" Jack asked the woman, leaning the tray toward her.

Her eyes rolled up and down his frame a second time before she finally said, "Would I ever."

Jessie lifted her hands and glanced at them, wondering if she was invisible to this woman or if she was always so rude.

"Ah, Jack, don't you need to stroll around the room with those?" Jessie asked, doing her best to pull his attention away from the surgery-stabilized woman.

"I suppose I should," he said.

Jessie nudged him, which resulted in a cheeky grin and a chuckle as he walked away.

Cougar-lady watched his ass as he left their side. "Yum," she whispered nearly to herself.

"He's a little young for you, don't you think?" Jessie asked.

Cougar-lady's eyes shot to Jessie, seeing her for the first time. "Oh, I don't know about that. I always make it worth their while."

The way she spoke, Jessie realized this woman used men like Jack to suit their needs, never worrying about appearances. Her dress and jewelry pointed to a fat checking account or a high limit on a credit card. Jessie wondered if Jack ever took women like this one up on their offers of sex, a good time, and probably some type of monetary gain from the whole arrangement.

What did that make Jessie? Here she was looking for love with a pocketbook, and the cougar-lady was looking for loving using her pocketbook.

Suddenly the wine in Jessie's glass tasted like vinegar. "Excuse me," she said, shifting around the woman and setting the near-empty glass on a table.

The room grew warm. Jessie wandered out to the twinkling lighted veranda where some of the guests mingled. Guilt and a little disappointment in her own agenda made her want to leave. She was using Jack and his good-natured way just as much as the cougar would if given the chance. When had she become so shallow?

Maybe this is a mistake?

Attempting to shake her abruptly shifting mood, Jessie took in the breathtaking view of the gardens and the lit pond with koi swimming around in circles. She leaned over the railing to see one of the orange fish disappear between two rocks.

When she stood up, she realized someone had joined her.

"Hello," the sharply dressed man said to her once their eyes met. He was tall, about Jack's height, slender, almost too much so. He had long fingers that looked as if he played the piano.

"Hi," she managed.

"I hope I'm not disturbing you." His easy smile was nice, but brief.

"No, just getting some fresh air."

"I'm Brad," he said, extending his hand.

"Jessie." She allowed him to shake her hand. He let go quickly.

"It is a bit stuffy in there. Are you out here waiting for someone?"

Testing the waters, Jessie thought, and flirting with her, if she wasn't too far out of the game to notice. His hair was darker than Jack's, but not in a bad way. He definitely wasn't from Texas; not a single twang to his voice.

"No, not really." Even saying that felt strange, like maybe she should say she knew one of the servers. Then again, she was there to meet someone. Hadn't Jack invited her to do just that?

"Good, then maybe you won't mind if I join you."

Did she want that? Brad wasn't unappealing, but there wasn't much about him that screamed attraction. When he smiled, the spark didn't reach his eyes, not the way Jack's eyes danced when he laughed.

She really needed to stop comparing the man to Jack. Jack was the waiter; this man was a guest. Still, her concern that Jack could round the corner and catch her talking to this guy made her feel wrong somehow. It shouldn't, she realized, but it did. Bad form to be wearing a dress one man picked out for her while another man was flirting with her.

"I'm actually about to leave, but it's been nice meeting you."

A flash of disappointment spread over Brad's face. "Are you just saying that, or do you mean that?" he asked.

"I mean it. It's late, and my...my sitter needs to get home." OK, that was a crock. Monica didn't need to go anywhere. Jessie had learned early on that talking about her sitter was a good way of telling a prospective date that she was a mother without the awkward *Do you want to date a single mom* conversation.

Brad glanced at her left hand.

"I'm not married," she informed him, saving him the trouble of asking.

He smiled again. No dimples, no spark to his brown eyes. At least she thought they were brown. It was hard to tell with the dim lighting.

"How old are your children?"

OK, he didn't run screaming. *Not a bad sign.*

"Child. I have a son. He's five."

Brad lifted his chin. "I'll bet he's adorable, just like his mother."

Hookay, time to go. "Thanks, he's the best." She scooted away, but only a couple of steps. She peeked over her shoulder, sure someone was watching her.

"Would you mind if I called you, Jessie? Maybe grab a cup of coffee or something?"

Jessie had to stop herself from saying no. *Why?* she asked herself. Jack.

Dammit.

"That might be nice," she found herself saying. "I like coffee."

He pulled out a pen from the inside of his suit pocket and a card. "I'm going out of town this week, but I'll be back the beginning of next."

Jessie rambled off her number, which Brad happily wrote down.

"I really should go."

He lifted his eyebrows and said, "I'll see you later, then."

"OK, bye."

Jessie pulled her wrap close and fought a chill as she stepped back into the busy ballroom. She walked about three yards before she noticed Jack's eyes on her. He glanced behind her, to the open patio doors, then back her way. Jessie had to force herself not to look behind her to see if Brad had walked in the room. She felt guilty as it was, which was stupid. She shouldn't feel bad at all.

She made her way to Jack's side, forcing a calm smile on her face.

"There you are," he said when she was within earshot.

"I needed to escape the cougar-lady after you left."

Jack was still watching the doorway.

Jessie shifted on her feet. "Um, Jack, I think I should work my way home." It was nearly midnight, and some of the guests had started to leave.

Something shifted in Jack's gaze.

Jessie turned toward the patio doors and noticed Brad watching the two of them. He nodded his head to her before turning to talk to one of the guests.

"Who's that?" Jack asked.

"Some guy."

"Some guy?"

"Yeah, we met outside. He said his name was Brad. Do you know him?"

Jack shook his head; all the while, he followed Brad's movements. "No, can't say as I do."

"He seemed nice enough." Because not telling him was eating her up inside, she blurted out, "He asked me for my number."

When Jack's head spun to her, she swallowed hard. Jack pissed wasn't a happy look. The sparkle she liked to see in his eyes when he smiled took on a whole new level when he was ticked. "Come on, Jack, you know I'm here to meet someone."

"Someone I know that will do good by you. That guy—"

"Brad."

"Brad, what kind of name is Brad? He looks like a lawyer."

Jessie was sure Jack meant that as an insult, but a lawyer spelled stability to her. "Brad is a perfectly normal name and I don't know what he does for a living."

"What do you know about him?"

"Nothing, really."

"And you just gave him your number? He could be some wacko. Why don't you let me do the matchmaking?"

Jessie laughed. "Stop it. I doubt he's a wacko."

Jack finally stopped staring at Brad and gazed down at her.

"Thank you for your concern, but I'm a big girl. My judgment in people isn't usually very far off." *As long as you weren't counting Rory or Mathew.*

"I don't know." He glanced back at Brad.

Jessie stood in front of him. "Don't go doing anything stupid when I leave. Harassing the guests will get you fired."

"You're leaving?"

"Yes, didn't you hear me?" No, of course he didn't. Testosterone truly poisoned men's brains.

"Is something wrong at home?"

"No, Danny is sleeping by now, I'm sure."

Jack set the tray he held down on a nearby table. "I'll walk you to your car."

"That isn't necessary."

"I insist." He placed his hand on the small of her back and pushed her to the door.

"What about work? Won't you get in trouble?"

Jack smiled. Some of it actually overtook his frown, and his eyes started to sparkle again. "I'm off at midnight anyway."

"It's not midnight yet."

He ignored her words and fell in step beside her. They dodged several people before making their way to the quiet lobby, then out into the entryway. "Did you valet park?"

"What do you think?" she asked as she turned toward the sidewalk, where self-parking was encouraged.

Jack nodded to the porter before catching up to her again. "You really don't need to walk me to my car."

"You can't accuse me of not being a gentleman."

No, she couldn't say that about him. Jessie weaved her way through the cars until she saw her old Toyota Celica. It looked lost among so many fancy, newer vehicles. It ran, and that's what counted.

"This is me," she announced as she fished her keys from her bag. She opened the door and tossed her purse in the passenger seat before turning to Jack. "Thanks again, Jack. For everything."

Jack shoved his hands in his pockets and rocked back on his heels. "It's nothing. I'm glad you came."

"I had fun. Be careful with the cougar-lady if you go back in there," she warned.

"Cougar-lady?"

"Yeah, the flashy woman with the shrimp. She looks like she eats waiters for breakfast, and she had you in her sights." Friends warn friends about bad choices for the bedroom, didn't they?

"You be careful with Braaad."

Jessie had to smirk at how Jack drew out Brad's name. "He said something about calling me next week. I'm not even sure I'll go out with him." Now why did she tell him that? Maybe because when he said the other man's name, he did so with a frown. Unease about the entire evening started to seep into her bones.

Jack stepped back. "Well, good night."

"Night, Jack."

Closing the door, Jessie was grateful for the easy exit. No drama, no fuss.

Famous last words.

When she twisted the key in the ignition, the car groaned, then moaned, then gave up trying to start altogether. She twisted it again, but the car made only a clicking noise in response.

Oh boy. Just what she needed. Jack watched her through the windshield. Jessie threw her hands in the air and tried to start it again.

Nothing.

Frustrated, she opened the door and swung her feet out.

"I don't get it; darn car wasn't acting up on the way over here."

"Pop the hood."

"You know about cars?" Jessie leaned in and pulled the lever.

Jack opened the hood, but the dimly lit parking lot made viewing the engine minimally possible at best. Jack fiddled with a couple of things anyway. "Try again."

Jessie did, but nothing changed. She pushed out of the car a second time and stood with Jack over the worn-out engine. "I hate this car. If it isn't one thing, it's another."

"How many miles are on it?" Jack asked as he stood and lowered the hood.

"Two hundred and some change."

"Thousand?"

"It's an old car, Jack."

He shook his head. "Here, give me the keys."

"Why?"

"I'll look at it in the morning, when I can see what's going on."

"You don't have to do that. I can have it towed. Have a mechanic check it out."

Jack kept his hand out, palm up. "Save your money, let me see if I can fix it."

Jessie vacillated over what she should do. "You've already done enough."

"Jessie, darlin', give me the keys."

She handed them over. "If it isn't simple, or it costs you money, I wanna pay for it."

Jack surveyed his greasy hands.

Jessie opened the back door and pulled out a package of wipes she kept there for her son. "Here," she said, pulling a couple wipes free and handing them to him.

Cleaning his hands, Jack thanked her. "Let's get you home."

"I can call my sister."

"And wake up your son? Come on." He grabbed her elbow and led her toward the front of the hotel. "A friend of mine borrowed my truck, so we're going to have to use a different car to take you home."

"You have a second car?"

"Not exactly."

Jessie walked faster to keep up with Jack's steps.

He stopped in front of the valet porter and smiled. "Hello, Wes."

Wes stood a little taller at the mention of his name. His eyes swept back and forth between her and Jack.

"Hello, Mr.—"

"Jack," he interrupted. "*Mister* is so formal."

"Jack," Wes said, his eyes continuing to shift almost as if he was nervous or something.

"Wes, it appears that one of the hotels guests is having a bit of difficulty with her car."

"Oh, I'm sorry, miss."

Jessie smiled and Jack continued to talk.

"Is there a car available?"

Wes took short steps as he walked up to his podium to check a book sitting on top of it. "There is, but Mr....Jack, it seems we are short a driver tonight. The other two are taking other people home at this time. No telling when they'll come back."

"That's fine. I can drive the lady home. Can you have one of your runners bring the car around?"

Wes's head bobbed up and down, his cheeks rippling slightly as he did. "Right away, sir."

Jessie grabbed Jack's arm and led him back a few feet. "What are you doing?"

"Getting you home."

"In a hotel car?"

"Relax, Jessie, we do this all the time."

First the dress, then the party, now this? Jack was sure to get canned, and it would all be her fault.

A few seconds later, a limousine pulled up into the circular drive and a porter popped out of the driver's seat. Wes opened the back door and extended his arm to Jessie.

Her feet wouldn't budge. This couldn't be the car Jack spoke of.

Jack pushed her forward. "Get in," he whispered under his breath. "Act like you do this all the time."

Jessie plastered a forced smile on her lips and quickly slid into the backseat of the stretch limo.

Bedded lighting roped around the doors and seats. Eight or nine people could easily fit into the space. A minibar sat below a flat-screen television; a moonroof displayed the stars twinkling above.

When the front door closed and Jack pushed a button, lowering the glass separating her space from his, Jessie hopped into the seat closer to him. "You know, Jack, you're crazy."

"Nice, isn't it?"

"Nice? It's amazing."

Jack pulled out of the drive and into what traffic milled about this late on a Saturday night.

"You were a guest at the hotel, and The Morrison takes care of their guests."

"I was an impostor, and you know it," she scolded as she ran her hand along the soft leather interior with a sigh.

"Darlin', there is nothing about you that's fake. Nothing!"

Chapter Five

Jack watched her from the rearview mirror. Jessie was grinning from ear to ear, pressing buttons and checking out the luxuries a limo provided. Adorable, there was no other way to describe it.

"Have you ever ridden in a limo before?" he asked, turning toward the airport.

"No, can't say as I have. I can't believe people live this way all the time."

"Some do."

"Can you imagine being able to do this anytime you wanted a ride?"

Jack swallowed and kept his eyes on the road. "I've met my share of silver-spooned kids...adults who have had access to limos all their lives. You'd be surprised how many of them are a lot like you and me." He glanced in the rearview mirror to gauge Jessie's reaction.

She shrugged her shoulders and petted the leather as if it were fur.

What would she think if she knew he had been riding in limos since before he was born? His dad couldn't be there for him all the time, and he'd needed to get back and forth to school. A driver had been assigned to him and Katie at an early age. When junior high started, Jack asked his dad if the driver could drive a "normal" car so the kids wouldn't get on him at school. Gaylord told him to cowboy up and set the kids right himself. He was a Morrison, and Morrisons had money. They spent it, too.

Jack took it upon himself to offer other kids rides all the time, ending the teasing and starting the party. In high school, Jack learned who his true friends were and who the moochers were. Mike, Tom, and Dean stuck; the others fell through the cracks.

"I guess anyone could get used to this. Lord knows I could."

Jack smiled and wished he could record her words to use later, when he could tell her the truth about himself. "Is there wine back there?"

"Champagne."

"If it's OK with you, I can park by the runways and we can watch the jets take off through the moonroof." The Morrison Hotel sat on the edge of the convention center, which was no more than four miles from the airport.

"Don't you have to get this back?"

"No, there's no one to drive her." Jack pulled down the dark street where other people parked to watch the jets take off. Ontario still wasn't overpopulated around the airport to the point where you couldn't watch.

He found a good spot, killed the engine, and joined Jessie in the back. Once seated, he flipped the switch and opened the roof.

"Wow." Her eyes sparkled.

Jack found the champagne and twisted off the metal covering. "Here," he said, standing up to poke his head through the roof. He popped the cork and it flew into the bush. The sparkling wine started to bubble over, and Jessie let out a tiny scream.

"Here." She thrust a towel at him before the beverage could spill onto the floor.

"Thank ya kindly, ma'am."

Jessie laughed again and handed him a couple of glasses once he sat back down.

Jack poured her a glass, then filled his own before returning the bottle to the chilled bucket. He lifted his glass and said, "To new friends."

"I can drink to that," Jessie said before clicking her glass to his. She sipped the wine and relaxed back into the seat next to him. Her gaze moved to the roof to catch the bottom view of a jet taking off. "You know, I've seen people park here all the time, but I never once thought to do it myself."

"It's amazing how they keep those hunks of metal up in the air."

"I don't get it, either. I'm surprised there aren't more problems with them."

"It's still the safest way to travel," Jack said.

"I wouldn't know. I've only been on a plane once."

"Really?" That was hard to believe.

"I was twelve; Monica, my sister, was nine. Mom met some guy who told her he was visiting from Seattle. She'd fallen head over heels for him in the course of two weeks during the summer."

"I take it your mom's divorced."

"A few times over," Jessie told him, without even a hint of a frown on her face. She was obviously used to her mom's ways. "Anyway, this guy gave her a line about how he'd love to be with her and us kids, but he couldn't live in Southern California. He had a business in Seattle to run anyway. He couldn't ask her to leave here and drag us girls up north…blah, blah, blah."

"Then what?"

"Mom bought us tickets, packed our bags, and took us to Seattle." She shook her head at the memory.

"I take it that didn't go over with Mr. Blowhard."

"No. Mr. Blowhard's wife wasn't too fond of opening the door and finding us there."

"Ouch."

"Monica and I never even had a chance to feel the Pacific Northwest rain they always complain about. Mom took us to the airport, where we stayed for nearly two days until we could get a flight home."

"Two days? Why so long?"

"My mother didn't have the foresight to buy round-trip tickets or even have enough money to buy our way home. A friend of hers wired money, but we still had to wait on standby in the middle of the night to catch a cheap flight. It was a mess."

"Kind of takes the fun out of flying," he told her.

Jessie sipped her wine again. "What about you? Your parents still married?"

"Ah, no."

"You don't sound too sure."

"Well, my mom took off when I was in my early teens. She kept in touch, in her own way—a phone call here, a letter there. She kept my dad on the hook until my sister graduated high school, then she filed for a divorce." He remembered that day. "It was June. The weather in Texas was starting to heat up. My dad was working too many hours. Then one day I walked in and found my dad sitting in the den, drinking whiskey."

"That doesn't sound too bad."

"It was one in the afternoon on a Wednesday."

"Oh. I take it that was out of character for your father."

Jack saw true concern lace Jessie's features when he glanced over at her. "My dad works hard," he said in a low voice.

"It sounds like you admire your father a lot."

"I do. He worked hard and managed two kids without the help of a mom. When my mom was around, he worked harder than anyone I knew. We didn't see him very much, which might be why she left him. I don't know. I don't remember her complaining. Once she left, he was around more. He took taking care of my sister and me to another level. A better level. Anyway, Mom filed for a divorce, and now we exchange Christmas cards. Sometimes not even that." Last year she was living in Italy with a guy named Pierre or some other god-awful name.

"Your dad took it hard, didn't he?" Jessie set her glass aside and sat farther back in the seat.

"I think he always wanted her back. Even after leaving him for all those years, he would have taken her back without even an ounce of explanation as to why she left." Which was sad beyond words. Why anyone would worship his mother was beyond any reason that Jack could see.

"Did your dad ever try to explain what happened with them? Why she left?"

"No. He's never talked about it. The only thing I came up with is that she didn't love him. He took care of her financially; she didn't really want for anything. They didn't fight. But what did I know…I was a kid."

"Has your father remarried?"

Jack shook his head. "No."

"He must still love your mom."

He thought so, too. He knew now it had been a one-way love from the beginning.

"If it makes you feel any better, I don't even get a card from my dad at Christmas." Jessie shifted in her seat, kicked her shoes off, and tucked her legs under her.

"Really?"

"Not a word since he walked out on us."

"Why did he leave?"

Jessie's eyes gazed beyond the moonroof as she spoke, her thoughts deep in the past. "He wanted nothing to do with parenthood or monogamy. My mom said he cheated on her from the beginning, but she was willing to look beyond it."

"Why would any woman look beyond that?"

"Having two kids to feed makes women do all kinds of things. But I'm sure she would have buckled eventually. Anyway, Mom filed for divorce and pinned him down long enough to get the papers signed. After that, he was gone."

When Jessie shivered, Jack pressed the button and closed the moonroof. He found a switch and clicked on the seat heaters. "Was that hard on her?"

Jessie shrugged. "I'm sure it was. But she quickly replaced him with husband number two, then three. Lately she just shacks up with them long enough until the new wears off, then finds another."

"That's cold," he said.

"It's the truth. She lives just outside of Fontana, but my sister would rather live with me and Danny than deal with her drama all the time."

Jack stretched his arm out along the back of the seat. "That's just smart. No one needs that kind of instability in their life."

"True."

"You and your sister are close, then?"

Jessie brushed away a lock of hair that had fallen in her eyes. "Very. What about you and your sister...close?"

"We get along, but I wouldn't say we're close. She's wild, doesn't want to grow up."

Jessie laughed. "This from the guy I met coming back from a weekend in Vegas with his buddies, 'borrowed' this evening gown and shoes for a near stranger, and sneaked the hotel's limo to give a girl a ride home. If you're calling her wild, I think it runs in the family."

Jack tossed his head back, laughing. He guessed he didn't exactly look like a choirboy in Jessie's eyes. "Since you put it that way..."

"Do you see your family during the holidays? I'm guessing you didn't for Thanksgiving since you're still here."

"I try and get home, but it doesn't always work out. What about you? Did you see your mom on Thanksgiving?"

"Couldn't avoid it. When Renee Effinger—that's my mom's name—invites you, you better go. If you don't, be prepared for some serious guilt the next time you see her. It didn't matter that I'd worked the morning before, didn't matter that none of us like her cooking, you'd better come."

"I guess that means you'll be with her over Christmas."

"Probably. Danny thinks she's funny. It's my sister and me that she rubs wrong. Everyone else loves her. Heck, you'd adore her." Jessie leaned her head forward onto her bent elbow resting on the back of the seat.

"Has she done anything awful?"

"No, not really. She tried her best raising us. Which isn't easy when there's only one income. I know that more than anybody does. I think maybe I'm ticked at her for not finding one guy and sticking with him. How hard can that be? Thousands of people manage to stay in a marriage for years and years. Why can't she?"

Jack felt her sadness and wanted to wipe it clean off her plate. "Thousands of people get divorced, too."

"I know. I guess I just want to see her settled. Safe."

"Stability is important to you." Now he understood her desire for a rich husband. Jessie thought that with money came stability. Hell, his parents' relationship proved her wrong. There were no guarantees, even when one of the parties was hopelessly in love with the other.

"It is."

"I understand. I remember waking on Christmas every year, dreaming that my mom was there. She'd tell us about some horrible thing that kept her away and how she wished she had been with us."

"But she never came."

Jack shook his head and cleared his throat. "Never."

Jessie reached over and covered his hand with hers. "Life sucks that way."

He watched her hand playing with his, liked the feel of it. "Enough of memory lane. What about your future, Jessie...what is your last name?"

"Mann, Jessie Mann."

"What do you see yourself doing in five years?"

Her face lit up and Jack was glad he changed the subject. "I don't know. I want to go back to school, like I said, maybe get into some type of event coordinating job."

"You said something about being a wedding planner."

"Not that I know anything about weddings. My mom's marriages at the county clerk's office don't count. But yeah, I'd love to help brides with what is supposed to be the happiest day of their lives." Jessie still rubbed her fingers over his. He wondered if she realized what she was doing.

"You do appreciate how weird that sounds after learning about all your mom's failed marriages."

"That doesn't mean I don't believe in marriage. I mean a real marriage, not the temporary state my mom plays in. I can plan more than weddings. There are anniversary parties, birthdays, corporate events. There's all kinds of things an event planner puts together."

"I'll have to find out what the lady at the hotel did to get her job."

"I'd love to know."

"I'll ask her for you."

She smiled. "Thanks. What about you, Jack, where do you see yourself in five years?"

Jack turned her palm over and rubbed the inside with his thumb. "I like the hotel business."

"You want to manage a hotel?"

"Kinda. I want to start a new concept in hotels. One geared for the typical family, with the typical family budget. Nothing over-the-top or high-end."

Jessie glanced around the inside of the limousine. "Nothing with limos and caviar?"

"That wouldn't be cost-effective, but minivans and car seats would work. I want to cater to the middle class, but give them some of the same perks The Morrison does."

"What kind of perks?" She leaned in a little while she listened.

"Room service with food geared for the family. Babysitting, dog sitting, even a spa priced right." That was his concept for the hotel he was in Ontario to build. "I'd place every hotel around airports, major family vacation destinations."

"So you want to start a chain of them, not just one? Those are some serious goals, Jack."

Jack cautioned himself about opening up to Jessie. "I'd start with one, see what works, what doesn't, then revise and go forward with the profits from the first hotel and build the next."

"You're talking massive capital, investors."

"I've been saving." Which was true.

"What will you name your hotel?" She was smiling, and not in a mocking, *Yeah, sure you'll do that...one day* kind of way, but in a sincere, *Here's hoping you do make it* kind of way.

"More for Less."

Jessie held back a laugh.

"What? You don't like it?"

"Well, 'More' is a rip from Morrison, isn't it?"

"My friends do call me Jack Moore."

She really didn't like the name. "Still, 'More for Less.' It sounds...I don't know, cheap. Like Pick 'n Save."

"It will be priced cheap, compared to The Morrison anyway."

She sat taller. "The name needs to be something people will brag about. Think of Nordstrom and Nordstrom Rack. Both sell Nordstrom clothing, but one is the cast-off store. If you had an in with The Morrison, I'd suggest you call your place 'Morrison West' or something like that. Or name it something completely ambiguous like 'Jack's Place.'"

Jack scratched his head and purposely didn't say anything about her comment concerning an *in* with The Morrison. "Jack's Place sounds like a bar to me."

Jessie waved her free hand at him while she spoke. "Or a friend's place. Think about it: *We're going to Disneyland and we're staying at Jack's Place.* Then again, *We're going to Sea World and we're staying at More for Less.* Do you see what I mean? The one sounds like a great time, the other sounds like a budget vacation with hard beds and leaky roofs."

Jack scratched his jaw. "I never thought of it like that." He wondered if anyone on his planning team thought the same thing but didn't want to reveal their concerns because More for Less was his brainchild. He definitely needed to talk to the marketing department on Monday.

Jack watched her lips as she spoke. "You have time to think about the name. It will take years and lots of connections before anyone like us can open up such a place."

Guilt sucker punched him hard in the gut. Jessie really had no earthly idea who he was or his net worth. If she did know who he really was, would she have been so open and honest with him? Probably not.

Jessie hid a yawn behind her hand and smiled when he caught her eyes. She glanced at their hands, both of which were rolling tiny circles with the other. Her hand skidded away when she realized it was engaged in a little mindless flirting.

Jack missed her touch instantly, but didn't say a word about it. "I better get you home."

Nodding, Jessie said, "Yeah. It's late."

Only he didn't want to take her home. He wanted to keep her up late, talking, and then a little kissing, then maybe some more touching. Her pink lips would melt against his, he thought. *Head out of the gutter, Jack. You'll blow it if you come on too strong.*

Ignoring his urges, he opened the door and stepped out.

"I'll ride in front with you, if that's OK," she said after slipping her shoes back on and following him through the door.

"Are you sure? It's much nicer back here."

"It's not as much fun when you're by yourself."

Conceding, Jack helped her into the passenger's seat and walked around the car to take the driver's.

Jessie pointed out which road to take to her apartment.

"When do you work again?" Jack asked.

"I'm off tomorrow, then on for three. If my car needs something big, my sister can take me back and forth. Do you have any idea what's wrong with it?"

"Might be your starter. I'll check it out in the morning." Jack glanced over at her as she opened her purse and took out a pen and a piece of paper.

"Here's my number. Call me and let me know what it's going to cost me."

"Friends don't charge friends for favors," he told her.

"You've done enough already."

She hadn't seen anything...yet.

Jessie placed the paper with her phone number in the cubby that divided the seats. "I'll have the dress dry cleaned and have it ready to go back to the store."

"You can keep it." He switched lanes as he spoke.

"Right, that would be stealing, not borrowing."

Jessie was too good for that. Jack had no choice but to hide the fact that he'd paid for the dress.

"I don't think anyone would notice."

"I would."

Pushing her to keep the dress was out of the question. He glanced her way and noticed the sparkle dangling from her ears. "I bought the earrings. So don't put those back in the box. Those you can keep."

Her slender fingers touched the elegant diamonds, and a smile touched her lips. "You bought them?"

"I thought they would look great on you." He thought of the knockoff pair in his room at the hotel. Nordstrom versus Nordstrom Rack. There simply wasn't a substitution.

"You didn't have to do that."

"I wanted to. Consider it an early Christmas gift." One of many, he hoped.

"I trust it didn't cost you a lot."

He shot her a frown. "It's impolite to ask what someone spent on a gift."

Jessie laid her hand on his arm. "Thanks, Jack. You shouldn't have, but thanks."

They drove the rest of the way in comfortable silence. It was nearly two in the morning when they pulled up to her apartment building.

"I can make it from here," she told him.

Jack ignored her and opened his door. "In Texas, a man never lets a lady walk to her door alone. Especially at night." Besides, how would he kiss her if he didn't walk her home?

She laughed, a warm, inviting sound that pulled on Jack's heartstrings.

"I don't want to tick off all the men in Texas."

"Good."

After opening her door and helping her out of the car, Jack let her lead the way to her apartment door. The floral scent of her perfume followed her down the hall. He noted the number on her door for future use.

Tresses of her hair draped over her slender neck as she glanced at her door.

"This is me," she said as she turned toward him.

Jack stood close, close enough to see surprise in her eyes at his being there. She didn't back away. When she caught her lip between her teeth, Jack's pulse shot high. Jessie's gaze slid from his eyes to his lips, inadvertently inviting his kiss.

He didn't give her a chance to protest.

Jack weaved his hand behind her head and lowered his mouth to hers. The simmering flame that had been on all night with her nearness grew into an inferno within seconds.

Jessie didn't pull away.

He captured her around her slim waist and held her closer.

She moaned and tilted her head a little more. He slipped his tongue between her lips and melted into her. Jack committed every sensation he felt, from how she smelled and how she smiled to how her lips slid over his, into his memory. Her hand moved to his arm; her fingers kneaded his flesh. Timid strokes of her tongue against his proved her attraction, her feelings toward him, more than any of her words could.

This was more than friendship, he thought.

This is what poets write about.

Jack wanted more, so much more than a stolen kiss at her apartment door.

The door behind her suddenly flew open, causing Jessie to fall back. Had Jack not been holding her, she probably would have ended up on her butt.

Jack's eyes snapped open and saw the shocked expression from both Jessie and the woman who had to be her sister, Monica.

"Oh, I'm sorry. So sorry." Monica's eyes were wide. Her hands covered her reddening cheeks.

Jessie stepped away from him. Her fingertips ran along her swollen lower lip. The glow of her cheeks was this side of delectable.

"It's OK. Jack was just leaving," Jessie finally spoke.

He'd better do so quickly, before Jessie started to regret their shared kiss. "I'll call you tomorrow."

Blowing out a sigh, Jessie chewed on her lower lip. "Right. My car. OK, I'll talk to you tomorrow."

"Good night, Jessica," he said as he turned and left both stunned women at the door.

Before he rounded the corner of the hall, he heard Monica giggle and say, "Oh my God. Is that Jack?"

Jack stood a little taller, his grin a little bigger.

Chapter Six

"That *was* Jack, right? Holy shit, is he cute or what?" Monica practically squealed when she spoke.

"That was Jack." *Lethal lips and all.* Oh man, his kiss had been to die for. Knock-her-on-her-butt delicious. And completely wrong. "Dammit. That shouldn't have happened."

"What shouldn't have happened?" Monica pulled Jessie down on the bed that doubled as a couch.

"That kiss. I shouldn't have…he shouldn't have." *I should have pulled away, reminded him that he's bad for me.*

"Is he a bad kisser?" Monica tucked her feet under herself Indian style and rubbed her hands together.

"He's an amazing kisser, but I shouldn't have let him."

"Why on earth not? He's gorgeous, and that accent…geez, makes me a big pile of goo just thinking about it."

"You know how I feel about dreamers, Monica. He's a waiter at The Morrison."

"So? You wait tables, too. You both have that in common."

Jessie rolled her eyes. "Great, so we'll save money so one day we might actually be able to buy a decent car that we'd have to share in order to get back and forth to our go-nowhere jobs. It wouldn't work." Falling for someone like Jack would break her heart. Then what? She'd end up like her mother, hopping from one man to another.

No, the kiss was a mistake. The next time Jessie saw him she'd set him straight, make him promise to keep his distance, or their friendship needed to end. She liked talking to him, listening to his plans, but kissing her needed to be something they did once.

One amazing time…but only once.

Jessie glanced at her sister and pushed off the sofa bed. "I'm beat."

"But I want to hear more about this date."

"It wasn't a date."

"He drove you home."

"That's because my car wouldn't start," she said, explaining the situation.

"He kissed you at the door, and it's almost three in the morning."

"We talked in the back of the limo, watched the planes take off."

"You were in a limo?"

Oh boy, not the information her sister needed to hear if Jessie was going to get any sleep before her son woke her up. "The hotel limo. Jack finagled it to give me a ride home. It wasn't a date."

"Sounds like a date to me."

Jessie had spent the whole night in Jack's presence, driven home with the guy, talked about their past, their futures. That kiss wouldn't be forgotten any time soon. "Not *quite* a date."

Monica pushed in between the covers of her bed with a catty smile. "If what I saw is 'not quite dating,' I want some." She air quoted the dating statement and then turned off the light.

"Good night, Mo."

"Night, sis. Have amazing, 'not quite kissing' dreams."

Jessie tossed a pillow at her. "Brat."

"If you want my advice, I'd suggest you send this wreck to its grave." Max Harper owned a small auto shop a few blocks from the hotel. He had happily towed Jessie's car and squeezed in time to work on it. Jack had met Max prior to Dean's bachelor party. He had wanted his truck road-ready, and Max had taken care of him.

"Can't do it," Jack told him. "The lady who owns it can't afford to dump this quite yet."

Max wiped his hands with a shop rag and pulled a pencil from his blue shirt. "I can get it up and running without too much fuss. Needs a new starter."

"It needs more than a starter." Jack noticed the worn-out belts, the overheating radiator.

"It needs to collect dust in a junkyard. But if you insist on limping her along, I'll get you out the door today with a starter."

"The battery looks ancient," Jack told him.

"It still has a charge, but I'd be happy to replace it."

"Do that."

Max moved around the car and to the back of the shop to gather parts.

The need to fix every possible problem with the car made Jack's skin itch. The thought of Jessie driving around town or breaking down at night…

"You know what I don't get?" Max asked.

"No, what's that?"

"How someone with your money is driving around in crap like this. No offense." Max was pushing sixty, weighed forty more pounds than he should, breathed too heavy for a man his age, and was honest to a fault. Dean had recommended the man and Jack knew now why. Even with the knowledge of Jack's deep pockets, Max didn't try and sell him more than he needed. Even now, as the two of them stared at the bleak engine in tandem, both of them agreeing the car should be shot, Max didn't push.

And he didn't hold his tongue, either.

"It's not mine, and like I said, I'm helping out a friend."

"You would help her by getting her something reliable. Not all mechanics are like me. And unless the woman knows something about basic auto repair, she'll end up overspending every time the car needs so much as an oil change. Hell, the mechanic wouldn't even have to be unethical working on this. He'd just have to start at one end and work his way to the other to find issues."

Didn't Jack know it.

But he couldn't tell Jessie that someone had left a new car at the hotel and she could keep it. No, he'd have to work in something that big a little differently.

"I couldn't agree with you more, Max. Just get her back up and running. If you can replace a few things my lady friend won't notice, by all means do it. If she notices that I've spent money on it, she'll insist on paying me." As it was, Jack worried about telling her he'd taken it to a mechanic. A friend working on the car was one thing...quite another to hire someone to do the job. But if he was put to the test at some point, he might find that lie hard to continue. No, he'd tell her someone had helped him if he had to.

He needed to keep the web of lies as thin as possible.

"A woman who doesn't want you to spend money on her? Seriously? I didn't think they existed."

Jack offered a smile. His did.

It was after noon when Jack finally picked up the phone and called Jessie. Although he'd thought of her all day it wasn't until he heard her chipper voice that he was reminded of their kiss all over again. The kiss to end all kisses. The mating of lips that promised amazing things should they ever find the right time to touch in other places.

Jack knew Jessie would be miffed about the kiss, so he planned on acting as if it hadn't happened unless she said something about it. He wouldn't apologize for something he wasn't sorry for and something he knew she'd enjoyed just as much as he did.

"Hey, darlin', how did you sleep?" He'd tossed and turned all night, but he wasn't about to tell her that and give her ammunition to hang up the phone.

"Hey, Jack. I-I, ah, slept good, fine." Her voice wavered, making him wonder if she spoke the truth.

"I should have your car up and running in the hour. Are you going to be home so I can drop it off?"

"Actually, I was taking Danny to the park around the corner so he can play with some of his friends."

Even better. "I can bring it to you there. What's the name of the park?"

She told him, then added, "You don't have to do this. I can get Monica to drive me over to the hotel to pick it up."

Only the car wasn't at the hotel. It was with a mechanic at a shop, getting a new starter and a new battery, an oil change, air filter…"Not a problem."

"You sure?"

"Jessie, please. I might not be able to help with much, but I can do this." The lie tasted sour on his tongue, but he blurted it out all the same.

"What was the problem?"

"The starter, like I thought. I, ah, just had to find the part."

"Was it a hassle?"

"No," he said too quickly. After a breath he added, "There's a place around the corner from the hotel that sells parts. It's just gonna take a little longer to get it in and clean up. You'll still be at the park in an hour?"

Jessie laughed. "Danny would make me stay there until dark if he could. We'll be there."

"I'll see you in an hour." Jack said good-bye and hung up.

———

A late November bite in the air was what Jessie referred to as a sweater-without-a-coat day. The sun was warm, but the air held a tiny nip. The kids filled the park while their parents sat on the benches next to the playground equipment and watched them play.

Danny concocted a game of follow the leader with three other boys. The kids led one another up and down the slides, hopped over the swings, and spun in circles in the sand. Within ten minutes of playing in the park, Danny was laughing, dirty, and jumping around. Days like this made her happy with her choice about working graveyard. She didn't miss out on her son's day-to-day life so long as she worked during his sleeping hours.

It didn't always work that way. Sometimes when he came down with a cold or had a nightmare, she missed being there to care for him, but Monica handled those times like a pro. If ever Danny really needed her, Jessie called in sick or would come home. By the time she was able to manage a day job, Danny would be spending his days in school, and Jessie could work while he was there. That was the plan, anyway.

"Hey, darlin'." Jack's voice purred behind her ear. She turned around and caught his grinning face only a few inches from hers. She pulled back, just in case he thought he was going to greet her with a kiss.

"Hey."

She was sitting on the edge of a picnic table and decided to slide between the seat and the table to further the distance from him. Without a glance, Jack sat opposite her.

He dangled her keys from his fingertips. "All fixed."

"So…it was the starter." She gathered the keys in her palm, grazing his hand in the process. That innocent touch reminded her of their fondling fingers the night before. Even holding hands with the cowboy held appeal.

His hat sat firmly in place. His button-up shirt covered his muscular arms that had held her so close the night before, and she remembered the hardness of his chest and the sound of his sigh when she dropped her inhibitions and allowed the kiss to continue. His lips were just as plump as the night before. The sweater she wore suddenly felt hot. Jessie shook her head and looked behind her to see where Danny was.

"Your starter was fried."

"Was that expensive?" She reached for her purse sitting beside her.

"A friend owed me a favor."

"So you had to have someone else do the work?"

"Had to; Max had the parts, I didn't."

How silly of her. Of course Jack didn't have the parts. She removed her checkbook, but Jack covered her hand with his.

"Max owed me a favor, Jessie. No charge."

"I can't let you do that."

"You have to," he insisted.

"What if you need Max's help for your truck? You'll have used your get-out-of-jail-free card for me." Jessie shook off his hand and started to write out a check.

"I'm not taking your money."

"You're right, you're not. You're giving it to Max. Now, how much does an average starter cost?"

Jack ignored her and peered over her shoulder at the kids playing on the playground. "Which one is Danny?"

"You're changing the subject."

He winked at her. A smile played on his lips. He wasn't going to tell her what it cost, wouldn't take the money willingly. Jessie knew she'd have to find another way to pay him back. She refused to mooch off someone's goodwill.

"He's five, right?"

"How much, Jack?" she asked, trying one last time.

"Not gonna happen, Jessie," he fired back with a grin.

The man was impossible. She shoved her checkbook back in her purse. "This isn't over."

"Does your son have your color hair?"

Again, changing the subject and blowing off her words. Brat. He and Monica would get along great.

Swiveling in her seat, Jessie pointed out her son. "See the boys playing follow the leader?"

"Yeah."

"He's the one in front, with the striped sweatshirt."

Jack's face lit up. "He looks like you."

"I think so, too."

Danny's head popped up to look over at her, then glanced beyond her to Jack. He said something to his friends before running her way.

"Hey, Mommy." Jessie wiped his hair out of his eyes. He needed it cut.

"Hey, buddy."

"Who's that?" he asked, pointing at Jack.

"This is a friend of mine. His name is Jack. Jack, this is Danny." It was strange watching the play of emotions stream over her son's face. He went from curious to a little scared in a few seconds.

"Howdy, Danny." Jack tilted his hat toward her son.

Danny's eyes grew wide. "Are you a real cowboy? Do you ride a horse and everything?"

"I'm from Texas and have been known to ride a horse on occasion," Jack told him with a tad more Texas in his voice.

Jessie sent him a *Don't encourage him* look, or at least she hoped he understood her body language.

"I want to ride a horse, but Mom says it's dangerous."

"People fall off horses and get hurt all the time," Jessie told him.

"I fell from my scooter; it didn't hurt very bad."

"Horses are a lot farther off the ground," Jack told him.

Good, Jessie thought, he was watching his words.

"But riding is easy to do and not dangerous at all with the right horse."

Jessie beamed Jack an angry look. "We don't know anyone with any kind of horse, so there's no need to get excited about something that isn't going to happen."

Jack met her gaze. "Actually, my dad lives on a ranch in Texas. He has lots of horses, young and old."

Jessie pressed her lips together. "We aren't in Texas."

"Could we go sometime, to your dad's ranch?" Danny asked.

"I think that's a great idea." Jack kept looking at Danny and ignored Jessie's facial expressions. "Maybe someday we can do that."

Danny tugged on Jessie's sweater until she lowered her eyes to his. "Wouldn't that be fun?"

"Texas is a long way away, Danny. You'll have to settle for the pony rides at the fair for now."

Disappointed, Danny turned toward his friends on the playground. "Hey, I wanna play," he called to the kids and then ran over to them.

"Why did you do that?" Jessie asked Jack the minute Danny was out of hearing range.

"Do what?"

"Encourage him to visit your dad's ranch? You know I can't afford a trip to Texas."

Jack actually started to look guilty. Which was good, considering the position he'd put her in. Disappointing Danny happened on a daily basis, from the toys she couldn't afford to the backyard he didn't have to play in. Promising pony rides in Texas was just mean.

"He seemed so excited."

"He's five. He gets excited about bubbles."

"Texas is a three-day drive from here," he told her.

Jessie crossed her arms over her chest. "Stop. OK. You know I can't go. Between taking time off work, the cost of driving... Maybe in the five-year plan that would be doable, but it isn't right now. I'll be lucky if I can scrape enough together to give Danny any Christmas at all. A trip to Texas isn't something I can make happen." Jessie hated to admit it, but things were too tight for words. She'd even considered taking on a part-time job, but that would mess up the schedule she and Monica had worked out. All the fun things in life would just have to wait.

Jack looked as if he wanted to say something, something profound, but instead he lowered his gaze and offered an apology. "I'm sorry."

The words sounded as if they were new to him, so Jessie didn't push it. "It's OK. I know you didn't mean any harm."

"No, it's not OK. I should have kept my mouth shut."

Jessie eased the tension with a smile. "Your dad really has a ranch?"

"Texas is a big state; lots of people have land there."

"Seems like no one in California has land, outside of the farmers midstate. Heck, I'd settle for a yard and a fence." She couldn't even get a dog for Danny if she wanted to.

"I have a feeling one day you'll get everything you want."

Jack. The ever-optimistic dreamer. Cute, great kisser, selfless, giving, ambitious, and, she needed to add again, dreamer. Dreamers fluttered to a different flower when the need hit.

"Listen, Jack, about last night..." Jessie looked away from his gray eyes to study a couple of ants that had found a crumb on the table to attack. "That shouldn't have happened."

"What, the ride in the limousine? I brought it back, no one even missed it."

Jessie's shoulders slumped. Darn the man, he wasn't going to make this easy. "Not the limo. You know that's not what I'm talking about."

"Oh," he said, acting surprised. "You mean that amazing kiss."

She shushed him and took in the people around them to see if anyone was listening to their conversation. "It was a mistake."

"It didn't feel like a mistake to me."

Although she knew she probably should tell him it felt wrong, Jessie knew he'd see right through her, call her out on a blatant lie. His kiss had been amazing. She-couldn't-fall-asleep-for-hours-after-going-to-bed amazing. "It can't happen again."

Jessie met his eyes long enough to see the smirk on his face. "This isn't funny, Jack. I told you before I can't date you."

"Right, and why is that again?"

"You know perfectly well why. You're a dreamer, Jack. You have great plans for a bright future, and something tells me you'll make all those lofty goals a reality...someday. But right now, you're still dreaming. Maybe if it was just me, if Danny..." She shot a glance over her shoulder to make certain Danny didn't hear her. He played on the other end of the playground, oblivious to her and Jack. "If I didn't have to consider my son, then maybe you and I could have dated, seen if we were good for each other. When you're a parent, and all your decisions affect another human being, you have to be smart about who you date."

The smirk faded from Jack's face. His brows pitched together briefly. "What is it you're afraid of, Jessie?" he asked softly.

"My mom said once, don't date anyone you don't see yourself falling in love with. I didn't listen to her advice when I was a teenager, and Danny is the result. I love him more than anything on this earth, wouldn't change him in my life for the world. But I can't do it again. It wouldn't be fair to him, or me. You're a great guy, Jack, but we need to just be friends. Friends who don't kiss. I'm sorry, but that's the way it has to be." So why did saying the words hurt already?

Jack leaned his elbows on the table and placed his head in his palms. "Nothing I can say will change your mind?"

"No. Please understand. I'd like to still be friends."

Rubbing his jaw, Jack let himself smile again. "I can't say I like it, but I understand."

She sighed. "So we're good?"

A hint of mischief sparkled in his eyes when he said, "Darlin', we're better than good. I've got to go, but I'll be in touch."

"I should have the dress ready to go back by Tuesday. I can drop it off at the hotel."

He waved a hand and said, "That isn't necessary. I'll stop by the diner. You said you worked on Tuesday, right?"

"Right."

He unfolded from the bench. "I'll come by. If something comes up, I'll call you."

"Sounds good to me."

Jack looked as if he wanted to say something else, but decided against it. "Have a nice day off, Jessie."

"Thanks, you too."

Then he was gone. Jessie watched his cute, denim-clad ass walking in the opposite direction. No argument, no counterpoints for trying to talk her into dating him. Nothing.

She should have been happy with how quickly he agreed to a platonic relationship, but somehow she wasn't. Maybe the kiss had affected only her in a profound *You'll never find another guy to kiss you like that* way.

Maybe Jack wasn't all that into her.

Jessie forced her gaze to fall on her son and to stop staring at the retreating man. Before she could turn in her seat, Jack glanced over his shoulder and caught her staring at him.

Without a doubt, there would be a smirk, hidden in the shadow cast by his hat, all over his face.

Chapter Seven

Jack sat in meetings most of Monday and half of Tuesday. Eric Richardson, his marketing manager of the Southern California region, ran with the suggestion of renaming Jack's new chain of hotels.

When Jack asked Eric why he didn't speak up earlier about his reservations, Eric told him he didn't want to step on Jack's ego since the new hotels had his name in the title.

"Step on it next time," Jack told him. "We pay you to know how to market what we come up with. If the name will keep people from coming, then these hotels will never get off the ground."

Eric sat opposite Jack in one of the conference rooms on the main floor. Eric was much younger than Jack and was probably worried about his job if he became too disagreeable. Jack had had to deal with those emotions from employees for years. It usually took some time and effort to help them relax and feel safe enough in their jobs to offer what they really felt.

"I'll remind you about this conversation next time," Eric promised.

"As you should. Have you considered a different name?"

Eric shrugged. "I haven't given it much thought. I'll put picking a new name for the hotel at the top of my list."

Jack thought of Jessie and her ideas. "What about the Morrison East?"

Eric wrinkled his nose. "Well, that might be confusing to our guests here out west."

"Jack's Place."

"Almost too casual, but I like that direction more. Oh." Eric shot up in his chair. "How about the Morrison Family Inn?"

Jack smoothed his suit jacket against his chest as he considered the title. "I like that. Gives people the Morrison name, a name associated with quality and leaders in the hotel business across the nation, but puts in the family twist. I think that will work."

"Shall I pencil that in?"

"Do it, but let's run a few market tests to determine if the public will see this the way we do."

Eric nodded. "I'll have my assistant get on this when I get back to my office."

"Get back to me next week on the results."

Eric stood and folded his papers before shoving them into his briefcase. "If there isn't anything else you need, I'll go ahead and return to San Francisco and meet with you before Christmas for the board meeting."

Jack stood and shook the other man's hand. "We'll see you then. Thanks for coming all the way down here."

"My pleasure."

"And Eric?"

He turned toward Jack.

"In the future, speak up. I'm not going to can you if your ideas differ from mine."

Eric nodded. "With the economy the way it's been, everyone fears for their jobs."

Jack understood his concerns. The hotels had gone through a couple of rounds of layoffs since the recession. The budget-minded hotel idea had bloomed because of the bad economy.

"The Morrison hotels are riding the storm. I don't foresee any more layoffs." It was the best Jack could do. He couldn't promise the man he'd always have a job, but he wanted him at ease enough to offer insightful ideas on something as important as the name of a hotel.

"Thank you, Mr. Morrison."

"Safe flight home."

As Eric left the room, Jack stacked his market analysis papers together and placed them in his briefcase. His cell phone in his pocket rang as he headed out of the room.

Recognizing the number, Jack answered with a greeting. "Hey, Mike."

"Good, you're answering." His friend's frazzled voice turned Jack's smile to a frown.

"What's up?"

"It's Dean. Has he called you?"

"Haven't spoken to him since Vegas. The construction end of the new hotels is a ways off, so I didn't think I'd hear from him for a while. Why?" Jack set his briefcase back down. Dean owned and operated a major western United States construction company that Jack planned to use to build the family inns. Dean was going to take on the oversight of the project personally.

"Damn. I thought he'd have called one of us."

"What's going on? Is he OK?" Jack rubbed a hand over his face and sat forward in his chair.

"Probably not. Maggie called off the wedding."

Of all the things he expected to come out of Mike's mouth, Maggie and Dean's engagement ending wasn't one of them. "Oh man. Dean must be devastated." For better or for worse, Dean had adored Maggie.

"He's disappeared."

"Do you know what happened? Why did she call it off?" Jack stood and paced the room. Dean was his best friend, and he had no idea what was happening with him. Damn, what kind of friend was that?

"No idea."

"Never mind, that isn't my business. Where do you think Dean went?" Jack could think of a few places to check out. Places they would escape to during Dean's early years in Southern California.

"He could be anywhere. He left on his motorcycle, according to Maggie."

Being pissed on a motorcycle never ended well. Dammit! "I thought he sold the motorcycle."

"Apparently not. Anyway, I don't think he went far. Maybe up to Arrowhead or possibly Mammoth."

"It's December. Mammoth is covered in snow." Dean could be wild, but he wasn't reckless. "I'll pick you up in the hour. We'll head out and find him."

"You read my mind, bro."

Jack hung up the phone, thinking about his friend. Dean would be distraught. Probably didn't want company, but if left alone, he might find himself drinking too much and having an accident. Jack and Mike could keep him safe while he wallowed for a few days.

Up in his suite, Jack tossed his case aside and stepped into his bedroom to change his clothes. Once he'd dressed down into jeans and a button-up plaid shirt, he plopped his hat on his head and started for the door.

"Damn," he said, thinking of Jessie. He picked up his phone and dialed her number.

She answered on the second ring. "Hello?"

Her voice was honey to his ears. "Hey, Jessie, it's Jack."

"Hi."

"Listen, I'm not going to be by the restaurant tonight. Something came up."

"Oh." Was that disappointment in her voice?

Jack smiled.

"I hope everything's OK."

"I'm not sure. Remember my friend Dean, the one who was getting married?"

"The blond guy?"

"Right. Well, his fiancée called off the wedding, and Dean's disappeared."

"Oh God, Jack, that's awful. He seemed all goo-goo-eyed over her—what I saw of him, anyway." The kindhearted sincerity of her words made him smile.

"He couldn't have taken it well. Anyway, Mike and I are headed out to see if we can catch up with him…keep him out of trouble."

"That sounds like a great idea. Is your work cooperating?"

His work? Oh, yeah, his "waiter" job. "They're great here. You know, though, they aren't great about personal phone calls. Let me give you my cell number so if you need to get hold of me, you can." The last thing he wanted was for Jessie to call the hotel asking to talk to Jack Moore and learn the truth. It was probably best to keep her from the hotel as much as possible. Jack told her his number, made her promise to put it in her cell. "How is the car running?"

"It's great. Thanks again."

"You're welcome. I've got to go."

"Go. Good luck."

"Thanks, I'll get in touch once I'm back."

"I hope you find your friend, and that he's all right."

She did sound as if she cared. "Bye, Jessie."

"Bye, Jack."

Boy, he thought, one relationship ending, while his and Jessie's was just warming up. There really weren't any guarantees when it came to love and life.

———

Two days later, Jessie couldn't handle the not knowing. She shouldn't let Jack's problems bother her, but for some reason they did. He hadn't called, hadn't shown up at the diner. Now it was her day off and she sat on the same park bench, watching her son play after school. Maybe the bench reminded her of him. Then again, she hadn't stopped thinking about Jack since they'd met. Twice she'd picked up the phone to call him; twice she'd chickened out.

How was his friend doing? Did they find him? If there was one thing she knew about Jack it was his loyalty to people he called friend. Look at her. They hardly knew each other and yet he'd put his job on the line for her...fixed her car when he didn't need to.

Sure, he might not have a kid to take care of or much in the way of responsibility, but he'd spent his money paying to have her car fixed. She hadn't bought into his saying he owed a friend a favor. Chances were he'd paid something to have her car fixed.

The oil light didn't even blink at her anymore.

Where was Jack now? Could she return the friendship favor and help him out? She had to do something other than sit here in the park and worry.

Friends call friends to see how they're doing.

Jack was a friend...right?

Jessie had a sudden feeling of déjà vu. She was in high school again, contemplating whether or not she should call a boy.

"Grow up," she chided herself.

She dialed Jack's number and held her breath until he answered. When he did, he sounded like he was still in bed.

"Jack, it's Jessie. Did I wake you?"

"Jessie? Yeah, hold on."

Muffled sounds permeated the line until Jack returned. "Hey."

"You're in bed?"

"Yeah."

"It's four o'clock."

Jack released a long sigh. "We couldn't get Dean off his binge until sunrise. Then the alcohol haunted him until noon. He was a mess, Jessie. One sorry son of a bitch."

Jessie sighed. "So you found him."

"We did. I might have to spike his cereal with whiskey to keep his head from exploding, but we did find him, drunk as any sailor on shore leave."

"Where are you?"

"Up in Arrowhead."

"Dean is taking the breakup hard, then?"

Jack's voice sounded more alert with every sentence. "He is. No man ever wants to believe the woman he pledged his life to isn't committed. But between you and me, I think it's for the best. Maggie was nice and all, but not for Dean. Better they figure that out now than get married and figure it out after."

"You didn't tell him that, did you?"

"I'm not an idiot, Jessie." He laughed. "I've seen Dean throw a punch, and I don't want to be on the receiving end of one."

"Good. Why did his fiancée break it off?"

Jack sounded as if he was moving around on a bed. "I don't think he knows. She just told him she couldn't do it. They were too different. Shouldn't she have figured that out before she said yes?"

"I've never been engaged, but I think that's what an engagement is all about. You have to spend time with each other, figure out if you work together outside of the physical."

"Dean said the physical was amazing."

"He's a guy. Of course it was. Did he know about the things that count? Did they mesh outside of the bedroom? Could they talk to each other about any and everything?"

"Damn...no. I don't think so. But I already told you I didn't think they worked. Dean thought they did, and for that I'm bummed for him."

Jessie watched her son on the playground and leaned on her forearms. "You're a good friend, Jack. You were ready to accept her regardless, and you're there for him when it fell apart."

"I've known Dean since we were kids."

"Did you grow up together?"

"Yeah. He's like a brother to me."

Jessie smiled. "You take care of the people you care about, Jack, and it shows. Dean's lucky to have you on his side."

"Ah, now, Miss Jessie, you keep talkin' like that and I'm going to have to get down to you and show you how much I appreciate your astute attention to my divine disposition." Jack's accent sang like a soprano in church.

"I'm paying you a compliment, not inviting you into anything divine."

Jack laughed.

She laughed with him. "OK, well, I'll let you go. Just wanted to check up."

"You just wanted to hear my sexy cowboy voice," he teased.

"I was concerned for your friend." The sexy voice was a nice bonus.

Jack laughed. "What are you doing today?"

"I'm at the park with Danny. We're going to the outlet center tomorrow, get some Christmas shopping done. How long are you going to be in Arrowhead?"

"We're going to try and get Dean off the hill later tonight. He'll stay with Mike for a while."

"If there is anything I can do for him, let me know."

"I will. Dean is pissed at your whole gender right now, but I'll keep you in mind."

She heard Jack yawn. "Get some sleep. I'll talk to you later."

"OK, thanks for calling."

She hung up and found herself smiling.

It was good to hear his sexy cowboy voice.

———

The outlet center was packed. Jessie held on to Danny's hand for fear he'd get lost in the crowd. People pushed, shoved, and seldom offered an apology for stepping into her personal space. Bah humbug!

"How long do we have to be here, Mommy?"

"Long enough to pick out something for Auntie Monica and Grandma." Her mother was the hardest person to shop for. What she really needed, Jessie couldn't afford, and what she wanted, love from a man, Jessie couldn't buy. There was no guarantee the outlet mall would have anything on her list.

"Can we buy something for Mrs. Ridgwall?"

"Your teacher?"

"Yeah."

Jessie wanted to say yes, but every dime really needed to go far. "How about we make something at home for your teacher? I'll bet she'd love some of our famous peanut brittle."

Danny nodded with enthusiasm. "OK. I'll make her a card, too."

Jessie knew she had skated out of that one. In the future he wouldn't be that easy to sway, but she was glad he was at this point.

Every toy store they passed, Danny wanted to go inside to see what he should put on his Christmas list for Santa. Jessie had explained to Danny that Santa had a lot of kids to take care of and to give Santa only a few things to choose from. Just in case the elves couldn't come up with his most favorite toy. Steering him away from the pricey items took a certain skill that didn't always work.

On the way into the third toy store, Jessie glanced up and noticed Jack's hat before she recognized the man.

Jack, in his signature outfit, leaned against the massive window of the toy store with a smile on his face. It was almost as if he was waiting there for her.

"Isn't that your friend?" Danny asked.

"It is."

"What's he doing here?"

"I don't know." But seeing him brought a smile to her face and gooseflesh to her arms.

"Hey, darlin'." Jack tipped his hat when she walked up to him.

"What are you doing here?"

He ignored her question and bent down to talk to Danny. "Hey, Danny. Are you dragging your mother through the mall today?"

Danny laughed. "She's dragging me," he revealed.

"She's dragging you, huh? Into a toy store? I didn't know your mom played with toys."

Jessie felt the warmth of Danny's giggle and couldn't hold back the grin on her face. "My mom doesn't play with toys. I play with toys."

"Oh, so you *are* dragging her into the toy store."

Danny shrugged. "I guess."

Jack stood and winked. His flashy smile and dimples matched his mood.

Closer to eye level, Jessie glanced up and felt the warmth of his smile slide over her. The crowded mall melted away and the chore of shopping in the holiday shuffle felt less bleak. "How's your friend?"

"Pickled, but he'll live."

"I'm glad to hear you found him and that your boss was gracious enough to let you help him out."

"My boss loves me. I make the customers in the hotel smile. Must be the hat."

She laughed. "The hat does have a certain something we don't see around here very often."

Jack reached up and pushed a strand of her hair out of her eyes. His smile wavered, and she bit on her lower lip.

"C'mon, Mom. Let's go in." Danny tugged on her hand, breaking Jack's deep stare.

"OK, OK."

Jack let his hand fall and held the door for them before following them into the store.

Danny lit up the minute he hit the aisle with the trucks and trains. "Oh, cool. Look at this one."

Jessie glanced at the toy Danny was cooing over while he pressed a few buttons, putting the truck into motion inside the box. Soon he moved on to another colorful rolling gadget.

She found herself smiling when only a few minutes prior she was tired of shopping and wanting nothing more than to leave the mall and go home. Something about Jack's presence warmed her from the inside. From the way Danny was smiling up at Jack, he liked his impromptu visit as well.

Jessie warned herself against any warm and fuzzies when it came to him. She glanced at his lips and remembered their kiss. She shook her head, dispelled the thought, and asked, "What are you doing here, Jack?"

"Christmas shopping."

Yeah, right! When Jessie looked down at his hands, she saw he wasn't holding a single bag. "Not very successful, I see."

"I don't see any bags in your hands, either."

True. They'd been there for over two hours and found nothing. The crowded state of the mall didn't help. "This time of year brings out all the shoppers. This place is always a zoo."

Danny glanced up to her and said, "What about the zoo?"

"I said this place *is* a zoo," she said a little louder over the noise of the toys and the overexcited kids.

"Oh, I thought you said we were going to the zoo."

"No, that's not what I said."

"Hey, that's a good idea," Jack jumped in. "Beats this place."

Danny's eyes lit up. "Can we, Mommy? I love the zoo."

"I don't know—"

"My treat," Jack said before she could utter anything about the admission price.

"It's kind of far away," Jessie pointed out.

"Which means we need to get a move on." Jack tugged her elbow. "C'mon, it'll be fun. I haven't been to the zoo in years."

"Your dad lives on a ranch. You probably see animals all the time."

"Horses and cows. Not lions and tigers and bears." Jack's expression was as hopeful as Danny's. She hated always being the spoilsport, the voice of financial reason. The bad guy.

"C'mon, Mommy."

Jack knelt down to Danny's level and smiled up at her. "Yeah, c'mon, Mom. Danny and I haven't been to the zoo in forever."

Oh lord...Jack's dimples combined with Danny's hopeful smile were her undoing.

"OK. Let's go."

Danny jumped up and down, grabbed Jack's hand, and raced for the door.

Jessie ran to keep up with them.

Chapter Eight

Danny munched on popcorn and peered through the animal nursery window at the baby monkey sleeping in a crib. Jessie stood back with Jack at her side.

He had insisted on driving, so they had dropped Jessie's car off at her apartment and taken his truck.

"We can take my truck," he'd said.

"Oh, I can drive."

"No offense, darlin', but I think my truck is in a little better shape than your car."

She'd tried to act offended when she said, "It's just old. Your truck isn't exactly young."

"Honey, your car is a senior citizen in a retirement home playing bingo while my truck is still young enough to line dance at a honky-tonk."

Jessie laughed, and then Danny had the final word.

"You have a truck?"

It was all over but the driving.

She offered to pay their way inside the zoo, but Jack refused. It was his idea, his treat.

Still, with him paying, him driving, it was starting to feel too much like a date. "This isn't a date," she told him once Danny moved to another window.

Jack slid her a sly look. "Of course it isn't. We're not dating. We're *friends*."

Oh, but he said "friends" in such a sensual manner, Jessie felt her knees wobble. "Right, friends."

Jack leaned close to her ear so no one could hear him. "Friends that *don't* kiss."

"Exactly." Only with his lips so close to her ear, she was having a hard time forgetting about his incredible kiss.

"Exactly," he parroted before pulling away.

"I wanna see the snakes. Hey, Jack, did you know they have a whole building with nothing but snakes in it?"

Jack winked at Jessie and reached for Danny's hand. "Lead the way, partner. I love snakes."

Danny led Jack around the snake pavilion and the monkey and gorilla habitats, and through the aviary. Jessie squirmed while viewing the snakes, which resulted in some serious razzing from the guys. "I'm a girl, girls don't like snakes," she'd told them.

Then in the aviary, Jack used her words to their advantage. "We're boys, we don't like birds."

But they walked inside the enclosure anyway. One flying friend left a tiny present on Jack's shoulder, and both Danny and Jessie laughed until their guts hurt. "You hurt the bird's feelings," Jessie told him, laughing.

Jack found the humor and tossed back the teasing every chance he got.

They had a late lunch/early dinner at one of the concession stands. The warmed-up hamburgers and fries were actually pretty good. Jack bought Danny a stuffed animal in the form of a snake, which he carried around all afternoon. "I'm going to call him Tex."

"Why Tex?" Jack asked.

"Cuz you bought him and you're from Texas."

The day couldn't have been more perfect. Danny was in heaven, and he led Jack around like a long-lost friend whom he couldn't get enough of. She realized him being drawn to Jack might have more to do with Jack being a man than anything else. No matter how much Jessie wanted to be able to be everything for her son, she couldn't be his dad.

Not that she was casting Jack in that role, but Danny needed some male influence. A friend like Jack in her life might help make up for some of what Danny was missing.

As the sun started to set and the zoo was about to close, Danny was holding Jack with one hand and Tex with the other. "I'm in a Christmas play at my school," Danny told Jack. "Can you come and watch it?"

Jack shot her a look. Jessie realized he was asking for her take on the invitation. She didn't mind, but didn't want Jack to say yes just to please her son. "Jack has to work sometimes, Danny."

"When is it?" Jack asked.

"Next Friday. It's at ten in the morning."

"Well, if your mom doesn't mind…" Jack held her gaze.

"If Danny wants you there, I don't see why not."

"Whoo hoo! My aunt Monica is coming, too. I go to Foothill Elementary, do you know where that is? It's really easy to find." Danny rattled on about the play and the songs they'd learned. Danny had them singing Christmas carols as they walked out of the zoo.

They piled into Jack's truck, giving Danny the whole backseat so he could sleep on the way home. He stayed awake long enough to see some of the Christmas lights on display in Griffith Park. Once they hit the freeway, he was out.

"He had a great time. Thanks for this, Jack."

He merged into traffic, which was incredibly heavy even though it was past seven.

"What about you? Did you have a good time?" he asked.

"I did. It was a nice day off. I can't remember the last time I stole a day to just have fun." Her feet ached from walking all day, her cheeks from smiling.

"You have a great kid, Jessie. You're doing a wonderful job with him."

She peeked into the backseat at her sleeping son. "He's a great kid. He adores you."

Jack smiled. "Feeling's mutual. Listen, about the Christmas play—"

"If you can't go, he'll understand. I can make—"

"No," he interrupted. "I want to go. Only if it's really OK with you. I saw how he latched on to me, which I'm fine with, but if it bothers you, I'll understand if you want me to keep my distance."

Jessie stared at Jack's profile for a few seconds and considered his words. "You really do get it, don't you? The emotional toll of any relationship I may have with someone and how that can affect Danny?"

"Didn't you tell me your mom brings men in and out of your life?"

"Yeah, she does."

"You must think about that when you bring friends around Danny."

"I don't bring 'friends' around Danny. I can't even tell you the last time I was on a real date. I refuse to be my mother. If you and I were dating, I'd probably have said no to the zoo today. For the very reasons you bring up. Danny is missing a father in his life. There's nothing I can do about that other than try and keep him away from the men I date. Or risk him getting attached and disappointed when things don't work out."

Jack managed to get into the carpool lane, and traffic flowed a little easier. "I guess it's a good thing we're not dating, then."

"Right."

Later, Jack hoisted a snoozing Danny from the truck up onto his shoulder and let the poor tyke sleep while he walked him into Jessie's apartment.

She led him through the tidy living room and into Danny's bedroom.

Jack laid him down on his bed, and Jessie removed his shoes and tugged off his jeans. Danny murmured in his sleep and rolled over with Tex in his grip.

Jessie kissed his forehead and led Jack back to the living room.

A Christmas tree stood in the corner of the room, up on a table to give it some height. There were a couple presents under it, a few strands of lights giving it some life. The apartment was tidy, but incredibly small. How the three of them lived in such a compact place baffled him.

"Would you like some coffee?" Jessie offered. "Or cocoa?"

"I haven't had cocoa in years."

She smiled and walked toward the kitchen. "First the zoo, now cocoa. I'm showing you all the good things in life."

More than she could ever know, he wanted to say. "Monica lives with you here?"

Jessie removed mugs from a cupboard and filled them both with water before placing them in the microwave. "There's a hide-a-bed in the couch. When I work, she uses my bed."

"How long before she's done with school?" Jack sank into a chair at the kitchen table.

"May. I'm so proud of her. She's done well in school, never complains about things here. She's going to be a great nurse."

"Big praise from the older sister."

The microwave dinged, and Jessie removed the steaming mugs and put generous portions of cocoa into the cups. She fished into the pantry and pulled out a bag of mini marshmallows.

"You're a serious cocoa die-hard."

"I have a five-year-old. Marshmallows are a must."

Jessie topped the mugs and handed him his cup. The first sip reminded him of snowy winter days and ice-cold noses. "Has Danny ever been to the snow?"

"No, I wish. The closest we came was a few flurries that hit the foothills near my mom's place. It didn't stick. I keep meaning to drive us up into Big Bear when it snows."

"Christmas in California is strange for me. I'm used to bundling up and knocking the dirt or snow off my boots before going into the house."

"I didn't think it snowed much in Texas."

"It does, some." He almost told her that he'd spent more than one Christmas in Colorado. Once his father realized how much he and his sister would pine for their mother's return during the holidays, he'd distract them with ski trips to Colorado. They had a cabin up there that Jack tried to visit once a season to get some skiing in. "A lot more than it does here."

"It's always a palm tree Christmas. Last year we actually ate on my mom's patio. The inside was too warm from the oven being on all day." Jessie blew into her cocoa and caught Jack's eyes.

Both of them sat there staring at each other. He'd give anything to know what she was thinking. What did she really see when she gazed at him? He saw an honest-to-goodness girl next door whom he was quickly learning he couldn't live without.

What was he to her? A dreamer, a wanderer. A liar. Jack broke their eye contact and glanced at his watch. "Wow, look at the time."

"It's late."

Jack drank the last of his cocoa and took the mug to her sink. He needed to get out of her place before he broke down and kissed her again. If he did, he knew she'd pull the plug on their "friendship." He wouldn't give her a reason to push him away. Jack's main goal in life was to wiggle under her skin until she couldn't live without him.

He already knew he could spend every day with Jessie and never get enough.

The beginning of the week sped by. Between work and a few stolen hours shopping for Christmas, Jessie's days ran into each other. Danny talked about Jack and the zoo so much that Monica told Jessie she felt as if she'd been there. "You will remember to introduce me to him on Friday, won't you?" Monica teased.

"Give me a break, Mo. You caught me kissing the guy, not exactly a family moment."

Monica laughed. "I know. Just doing my sisterly duty and giving you a hard time."

Jessie was getting ready for work while Danny settled into the couch for movie time with his aunt. Danny never made it through the first hour without crashing, but it was his routine, and it worked for them.

The phone rang, surprising both Jessie and Monica. They didn't usually get calls after eight.

Jessie answered it when she didn't recognize the number. "Hello?"

"Is this Jessie?"

The voice was slightly familiar, but Jessie couldn't place it. "This is. Who's this?"

"Hi, Jessie, it's Brad, from the Christmas party at The Morrison."

Jessie was stunned. She'd completely forgotten about the man. "Right. Hello."

"I haven't called at a bad time, have I?"

"No, um, hold on." Jessie covered the receiver of the phone and spoke to Monica in a hushed voice. "It's that guy from the party. Brad."

Monica narrowed her eyes at her. "What about Jack?"

Talk about guilt. Instead of saying anything else to Monica, Jessie stepped into the privacy of her bedroom to take the call, keeping the accusing eyes away. "Sorry about that. I was getting my son settled."

"I can call another time if it's better."

"No, now's good."

"Good." His voice was kind, and somewhat flat. No real humor in it, but nothing that stood out as creepy, either.

"How was your trip?"

"My trip?"

"Didn't you say you were out of town last week?" She remembered that much from their conversation.

"Right. Fine, I have a few clients back east that needed attention."

OK, so he was a businessman. That was good. "Oh. What do you do for a living?"

She told herself she was just making conversation.

"I'm an attorney."

She cringed. Didn't Jack say he looked like a lawyer? "I'll bet that's exciting."

"Corporate law is quite boring, actually."

"I wouldn't know," Jessie told him, trying her best to push Jack's voice out of her head.

"If you wouldn't mind being bored to tears over my stories of work, I'd love to take you out."

"I'm sure it isn't that bad."

"Is that a yes?"

What did she have to lose? She hated that she felt guilty, and tried to push the emotion aside. "I'd like that. Something casual, if that's OK with you."

"I know just the place. How's this Saturday?"

She had to work Friday night, but she could manage Saturday as long as Monica could stay with Danny. "I'll have to check with my babysitter, but Saturday sounds good."

"Let me give you my number and you can let me know once you talk to your sitter."

Jessie jotted down his number. "OK, I'll try and call you tomorrow."

"I'll look forward to it."

They said their good-byes, and Jessie sat on the edge of her bed with a mixture of emotions rolling in her stomach.

One the one hand, Brad did seem like a nice person, a professional man who could offer some stability to Jessie's life. She couldn't say she was all that attracted to the man. She was excited to get the call, but not in an anticipating kind of way. More of a nervous, *Should she or shouldn't she* kind of way.

Jack wouldn't leave her mind. He was there, shaking his finger at her, telling her the man looked like a *lawyer*. The way he said "lawyer" sounded dirty and unacceptable.

Jessie tried to shake the sick feeling in the pit of her stomach as she left her bedroom.

Monica met her in the kitchen with her hands perched on her hips and a scowl on her face. "You're going out with him, aren't you?"

Jessie glanced over to Danny, who wasn't paying any attention to them. "I'd like to. Can you sit with Danny Saturday? I'll be home by ten." Having an end time on a first date was a good safety net in case the evening was a complete bomb.

"What about Jack?"

"Jack and I aren't dating, Mo. You know that. He's a friend."

Monica wasn't buying it. "Then why do your eyes light up every time you talk about him?"

"They do not."

"Do too."

"Stop. Will you watch Danny or not?"

"I'll watch him. But I think you're making a mistake."

"I already told Jack about Brad." Which was met with the same ugliness Monica was giving her.

"So you'll tell him about this date, too?"

"Maybe, if the subject comes up." *Not likely.* She didn't need the third degree from him as well. "I've got to go." Jessie grabbed her purse and kissed Danny good night before sailing out the door.

It was one date, for crying out loud.

One lousy date.

———

Danny, dressed in a big jacket, mittens, and a scarf, sang his little heart out in the kindergarten Christmas play. Parents sat in the audience, snapping pictures and taping the entire performance to rewatch for years to come.

Jessie sat between Jack and Monica, who both hit it off wonderfully, which Jessie knew would backfire on her at the first opportunity.

When the performance was over, the excited kids made their way off the elementary school stage and melted into the audience to find their proud parents. Danny ran to Jessie, threw his precious arms around her, and graced her with a huge smile. "Did you see me up there?"

"You were great, Danny. You must have practiced for a really long time to remember all the words to the songs," she told him.

"We sing every day in class."

Danny pulled out of her arms and hugged Monica.

He slipped into Jack's embrace just as easily. "Hey, Uncle Jack. Wasn't that cool?"

Uncle Jack, that was new. Jessie narrowed her eyes and watched Jack's expression. When it didn't change, she wondered if Jack had caught Danny's title.

"Cool for days, partner."

"Do you want some cookies? There are cookies in the back." Danny grabbed Jack's hand and pulled him toward the back of the room, where the teachers and the parents had set out the refreshments.

"Uncle Jack?" Monica asked under her voice.

"New to me."

"Danny loves him. Look at them."

Jessie couldn't stop staring. Danny was chatting up a storm, and Jack was listening and laughing alongside him.

"It's natural," Jessie told her sister. "Danny doesn't have a man in his life. Jack has been around a few times, so he's gravitating toward him." She really hoped she wasn't making a mistake by letting the two of them get to know each other. Jack was an all-around good guy, and she trusted him. Trusted that he wouldn't do anything to hurt her son in any way. However, who knew how long Jack would be in their lives. It was a chance she wasn't willing to take.

"I don't know why you'd bother dating anyone else."

"Jack and I aren't dating." Was no one listening to her on this subject?

"Lawyers are boring."

"You can say that again." Jack snuck up behind them. Jessie jumped when she heard his voice. She turned and noticed the candy cane sticking out between his lips. The smile on his face was simply priceless. "Are we talking about a *particular* lawyer?"

Guilty. God, she felt so guilty. "No. Hey, Danny, do they have any more of those candy canes?"

Her son nodded and pulled her away from Jack and Monica. The farther away from her sister and Jack she walked, the more she worried about their topic of conversation.

At the refreshment table, Danny greeted one of his friends, and the child's mother turned to Jessie and started chatting.

A few minutes later, Jessie meandered her way through the thinning crowd and back to Monica and Jack's side. The two of them were laughing. Mo held her side as if the laughing pained her.

"What's so funny?"

"Nothing." But Monica was hiding her grin behind a hand.

Jessie's sister radar was flying high. Monica was up to something. "Sure. Nothing."

Danny pulled on her hand. "My teacher said we can go after the show."

Jessie glanced down at her son. "Are you ready to leave?"

People were already filing out of the auditorium. "I need to get my backpack from my room," Danny told her.

Monica placed her hand on Danny's shoulder and said, "Why don't you take me with you so you can show me your classroom."

Before Jessie could say anything, Monica and Danny were walking away, leaving Jack and her standing alone.

"It was really nice of you to come."

"I enjoyed it," he said as they started to walk out of the busy room with the other parents. "I haven't been to something like this since I was Danny's age. They haven't changed much, have they?"

"More treats, but that's about it."

He smiled. "I remember a cookie and, if we were lucky, one candy cane. Seems as if they had an entire bakery in the back."

"Lots of the parents bring treats for the kids."

Loads of adults were crammed into Danny's classroom, so Jessie decided to stay outside. Through the window, she saw Danny pointing out some of his "artwork" to Monica that hung on the walls.

"Danny seems to like his school."

"He loves it. Such a social kid. You would think living in an apartment building would mean there were lots of kids he could play with, but there aren't." Her apartment building wasn't loaded with nasty people and big parties, but it wasn't loaded with families, either. "One of these days I'll be able to put us in a house in a neighborhood. Ever since he saw that movie with the golden lab, Danny's bugged me about getting a dog."

"I take it your landlord doesn't accept pets."

"Right. Big dogs don't belong cooped up inside all day, anyway."

Jack patted her on the back. "Give yourself a break. You'll get there."

Jessie forced a smile onto her face. "I know. Someday."

Danny ran from his classroom and up to them. "I'm ready," he informed them.

"I have to get to class," Monica announced. "Thanks for showing me your classroom, buddy." She knelt down to talk to Danny. "Watch your mom for me, will ya? Make sure she takes a nap."

Danny giggled.

"Are you staying late?" Jessie asked her sister.

"We have a huge test on Monday, so we're going to have a long study session. I'll be home before you go to work. I'm inviting Lynn over to study Saturday while you're gone."

Just the hint of a mention about her being away from home on Saturday was enough to have Jessie glancing over at Jack.

"I thought you were off Saturday," Jack said.

"Mom has a date," Danny spit out.

The expression on Jack's face froze. "Is that so?" Slowly his gaze moved to Jessie.

"You remember Brad from the party." Full disclosure. She shouldn't feel guilty, but the feeling rolled off her in painful waves.

"Right." Jack drew out the word in a long sigh. "The lawyer-looking guy."

"He *is* a lawyer, actually." She sounded defensive.

"He's not your type," Jack said with absolute certainty in his voice.

She shifted from foot to foot. "How do you know what my type is?"

"You'll be bored within thirty minutes."

Monica turned to Jack. "Do you know this guy?"

Jack never stopped staring at Jessie. The gaze made her fidget. "I see his type all the time at the hotel. Stuffy, not a lot of fun."

"Why do you want to date someone who isn't fun, Mommy?"

Jessie pulled her eyes away from Jack's and said to Danny, "Jack doesn't know if Brad will be fun or not; he's assuming."

"What's assuming?"

"It's when someone thinks someone is a certain way when they don't really know if they are a certain way." Dammit, she shouldn't have to be defending a date to her son, or Jack, or Monica for that matter.

"You should date Jack," Danny said, smiling. "We know he's fun."

Three sets of eyes pinned her down. "Jack and I are just friends, right, Jack?"

Jack didn't say a word, just stared at her with a tiny lift in his lips.

"What's a date, anyway?"

"It's when two people go out to dinner or do something to-gether to get to know each other." And why wasn't Jack helping her here?

"We went with Uncle Jack to the zoo. That was kinda a date."

"Not quite a date." Jessie shifted her attention to her son.

"Oh." He wasn't convinced. Confusion marked his expression.

"It's complicated, Danny. You'll understand when you're older."

A few moments of awkward silence filled the air, then Monica said, "On that note, I've gotta go."

"So do I," Jack said, a smile returning to his face. "Thanks again for inviting me, Danny."

Danny gave Monica and Jack hugs.

"Have a nice time with the lawyer, Jessie." Was it opposite day, and Jessie had somehow missed the memo? Jack actually sounded sincere.

"I'm sure it will be fine." Only now, she wasn't positive of anything.

Jessie watched Jack and Monica walk away, the two of them talking. She could only guess what about.

Chapter Nine

"I don't plan on staying out late," Jessie told her sister for the second time that night.

Dressed in a pair of slacks and a sweater, Jessie was comfortable and casual but not too casual. Wearing small heels with the slacks dressed up the outfit. Besides, Jessie didn't have the occasion to wear heels very often, so she jumped at the opportunity whenever she could. Something about wearing heels reminded her that she was a grown-up, desirable woman.

"Where are you two meeting?"

"He picked an Italian place by the mall. Antonio's."

"I've never heard of it." Monica reached over and tucked a stray lock of Jessie's hair back into place.

"We've passed it a few times. I've never eaten there," Jessie said.

"Call me if things aren't going the way you want them to and use me as an excuse to come home early if the date sucks."

Jessie dropped her chin and smiled at her sister. "Thanks. I don't think I'll need to use an excuse, but it's nice to know you've got my back."

"Always." Monica handed over the black purse Jessie had picked out for the night. "I still think it's Jack you should be meeting for dinner and not this Brad guy."

Throwing up her hand, Jessie said, "Enough. You've told me this a dozen times since yesterday. I know you don't approve, but this is what I need to be doing."

"Because Jack is a waiter and not a lawyer. You're not that shallow, Jessie, and I know it. Jack likes you. A lot!"

"Did he tell you that?" Jessie had been trying to pry out of her sister the meat of her conversation with Jack for the last twenty-four hours. Monica wouldn't give up one syllable of their discussion.

"I could see it in his eyes. The way he looks at you is magnetic. Even if you won't admit it, you look at him the same way."

Jessie did her best to ignore the energy between them. She could look past the man and not dwell on their one kiss, most of the time. She could wipe the images her mind dreamed up of the man, even the naked ones, most of the time. She could ignore how her heart sped up when she saw him walking into the diner, or her son's school, or the park, most of the time.

OK, maybe not most of the time, but for a few hours at a time. Or a few minutes.

She shook her head. *You're hopeless, Jessie.*

"I need someone stable, someone who has a real job, a real future. Not some temporary employee of a local hotel who will probably be traveling back to Texas after the holiday season is over. Have you forgotten Rory, Danny's father? Or Mathew?"

"Mathew? Oh, that guy you dated for, what, ten minutes?"

"It was two months, and he moved in with me, if you remember. His idea of helping out was to take my rent money and leave." Mathew was an expensive mistake.

She swung her purse on her shoulder and walked out of her bedroom and into the living room, where Danny was talking with Monica's friend Lynn.

"I'm leaving, Danny. Can I get a kiss?"

Danny pushed away from his Legos and Lynn before putting his arms around her.

"Will you be home before I go to bed?" he asked.

"I don't think so."

Danny's normally happy smile slid into a tiny pout. "Can I go on your next date with you?"

Oh boy. "I'm not sure. I guess we'll have to wait and see." The guilt was coming back tenfold.

"I went on your date with Uncle Jack."

Arguing with him about the dating status and Jack was pointless. He didn't understand, and Jessie was going to be late if she tried to explain the point again. "I'll think about it," Jessie said instead.

Danny took his frowning face and plopped on the sofa.

Jessie waved to her sister. "I'll see you in a few hours."

"Call if you need anything."

"I will. Bye, Monica. Bye, Lynn." Jessie turned to her son. "Bye, buddy."

Danny gave her a quick wave but didn't look at her.

Jessie walked out of the apartment, wondering if she was doing the wrong thing.

———

She found the restaurant easily enough. Parking was a little tight, but she managed to cram her car into the lot between a huge pickup truck and a Lexus. Glancing at her watch, Jessie realized she was five minutes early. She hoped Brad was already waiting for her inside so she wouldn't have to wait in the lounge or reception area by herself.

Inside the small Italian restaurant, the heavy smell of garlic and tomato sauce tickled her nose and made her mouth water. The dim lighting shed a nice romantic glow over the dark red booths.

"Welcome to Antonio's," a leggy, tall blonde woman about Jessie's age greeted her.

"I'm meeting someone here. His name is Brad."

The hostess glanced at her reservation list and smiled. "Your party hasn't arrived yet, but your table is ready if you'd like me to seat you."

Jessie sighed in relief. "You can seat me."

Several couples talked quietly in their intimate booths, drinking wine and eating breadsticks. At the table, Jessie removed her light jacket and placed it beside her.

"Would you like something from the bar while you wait?"

"Water for now."

The blonde left and Jessie went ahead and opened her menu to glance at the selections.

A busboy brought water and a basketful of breadsticks and then left her alone to watch the time pass.

Every minute that ticked by while Jessie waited felt like an hour.

Ten minutes past seven, Brad walked up to the table.

"I'm sorry I'm late," he said as he undid a button on his jacket and slid into the booth beside her. "I had a heck of a time getting through traffic, and the parking out there is a mess."

Jessie smiled and waved away Brad's concerns. "I'm glad you made it." And she was, she realized, despite her reservations about the date. Brad wore a well-pressed suit, his jaw was clean shaven, and he even smelled good. More because of the froufrou cologne he wore than his natural scent.

Jack always carried a little spice and pine wherever he went. *More masculine.*

"I hope you haven't been waiting long."

Fifteen minutes, thirty seconds. But who is counting? "I was only ahead of you by a few minutes," she lied, hoping she didn't appear too anxious.

Brad signaled the waiter as he walked by and ordered a bottle of wine and two glasses.

Strike two, Jessie found herself thinking. First, he was late for the date, and although traffic was a factor, she had still managed to get there on time, and it wasn't exactly rush hour out there. Second, Brad didn't even ask her if she drank wine. Then again, maybe that's what people with money did to impress their dates.

"The food here is excellent," Brad said as he pushed his menu aside. "You said you've never eaten here before, isn't that right?"

"I've passed here many times but never stopped." Jessie went ahead and reopened her menu and then pretended to look over what the restaurant offered.

"I can select the perfect dish for you, if you like."

"Ah…" She wasn't sure what to say.

Brad gently removed the menu from her fingers and folded it on top of his. "You have to have the lasagna. I don't think I've tasted better outside of New York."

"Ah, OK." Looks like it was lasagna, whether she wanted it or not. What was wrong with her? Brad was trying to be thoughtful, and here she was taking offense at nearly everything he was saying or doing.

The wine arrived and saved her the trouble of coming up with small talk. Jessie watched Brad's profile while he went through the process of tasting the wine and approving it. His features were just as she remembered: nice but not overly strong. His face was a little narrower than she remembered. There were no dimples when he smiled, and the smile did seem to lack something.

Jessie sipped her wine and watched him over the rim of the glass. The wine tickled the back of her throat, then slid down easily.

"What do you do at the hotel?" Brad asked.

"I'm sorry?" She didn't understand his question.

"You do work at the hotel, don't you? I thought for sure you were a waitress there." He cocked his head to the side when he spoke.

"No, I don't work at the hotel, but I do wait tables." She couldn't for the life of her figure out how he knew what she did for a living.

"You must know someone at the hotel who managed to get you a ticket to the party, then."

Jessie couldn't help but feel as if she were under interrogation. She thought of Jack and the risks he'd taken to get her in the door.

"Is being an investigator part of a lawyer's job?" she asked with a little laugh.

Brad let a sly smile pass his lips before he abruptly steered his words in a different direction. "You seemed a bit lost that night."

"A friend of mine forfeited his ticket for me," she explained.

Brad tipped his glass back again. "A friend who is a man?"

"Yes."

"I don't think I can call any woman in my life a friend. An ex–romantic engagement, a sister, a family member, a colleague, maybe, but never simply a friend."

"What about the wives or girlfriends of your male friends?"

"I don't consider them personal friends, more like how you just explained them...the *wife* of a friend of mine. Is this friend of yours married?"

Strange how this date had a third person at the table the entire time. Jack may not have been there in person, but he certainly was in spirit. "No."

The waiter arrived, and Jessie wanted to kiss him for his timing.

"Have you decided?" Their waiter was a man around forty-five, maybe older. His waistline looked as if he enjoyed the food at Antonio's, and his Italian accent kept her guessing if he was any relation to Antonio himself.

"I think so," Jessie said.

He smiled at her and poised his pen over his order slip.

"The lady would like the lasagna," Brad said before Jessie could open her mouth. "With the antipasto salad, and I'll have the same."

Jessie had the strong urge to glance at her watch, but squelched it.

Jack looked at his watch for the third time in fifteen minutes. Jessie was out with that lawyer. Brad Leland, to be exact. Jack had checked out the guest list of the benefit party and found only one Brad in the invites. A quick online search resulted in a name, the name of his practice, and a few hits on cases he'd tried recently. Jack had hoped to find a little dirt on the guy, but he didn't see any. Not married, his romantic entanglements were private at the current time. Jack did find an old girlfriend, one whom Brad had been engaged to. There was a write-up in an archived paper about the engagement, but it had been nearly two years ago. All the current information on Brad pointed toward a single status. As a corporate lawyer, Brad had a full plate of clients, and from the look of the pictures of his office, he wasn't hurting for cash.

There was even a picture of the guy on the website for the law firm he worked with.

Dull and boring. Jack couldn't imagine Jessie finding him remotely attractive.

Still, Brad the Boring was out on a date with Jessie, and Jack was in the penthouse, stewing. He would have to wait until Tuesday, the next time Jessie worked, to find out how the date went. Unless Jack wanted to come off as a jealous, jilted lover.

No matter how many sexy dreams Jack had experienced since meeting Jessie, he couldn't call himself her lover.

Not yet anyway.

Jack had turned toward the bar in the suite, intending to pour himself something big and strong, when his cell phone rang. His phone sat in the pocket of the suit hanging on the back of a chair.

Jessie's home phone number popped up on his caller ID. Maybe she had skipped out on the date after all. His lips slid into a grin.

"Hello?" he answered, trying to sound bored.

"Jack? Is this you?"

Not Jessie.

"This is. Who's this?"

"It's Monica, Jessie's sister." The alarm in her voice made Jack drop his bored demeanor. "I hope it's OK I called you."

"Is Jessie OK? Danny?"

"They're fine. Sorry to worry you. Jessie is out with that guy, the one from the party."

As if Jack needed to be reminded.

"And Danny is right here. It's…ahh…Danny suggested I call you." Monica was bothered about something.

"What's going on, Monica?"

"I'm at the apartment, with a friend, studying. Anyway, Lynn got a call a few minutes ago…her mom was in a car accident. Lynn's shook up, shouldn't be driving. I need to get her to Pomona Valley, but I'm babysitting Danny. I'd take him with me, but the emergency room is full of all kinds of people, illness."

"Did you call Jessie, tell her to come home?"

"She accidentally left her phone in her other purse. I called it and it rang in her bedroom."

Jack walked into his bedroom and pulled a suit jacket off a hanger. "You want me to come over, stay with Danny so you can drive your friend?"

"God, would you, Jack? I know it's sudden, but Jessie doesn't use many sitters. Only Mrs. Hoyt, but she's visiting her family. I didn't know who else to call. I know she trusts you, Danny knows you."

"I'll be there in ten minutes." Jack hung up his phone and shoved into his jacket as he walked out the door.

The ride to Jessie's apartment was short, and Jack didn't take it slow.

Monica met him at the door. "Danny goes to bed at nine, falls asleep on the couch most nights before then."

Danny jumped up from the couch, ran over to Jack, and pulled him into a fierce hug. "I knew you'd come. I told Auntie Monica to call you."

"You can always call me, Danny." Jack ruffled Danny's hair and glanced at Monica's friend whom he'd never seen before. "I hope your mom's OK."

The girl held back tears. "Thanks."

"Thanks again, Jack. I owe you." Then they were gone.

"Monica's friend was really sad. They said her mom was hurt in a car crash."

Jack walked with Danny over to the couch, where they both sat. The television was on and a cartoon played on the screen. "She's probably just fine, partner. Nothing for you to worry about."

"My mom drove our car tonight," Danny offered, catching Jack off guard.

Good, he thought. She met her date instead of giving him her address.

Danny's eyes narrowed. Jack realized that Danny's concern for his mother's well-being prompted the comment. "I'm sure your mom is a safe driver," Jack said, trying to assure the boy.

"Our car is always breaking something."

Yeah, Jack knew that already. The thought of Jessie out there without her cell phone bugged the crap out of him, too. *What if she broke down on one of the back roads?* After ten, Ontario had plenty of stretched-out, deserted, dark roads. It was only eight fifteen.

"What time did your mom leave tonight?"

"An hour ago. I think."

Great, Jack had to depend on Danny's memory. Still, odds were Jessie was eating dinner.

With *him. Brad!* Probably short for Bradley. What a wussy name that was.

"What are we watching here?"

"SpongeBob. He's funny. That's Patrick and Sandy..." Danny pointed out the key characters and Jack listened. He'd heard of the show, but couldn't say he'd ever sat and watched an episode. He found himself laughing at the jokes and some of the adult humor laced into the cartoon.

At eight thirty, Jack suggested Danny jump into his PJs and brush his teeth so he wouldn't forget before going to bed.

Danny bounced off the sofa and to his room.

Jack went into the kitchen and noticed Monica and her friend's books spread out all over the kitchen table. Among them were plates filled with half-eaten pizza and snacks. Jack rolled up his sleeves and realized he was wearing a suit, minus his tie. Maybe Monica would return before Jessie. Or Jessie would be so frazzled to see him there she wouldn't notice his clothes. *Can't change now.*

Jack straightened up some of the clutter and rinsed off the dishes before placing them in the dishwasher.

Danny bounced into the room, all smiles and giggles. "All done."

"OK, sport, now what do you want to do?"

"Do you play cards?" he asked.

"I know a few games." But Jack doubted they were the ones Danny knew.

"Cool," he said as he flew down the hall again and returned in seconds with a deck in his hand. "We can play Go Fish or War. Do you know how to play War?"

Not a clue.

"I'll bet you can teach me."

Back in the living room, Danny sat on his knees on the floor and dealt out the cards. He explained the rules, which Jack seemed to remember vaguely, and the two of them proceeded to play.

It was five past nine when Jack realized the time. "Dude, it's past your bedtime," Jack said.

Danny pushed his lower lip out. "But I usually fall asleep on the couch."

Right, Monica said that. Jack guessed it wouldn't be the end of the world if he let the kid stay up a little later than he normally did.

"OK, but we need to put the cards away and settle down."

Danny tossed the cards on the coffee table and curled back on the couch next to Jack.

"I like having you babysit," Danny informed him. "Maybe you can come over again."

The insides of Jack's chest swelled with warmth. "I like you too, partner."

Jack didn't even flinch when Danny leaned his head against his shoulder. Twenty minutes into another crazy animated show, Danny was snoring little logs and practically lying in Jack's lap. Jack smiled to himself and stroked the back of Danny's head.

With the remote, Jack switched on the evening news and set the volume to low.

To the side of the TV was the Mann Christmas tree. A few more gifts were scattered under it. Two Jack easily realized were from Danny to his mom and his aunt. The homemade wrapping paper, which was really a paper bag painted green and red, adorned gifts proudly piled in front. Danny's stocking was tacked to a wall.

The tree in his childhood home had been set up and taken down by his father's staff. The gifts wrapped by the department stores before they even made it home. When he stopped and thought about it, Jack wondered if his father had ever gone out and shopped for him and Katie, or had he sent his secretary to do the job? Probably the latter. Yet that had changed in the last few years, which was a good thing. Gaylord had never been cruel, just clueless about his children.

Jessica had created a home and holiday with love. The apartment might be small, but it screamed Christmas and family. Sitting on the worn sofa felt as comfortable as any leather variety he'd ever had the pleasure of planting his butt on.

The news announced the time as ten o'clock and Jack couldn't help but shift his thoughts to where Jessie was and what she was doing. A cloud of worry stretched over his earlier happy thoughts. She might not be out with *Braaad* if Jack had revealed certain truths about himself.

Part of him wanted to tell her the truth, and the other part reminded him that if she suddenly decided he was worthy enough to date, spend time with, make love to, that he'd never truly know if it was his money or him she wanted.

The guilt in her eyes when she'd said she was going on a date with that loser had said so much. Jessie worried about what Jack thought. He smiled at the thought. Without a doubt, there was heat in Jessie's gaze when she looked at him. He felt it every damn time he was around her. Someone upstairs really should offer him sainthood or some such thing for the restraints he'd placed on himself where Jessie was concerned.

Danny sighed in his sleep; a little drool fell from the boy's mouth and onto Jack's pants.

Jack was about to pick the boy up and put him to bed when he heard a key turning in the lock of the door.

Jessie walked in with her eyes to the floor. She held her shoes in one hand and the keys and her purse in the other. She turned toward the door and secured the dead bolt and the chain lock without even realizing Jack was there.

She rested her head against the door and dropped her shoes to the floor. "God, Monica, you won't believe this date."

Jack was proud to say that Jessie's tone didn't sound happy or dreamy.

Slowly Jessie turned around and lifted her gaze. She let out a quick squeal and stifled it before it became a full-on scream. Her hand flew to her mouth, her eyes to her son who lay in Jack's lap.

Lifting a finger to his lips, Jack said, "Shh, Danny's worn out."

"What are you doing here?" she asked in a curt, hushed tone.

Chapter Ten

"Let me put him to bed," Jack whispered before he lifted Danny into his strong arms, cradled him against his chest, and walked to Danny's room.

Jessie's heart was thumping faster than a jackrabbit's. What was Jack doing in her apartment, and where in the world was Monica?

Two hours earlier, Jessie had realized she'd left her phone at home and nearly asked to use the restaurant phone to call in. Instead, she kept on with the disaster of a date until she couldn't handle it any longer.

Standing in the doorway, Jessie watched Jack tuck Danny in bed as if he'd done so a hundred times.

Danny rolled over in his sleep, dragging Tex, the snake, with him.

Jack silently tiptoed away and squeezed between Jessie and the door before standing in the hall. She closed the door and motioned for Jack to follow her.

"What are you doing here?" she asked again.

"Monica called me. Her friend, the girl who was here tonight…"

"Lynn?"

"Right. Lynn's mother was in an accident and Monica needed to drive her to the hospital. Your sister didn't think it would be a good place for Danny, and you didn't have your phone, so she called me."

"Why you?" Who else, Jessie thought. Their mother was too far away and didn't take to watching Danny all that often. But she would have in an emergency.

"I was close and available. It was Danny's idea."

The explanation was reasonable, but Jessie wasn't happy to see the man who'd unknowingly wiggled into her date before it had even gotten started. Jack shot her a smile. His dimples peeked through. Dammit.

She'd thought of that smile for the past half hour. The past thirty minutes, as she'd walked from where her car had broken down, the crappy thing. "Could this night get any worse?" she said as she turned away from Jack's easy smile and sparkling gray eyes.

"What was that?" Jack asked.

"Nothing, nothing." Jessie picked up her shoes from where she'd dropped them and unlocked the dead bolt and chain so Monica wouldn't be locked out.

"Are you OK?" he asked. His voice had dropped the laughing tone, and suddenly Jessie was on the verge of tears. No, she was absolutely not *OK*.

But, darn it, she didn't need her bleeding heart, and probably feet, crying to Jack about it. Seemed like she was continually indebted to Jack already, and she'd hardly known the man for a month. "Fine!" she nearly barked out at him.

"You don't seem fine, Jessie."

"And how would you know whether I'm fine or not? I've known you for, what, a month?" She verbalized her frustration and her feelings. "A month, and already my family calls you when there's a crisis."

"I'd like to think we're friends," Jack said as he inched closer.

What a crock of horseshit. Jessie didn't fantasize about her friends. All night she'd compared Jack to Brad.

Jack had dimples and smiling, genuine eyes. Brad's were dull and less than convincing.

Jack would have been on time. Brad was late.

Jack considered what she wanted and wouldn't have ordered for her the way Brad had.

Jack asked her about her life, got to know her through long talks and not a continual drilling of questions that made her feel as if she was on the stand in a court of law.

More than any of that, Jack would never have said or pulled what Brad had tried once they'd finished their meal.

Jack was too much of a gentleman, too nice a guy. He respected her wishes even if he didn't believe in them.

The man of the hour stepped closer to her, took his finger, and lifted her chin so they looked at each other. "We are *friends*, Jessie."

"Really, Jack. That's what we are…friends?"

"Of course."

"Just friends. Are you saying that if I took my clothes off right now and offered myself to you, you wouldn't take me up on it?"

The words first widened Jack's eyes. A hot current of need flashed on his face; the effect shot molten heat straight to her core. Then those sparkling gray eyes narrowed. "I'm not a saint, Jessie, and you know how I feel about you." His husky voiced confirmed what his expression had already said.

"Friends don't sleep with friends." Her words were weak.

"Say the word, and I'll turn this friendship into a relationship faster than a rattlesnake can strike his prey." He would, she knew he would. The fire in his gaze said more than any of his words could.

"To what end, Jack?" Jessie pulled away from him, felt tears sting her eyes. "What is wrong with me? There has to be more out there than dreaming fantasies in cowboy boots and lawyers who peg me as a quick roll because I wait tables and have a kid."

Jack grasped her arm and swung her around to face him. His face grew stone cold. All fire and heat forgotten.

"What did you say?"

"Nothing." She tried to pull away, but he wouldn't let her go.

"Did he hurt you, Jessie? By God, he'd better not—"

"No. My pride. My ego. But not me physically." Why couldn't she find a combination of man that had it together financially like Brad but had all the qualities of Jack?

A sob escaped her throat and Jessie dropped her forehead on Jack's chest. The comfort of him, his heat, helped a few tears run down her cheeks.

Jack brought his other hand around her and pulled her closer.

She wanted to cry, a big sob session with tissues and blotchy eyes. Brad had dominated their meal, talked about his work, his worth, then asked her if she wanted to go home with him for a few hours and "finish up their date."

She was stunned by the proposition, didn't quite know how to act afterward. Jessie told him she didn't work that way. Brad appeared offended. His mountain-sized ego had escaped her until that moment. He couldn't believe she was blowing him off. There wasn't even interest to go on a second date with the guy, let alone sleep with him.

With as much dignity as she could muster, Jessie estimated the cost of her meal, tossed a few bills on the table, and walked out of the restaurant. When her car died halfway home, she screamed and pitched a hissy fit, dash-hitting and all. Truth was the walk home, in heels, probably helped burn off some of her anger.

Then to find Jack sitting on her couch, Danny curled in his lap, brought a whole new wave of emotions over her.

Jack was so…Jack.

Here she was, sobbing in his arms. Arms she had no business enjoying.

Jessie lifted her head from his white shirt and saw the mascara stain on his shoulder. "I'm a mess. Look what I did to your shirt."

Jack brought both hands to her face and forced her eyes to his. "It's just a shirt."

She realized that it was a dress shirt and that Jack wasn't wearing his normal jeans and hat. Had Monica called him off a date?

She wanted to ask but didn't really want to know.

Using his thumb, Jack wiped away her tears. "You want me to beat this Brad guy up?"

She laughed, despite herself. "He's a lawyer."

"Probably a sissy in a fight."

"He'll press charges and have the last laugh." The testosterone kick of Jack's words sure was nice to hear. "Thanks for the offer."

Jack's grin slowly faded as he stood there holding her. His eyes roamed her face; his thumbs went from wiping away her tears to stroking the outline of her bottom lip. It was as if he were memorizing her. Taking in every detail, every line, and committing it to memory.

Jessie found herself studying him. Gray eyes held silver flecks that sparkled from time to time. Running a finger along his jaw, she noticed the bristles of a five o'clock shadow. He was clean shaven most of the time, but his jaw took on a more rugged appeal when he was like this. She liked it. The hard edge of Jack that made him want to stand up for her and kick Brad's butt.

Her eyes focused on Jack's soft lips, next to his bristled chin.

Kissable lips. She wanted those lips against hers in the worst way.

Jessie trembled in his arms and pulled her lower lip between her teeth.

A questioning expression spread over his face, his hands tightened, and she swayed forward and placed her lips to his. There was no slow boil, no simmering steam. They went from hot to hotter instantly. Jack tilted his head and deepened their kiss. Fingers in his hair, Jessie enjoyed the silky feel of it, of him.

Their tongues fought for control as they explored each other.

He was perfect. Strong and hard in all the right places and so soft and caring in others. His mouth assaulted hers, but his hands slowly stroked her back and waist. Desire and need for this man, this dreamer, ate away at her resolve. Already her nipples pebbled to tight buds and her body hummed.

Jack's hand traveled low on her back until she felt it round over her bottom. The intimate touch held both relief and frustration. Relief because Jack's hands were on her, and not only in a dream. Frustration because of how she shouldn't be enjoying his kiss, his touch, so much.

Jack tore his lips from hers and moved to explore her neck, her ear.

She gasped and tilted her head back. Her clothes suddenly felt too tight, itchy.

Friends with benefits. They could do that...right?

But they couldn't. It wouldn't be fair to Jack. It would be easy for her to take him to her cold and lonely bed, but then what?

What about tomorrow? Jessie hated that she couldn't remove these lurking thoughts from her head and just enjoy the man's touch.

What if it didn't work out? How could their friendship survive?

Jessie realized her hand had slipped into his shirt and was clutching his bare skin. She pulled her hand away. "Jack," she whispered.

He stopped kissing her neck and focused his gaze on hers.

"We...we shouldn't be doing this." Not now, not after a date from hell, not with her emotions running high. She needed to think, make educated decisions about the man in her arms.

"You want this as much as I do," Jack stated the obvious.

There could be no denying that. "I don't want regrets, Jack. You evoke so many emotions inside of me, I can't see straight."

"Darlin', that makes two of us."

"But...we'd have regrets. Maybe not today, but tomorrow or the next day." When Jack took his fill and left to follow his next dream. She'd have a heaping boatful of regrets.

"I have never, nor will I ever, regret any time I spend with you." His sober words made her realize how many regrets she would hold.

"I value our friendship...If we do this, there would be no friendship."

Jessie knew he couldn't deny her words.

Jack groaned and kissed her forehead before breaking their contact.

Her body cooled instantly, a root of reality already reaching its fingers around her heart and giving it a tight squeeze.

Jack gathered his jacket and pushed his arms into it. At the door, he turned to her. "You have my number."

Which meant she'd have to make the next move.

"Thanks."

Jack nodded, passed her one long, heated stare, and walked out her door.

———

Jack slipped into his shower and blasted the water on cold. There was nothing remotely satisfying about a cold shower. The only thing it served was cooling his enraged hormones that were on a continual high cycle when in the presence of Jessie.

She'd been so vulnerable tonight. In hindsight, he was happy she'd pulled away. Left to himself, he wouldn't have. They would have both enjoyed each other in bed, but he could see the pain in Jessie's eyes; she would have regretted it.

She would have been right. Once they slept together, this pseudofriendship would blow up like smoke and Jack would hold on to her as tight as he could. No more misfit dates with lawyers who took her as easy. No more pretending not to care if another man looked at her with desire. Jack Morrison was a good many things, but he didn't share his women, and none had meant as much as Jessie did.

Jack let the cool water run over his face before turning and allowing it to drip down his back. He started to cool his jets, but his insides still flamed. Only now, they were in an all-fire pisser about Brad the snake. How dare the man expect something from a first date with a woman he barely knew?

How could the man ever mistake Jessie for that kind of woman? Kind and caring, Jessie deserved respect. Jack knew she was worried about his feelings when she'd backed away from sleeping with him tonight. She didn't want him falling for her because she wasn't ready to return the sentiment. What Jessie didn't realize was her efforts were already too late.

Jack turned off the water and stepped out of the shower. Grabbing a towel, he dried himself off.

Too late. Jack had it bad.

Then there was Danny...Lord, that kid had grown on him. How his real father could walk away and never look back ticked Jack off.

He wrapped the towel around his hips and ran his fingers through his wet hair. "Be patient," he told himself in the mirror.

Patience was entirely overrated.

———

Jessie jumped whenever a pickup truck pulled into the parking lot at work. Disappointment ran high when Jack didn't emerge from any of them.

She'd worked a couple of extra hours each morning for one of the day-shifters to make it easier on Monica, who was schlepping Jessie back and forth to work since they were down a car. Her car would be out of the shop in a couple of days, but boy did the extra expenses bite into Christmas.

Danny deserved much more than she could provide.

A man like Brad might have been able to provide some financial means, but he would have come up short on the emotional ones.

What was worse, she wondered, a man who cared with all his being who would only be around a short while? Or a man who didn't care at all?

Would the money last longer than the memories?

Would the heartache last longer than the money?

It was midnight on her first night off since the disaster date with Brad. Jack didn't call, didn't stop by. Monica had finished her semester and was enjoying a long-overdue break by going to Big Bear, where the snow had come down in feet rather than inches. Monica didn't ski, but she took pleasure in the snow and the guys who flocked to it.

Jessie stared up at the ceiling in her room, unable to sleep.

Danny had gone to bed early with a small cough.

Slipping out of bed, Jessie tossed her robe over her shoulders and shoved her feet into her slippers.

On her way to her kitchen to try some warm milk to help her sleep, she heard Danny coughing in his room.

She pushed open his door and noticed that he'd pushed off all his covers. She stepped in and went to cover her son up. The sweat on his forehead stopped her. Placing the back of her hand to his face, she realized how hot he was.

Danny started to cough again, and this time his eyes opened, glossy and unfocused.

"Hey, handsome."

Danny's little eyes instantly watered. "I don't feel good, Mommy."

Jessie lifted him into a sitting position and he started to cough even harder. Under his pajamas, his skin burned with fever. "Wait here," she told him before rushing to the bathroom to find the thermometer.

"Here, buddy. Let's see where you're at."

She stuck the gauge between his lips and under his tongue. He coughed around it while she stripped the hot pajamas from his tiny body. The coolness of the room had him shivering, but Jessie remembered Monica talking about the kids who arrived in the clinic ill. *"It's not cruel to strip a burning kid down to his underwear. It's much worse to let the fever stay high and keep all that heat in."*

Danny kept coughing, only it didn't sound like he was bringing anything up. He even had a squeaky noise when he pulled in a breath.

Inside, Jessie started to panic. Outside, she smiled and stroked Danny's head. Her car was in the shop and Monica was out of town.

It was late at night, and the only place open was the emergency room at Upland Community.

Jessie pulled the thermometer from Danny's mouth and tilted the glass tube until she saw the red line: 104.2.

Now it was time to panic.

She hurried to the bathroom and found the chewable children's Tylenol and glanced at the box to see how much to give him. The weight chart said two tablets, so she poured two in her hand and hurried back to Danny's side.

Danny whined when she handed him the medicine, his body shook, and his coughing never stopped. "Here, baby. Take these."

"Do they taste bad?"

"They're good, try 'em. They'll make you feel better." But 104.2 wasn't good. She had to get him to a doctor. The cough worried her even more than the fever.

She wished her sister were there helping her.

Jessie ran to her bedroom, grabbed a cordless phone, and dashed back to Danny's side.

Her mother was too far away.

Her fingers flew over the numbers, never hesitating.

Jack answered on the first ring.

"Jack, thank God you're there."

"Jessie? What's wrong? Are you OK?" There was panic in Jack's voice, and her own heightened in response.

"It's Danny." Danny started to cough again. "He's sick and my car's in the shop. He needs a—"

"Stay calm. I'll be right there."

"Hurry." But he'd already hung up the phone.

Jessie tossed a T-shirt over Danny's head and propped him up on a few pillows on the couch. In her room, she stepped into the clothes she'd worn the day before and grabbed her purse from her dresser.

Back in the living room, she unlocked the door and then had to wait. Danny's eyes kept drifting shut between his fits of coughing. Jessie had never felt more helpless in her entire life.

She rocked her son back and forth while he clutched Tex to his side. Jessie did her best to ignore his shaking body. This part of parenthood really sucked. Why couldn't she be the one to get sick? Why Danny?

She heard Jack's footsteps running down the hall before her door swung open. He was there, thank God. Jessie wanted to cry in relief.

Jack slowed his steps and reached down to take Danny from her arms. "Hey, partner." He greeted her son first.

Danny tried to smile, but he coughed instead.

"See, that cough is bad," Jessie said in alarm.

Jack shook his head. "Shh, I got him. Grab your purse and lock the door."

"OK," she said, following his instructions and taking her place at his side.

The cool air outside hit her hard. Jack opened the passenger door and buckled Danny in the center seat. Jessie stepped in beside him and Jack ran around the truck to the driver's side door.

"Where is the nearest ER?" he asked.

Jessie gave him directions and Jack drove. There was no small talk, no smiling. Jack looked just as concerned as she felt.

At the hospital, Jack carried Danny inside. The lobby was a quarter full with mostly slumbering people who looked like they were waiting on family members.

"Hello," the lady behind the bulletproof glass said with a smile as she pushed a sign-in sheet in front of them.

Jessie wrote down Danny's name on autopilot. "He has a fever over 104, and his cough is making it hard for him to breathe."

The lady gave a sympathetic look and said, "I'll get the triage nurse."

Jessie glanced up at Jack, who hadn't sat down. Danny coughed on his shoulder.

"What's taking so long?" he asked, though the woman hadn't been gone but a minute. When she walked back to the window, another, older lady stood there with a stethoscope around her neck and a pen in her hand. She looked through the window at Danny and motioned with her hand. "Come on back."

Around the corner, Jessie and Jack were led into the busy ER and placed in a small room. Jack sat next to the desk and placed Danny in his lap. Jessie grabbed a chair and moved it closer.

"I'm Teresa, one of the nurses here. How long has Danny been sick?"

"Only a few hours. He didn't feel well before he went to bed, but he wasn't coughing like this."

Teresa placed a sensor with tape on Danny's finger. "How high was his fever at home?"

"104.2. I gave him Tylenol right before we left."

"Good. Most parents just rush in and don't think."

Teresa asked a series of other questions. Danny's weight, previous illnesses, immunization status. Allergies to medicine. Jessie answered everything while the nurse wrote feverishly.

She unplugged the sensor attached to Danny's finger from the machine but kept it dangling on him. "His pulse ox is low; it's a good thing you came in."

"Is that a bad thing?" Jack asked.

"If left alone," she confirmed. "Don't worry, we'll take care of your little boy."

Neither Jessie nor Jack corrected the nurse.

"His temperature is still high, 102.5. I'm going to give him some ibuprofen."

"Is that OK after he had the Tylenol?"

"It's perfectly fine. Both medications have the same goal, but they work differently. Lots of kids have high fevers, and we bring them down with both medications all the time." Teresa stood and waved her hand. "Come on, Dad, follow me." Jack followed the nurse with Danny while Jessie followed Jack.

Chapter Eleven

The nurse led them into a room where she turned on a monitor and plugged in the oxygen sensor Danny wore on his finger. Jack saw the number—ninety-four—but didn't understand the significance of it. When the number dipped to ninety-two, the machine started beeping, which he didn't think was a good thing. At some point, the nurse left the room to find a doctor, and Danny reached for his mother.

Jessie pulled him into her lap and sat on the gurney with him. She swayed back and forth and spoke softly to Danny, who was more awake now and anxious about where he was and what was going to happen to him.

"Are they going to give me a shot? I don't want a shot."

Jack paced the room.

"Let's not worry about that, buddy," Jessie told her son. She glanced over at Jack. "Hey, did you notice that Jack gave us a ride in his truck? Cool, huh?"

Danny looked up at him. "I like your truck," he said, glossy eyes and all.

Jack knew Jessie was trying to distract her son. "When you're all fixed up, we should go mud wampum in my truck," he said. "That's lots of fun."

"W-what's that?" Danny asked through a cough.

"It's when we go out in the dirt after it rains and splash the truck in the mud puddles. In Texas, mud puddles get really big."

"I'd"—cough, cough—"like that."

The nurse returned with a doctor at her side. "Hi, folks, I'm Dr. Shields. This must be Danny."

Dr. Shields asked a bunch of questions while he listened to Danny's lungs and examined his ears and throat. He glanced at the nurse and said, "Let's get some Albuterol treatments going. When he's finished with the first one, we'll send him to X-ray to have a look."

Teresa left the room and Dr. Shields started to explain what was happening.

"Danny's never had asthma, allergies?"

"No. Not really."

"He started kindergarten this year?"

"Yes."

"Kindergarten exposes kids to all kinds of new and fun illnesses, I'm sorry to say. I'm going to give him a breathing treatment to open his airway, make it easier for him to breathe. Once his fever is down, he'll probably relax and his oxygen saturation will improve. He has an ear infection, which I'll send you home with antibiotics for, but I'll want you to follow up with your pediatrician later this week."

Jack's head spun. "Does he have asthma?"

"I doubt it, since this is the first time he's had these symptoms. Different things are blooming this time of year. Spring isn't the only time allergies can cause issues. The winds that blow here cause havoc on many of us, even those who don't have asthma. Let's be safe and have his doctor follow him. We'll take a chest X-ray to make sure we're not missing anything and send you home with a copy on a disc."

"OK," Jessie uttered.

"I'm jumping ahead. Let's get Danny more comfortable. I'll be back in a little bit, and Teresa will be in here in a few minutes with his treatment."

Jack held out his hand and shook the doctor's. "Thank you."

"My pleasure."

"Do I have to have a shot?" Danny asked from Jessie's arms.

"Not this time. Unless you want one," Dr. Shields said with a hopeful expression, teasing the boy.

"No way."

Danny's words made everyone laugh.

Within minutes, Danny held a steaming plastic pipe in his mouth and was inhaling the medicine deep into his lungs.

The tension in Jack's shoulders eased, and Jessie's frown and the lines of worry on her face faded.

Soon Danny wanted to sit on the gurney without his mom holding him. Jessie sat him down and took a seat next to Jack. Poor Danny, Jack thought. He must have felt like he was under a microscope with the two of them staring at him, waiting for his next move. Once Danny finished inhaling the medicine in the plastic pipe, the nurse returned and turned off the oxygen.

One of the clerks stepped into the room and gathered insurance information from Jessie, which she handed over quickly. The whole process of documenting her state-funded insurance and the billing for her part of Danny's expenses was quickly finished up and pushed aside.

By now, Danny had curled up on his side and closed his eyes.

"Thanks for coming, Jack," Jessie said, sitting beside him.

He glanced down at Jessie's tired face and put an arm around her. "I'm glad you called me."

She settled into his arms, much to his surprise.

"Monica is away and I still haven't got my car back."

"When did it break down again?" He should have had Max take care of all the issues with her car.

"Remember my date from hell?"

Like he would ever forget it. "Saturday?"

"Car died on the way home. I walked the last three miles."

Dammit. He shuddered, thinking of her walking at night by herself. Jack squeezed her closer to him, trying to take away all her misery. "You should have told me."

She yawned. "So you could come to my rescue again? It has to be getting old by now. I'm not usually so darn helpless."

"Are you kidding? You feed my ego, lady. There's nothing better for me to do than to take away all the bad things that happen."

Danny had fallen asleep, and for the first time since he walked through the door to Jessie's apartment, the boy didn't look like he was struggling.

"You do. Take away the bad. Tonight I started to panic. If you hadn't answered…"

"Hey, I did. We're good. Danny looks better already."

Jack settled in and stroked up and down Jessie's arm until both mother and son were nodding off and falling asleep.

Jack placed Danny into his bed and pulled a sheet over him. Jessie kissed her son and stepped out of the room.

It was three in the morning.

"I don't know how I'm going to make all this up to you."

"You already have, Jessie." Jack glanced around the living room. "I'll just rest up here on the couch."

"You don't have to do that. I'm sure Danny is going to be fine now. The doctor thought he'd sleep till morning without any problems."

Jack sat on the sofa and toed off his shoes. "If it's all the same to you, I'm staying. Save me the trouble of turning around and coming back should there be a need."

Jessie looked as if she wanted to argue, then shook her head. "OK. The sofa pulls out into a bed."

"I'm fine on the sofa."

Jessie disappeared for a few minutes and returned with a pillow and a blanket. "You sure?"

He took his jacket off and winked. "Positive."

"OK," she said. "G'night."

"Good night, sweetheart."

Jessie smiled before turning and walking to her bedroom.

Jack tossed the pillow on the side of the sofa and unfolded the blanket. Too keyed up to lie down, he sat there for a few minutes and listened to Jessie walking around in her room.

The dark Christmas tree was nearly as bare as it had been a week ago. It was wrong. The lush one that sat in his penthouse suite at The Morrison was what Jessie and Danny deserved. He was starting to forget why he kept his disguise as a poor dreamer. All his half truths and bald-faced lies were getting too carried away.

Tonight while Jessie slept in his arms and Danny snoozed on the gurney, Jack realized how much he'd fallen for her. For both of them.

All of the signs of falling in love were there. For some strange reason, the "L" word didn't worry him in the least. Perhaps with a different woman he'd feel closed in, trapped, but not with Jessie. The way she looked at him, called him when she needed him. She laughed at his jokes and listened when he needed to talk. The gentle sway of her hips and toss of her hair fired his blood with want.

Even now, Jack heard her tossing in her bed in the other room. He should just go in there and tell her the truth.

Jessie, he'd say. *All my life all I ever wanted was for a woman to want me for me. For who I am and not my name or the money I make. Then I walked into your diner, and you took my breath away. I had to know that you would love me for me. I can't let you go on thinking*

I'm some dreamer who couldn't make you happy if you gave me half a chance.

How hard could those words be? They sounded good to him, and he'd been fantasizing about saying them for weeks.

Jack heard the coils in her bedspring squeak and he stood.

Get it over with.

Yet the closer he moved to the door of her room, the more his stomach twisted.

The door was open. Probably so she could hear Danny if he called out.

She shifted on the bed and punched her pillow.

Jack watched her do this a couple of times and smiled. At least he wasn't the only one having trouble getting to sleep. Jessie shifted again and then tossed her covers off. "Dammit," she whispered.

"Trouble sleeping?" he asked, his voice low.

She turned and noticed him standing in the doorway. She clicked on a bedside lamp and illuminated the room with a soft glow.

"This is crazy," she whispered.

She tossed back the covers, revealing a long T-shirt with a snowman eating his nose. The image shouldn't have been sexy, but it was. Then again, the way Jessie lifted her frame from her bed, and the sultry look in her eyes when she approached him, knocked his brain clear away from his head. Cognitive thoughts fled as his pulse lunged into high gear.

Standing toe-to-toe, Jessie pulled him into her room and closed the door behind him. He'd come in there to tell her something, but he couldn't remember what.

Her perky breasts pushed against the snowman; her nipples poked against the thin fabric. Jessie ran a hand up his arm and back down.

"What are you doing, Jessie?"

"If you have to ask, I'm losing my touch," she said with a smile. Hadn't he used a similar line on her not so very long ago?

"But you don't—"

She silenced him by placing her finger over his lips. "No more talking. I've talked until I'm blue. I want to feel, Jack." She stepped back, crossed her arms over her shoulders, and tugged her night-shirt away from her body.

She stood in pink lace panties and nothing else. The heat in her stare shot straight to his groin, and his heart started to sing hallelujah.

Her porcelain skin dipped and swelled in all the right spots. Jack actually felt in awe of being next to her like this. Reaching a hand out, Jack gently touched her shoulder before letting his hand slide over her arm. He watched his fingers trace over her skin and noticed when Jessie visibly trembled at his touch.

Jack felt as if he'd waited a lifetime to touch her, to taste her. Their two kisses had sated nothing and fueled everything. His fingers lingered on her elbow before reaching for her waist. He fanned his fingers and touched as much of her skin as possible but still didn't have enough. Jack allowed his other hand to follow the curve of her soft, welcoming hip. Real gooseflesh rose on his arms. When Jessie sucked in a tight gasp of pleasure, Jack glanced into her hazel eyes, eyes that darkened when she was aroused as she was now. She stood there, enjoying his touch and demanding nothing.

Her lips parted when he followed up the curve of her waist and touched the underside of her generous breast with his knuckles. Her nipples hardened into aching pebbles of flesh asking to be touched.

"I want to be everything for you," he found himself saying.

Jessie reached up to his shirt and undid the buttons, slowly. With shaky hands, she managed to push the last piece of round plastic through its hole and brush his shirt off his chest until it pooled at their feet.

Her fingers spread over his chest and buried into the light dusting of hair she found. One tantalizing thumb rubbed over his nipple and provoked multiple firings of nerve endings that had sat dormant for a very long time.

They hadn't even kissed and already his erection strained against his pants.

No matter how much he wanted her, he wouldn't rush this moment.

No, this moment was meant to explore, feel, touch, taste, and experience with his whole being.

Bending his head, Jack pressed his lips against her neck and found her pulse beating hard. He nibbled, licked, and kissed a path to her collarbone until he felt Jessie mold her body to his.

Jack wrapped his arms around her. His lips lifted from her sweet skin and found her mouth. She groaned into their kiss but made no move to rush the moment. It was as if they had an agreement not to hurry, to make love slowly, thoroughly.

Her lips were soft, savory. Jack's mouth lingered on hers, exploring first with his lips, learning every curve, every motion that made Jessie moan, then he offered something deeper and mated his tongue to hers. Nails, hers, dug into his back as she pressed closer. Her breasts flattened against him as she gave in to sensation and let him ravish her with his needy mouth. Heat built and Jessie started to melt in his arms.

Jack backed her up to the bed and followed her down to the mattress. Jessie's hands were free to roam over his flesh, and she did so with bold, long strokes, down his back and over his jeans-clad ass and thighs. If he wasn't clothed, he'd be inside of her already; best to keep his pants on as long as he could stand the wicked torture of her touch.

Jessie was on fire. The weight of Jack pressing her into her bed was just as pleasurable as his hands roaming over her hip, past her panties, and down her thigh. His lips were lethal weapons; his tongue, ammunition that threatened to undo every restraint she possessed.

He kissed her until she was breathless, and then left her mouth to kiss her neck, her shoulder. His hands cupped her taut breasts, and waves of desire shot to her belly and settled between her legs.

Jessie lifted one leg and laid it over one of his until his knee settled firmly against her core. It was so delicious having him in her arms. Thoughts of stopping didn't penetrate her brain. Only the desire to feel him touch her everywhere ruled her thoughts.

When Jack's mouth touched her nipple, she lifted off the bed and pushed her hips up and against his thigh. That tiny motion and friction, that connection, needed repeating.

She wanted him so desperately but wouldn't speed them up any more than he would.

Jessie slid her hand down his thigh and pulled it up between her legs. Jack laughed over her breast. "You laugh now," she said as she shamelessly tilted her hips against his leg. "I know what you're doing."

"Do you?"

"Holding me off, making me pay for all the times I've denied you." He pinched her breast, tossing the words from her mouth and brain.

"Holding you off, but not for payment…for pleasure." His hand snaked down her taut stomach and teased the edge of her panties.

She held her breath, waiting.

When he hesitated, Jessie opened her eyes and found him staring at her. The smoky flecks in his eyes glistened in the dim light of the room. He moved his fingers between the lace and her skin and slowly sought her wet, throbbing core. There was no way to keep her eyes open when he opened her to pleasure. It had been so long since anyone had touched her, and if she was honest with herself, no one had ever taken such care of her needs.

His hand moved with her hips. Her breath grew shallow as her body started to tighten and strain. Slowly, Jack backed her down from the growing tidal wave of ecstasy, leaving frustration. "You are a brat, Jack Moore."

"Good things come to those who wait," he quoted.

Wait? Hadn't they waited long enough?

I'll show you wait.

Smiling, Jessie ran a hand up Jack's thigh. Her fingers grazed the inside of his waistband until she felt the button snap free.

"Oh no," Jack moaned when she grazed the outline of his arousal through his jeans. "I'm in trouble, aren't I?"

Jessie pushed him off her and leaned over him for a change. "Big, heaping mounds of trouble, cowboy."

Those sexy dimples of his poked through his smile as his hand lifted to her face and stroked her cheek. "I can take it," he said.

We'll see about that.

Jessie took her time undoing the series of buttons holding his pants together. She purposely stayed away from the hottest part of his body when she inched his jeans down his hips.

Jack lifted and helped in taking off his jeans. Once they were kicked free of his body, Jack settled back with a grin and wide-open eyes.

He wears boxers, Jessie thought as she stroked his hip and butt before coming around and purposely avoiding his impressive length. Leaning in, she set her lips to his and opened for his questing tongue instantly.

Jack's hand returned to her waist and pulled her closer. Her leg settled between his, and now it was Jack's turn to ride her thigh. Moving quicker, Jessie smiled under his kiss and reached between their bodies to cup him through the cotton of his boxer shorts.

Tearing his lips away, he hissed out, "Damn, darlin', this is going to be over too fast if you continue that."

Jessie eased her hand into the fly of his shorts and took him in her firm grip. "Good things come to those who wait," she mimicked, teasing him.

Something inside Jack snapped, and Jessie was pinned beneath him in the space of one breath. Jack had her wrists in his hands as he held her away. He kissed her hard, and Jessie had never felt more aware of a man before in her life.

Shaking with desire, Jack lifted his hands from hers, leaned down her body, and removed the scrap of material between her legs.

Lifting from the bed, he tossed his shorts with her panties and reached for his jeans. From his wallet, he produced a condom and quickly covered himself with it. Even that was sexy as hell.

When he returned, Jessie opened for him, cradling him amid her thighs. He leaned in and kissed her softly, the tip of his erection sliding against her, intimately, teasing.

Neither of them could stand the wait any longer.

Jessie ran her hand down his torso, his hip, and rounded in front to position him.

They stared into each other's wide-open eyes as he took her in slow, satisfying degrees.

Her body fluttered awake; dormant for so long, she knew her body gripped him tight.

"Lord," he gasped once he was fully seated.

Full and still hungry, Jessie waited for Jack to catch his breath before she rocked up against him.

Jack found her lips and kissed her as they began to move and her body tightened around him. Both of them fought to breathe, an effort in their goal of pleasure. Jessie gloried in the feel of him sliding against her, bringing her higher with every pass.

She lifted her legs around his waist, and he stroked her perfectly over and over.

"Yes," she said in a rough whisper. So close to exploding, so close, and then she was there, stifling her moan into Jack's shoulder and feeling her body spasm around him, draining every nerve ending that had held back for so long.

Jack rode her, prolonging her orgasm, until his breath caught and he moved faster.

"Jessie," he cried as he found his release and his strokes became slower, longer, until he collapsed on top of her.

Glorious. There was no other way to describe what the two of them were together. She hugged him close and pushed away rational thought.

There was only now. The afterglow of their loving.

Jack shifted to her side and pulled her back up against him, holding her close.

Jessie weaved her fingers with his and closed her eyes. She wanted to say something, but words escaped her, so she settled on silence and Jack's warmth as they fell asleep in each other's arms.

Chapter Twelve

The smell of coffee woke her. Jessie's eyes fluttered open to find the space next to her in bed empty. Surprisingly, the clock on the dresser told her it was after eight in the morning. Danny usually bounded from bed by seven, but either the lil' guy was still sleeping or he was doing a superior job of keeping quiet.

The previous night brought an immediate smile to her face. She stretched and felt a slight ache in the muscles she'd used. Oh, but the pain was a very good thing.

She rolled off the bed, tucked her feet into her slippers, and slipped on her bathrobe.

Walking out of her room, she heard the sound of the television running some type of cartoon. In the living room, Danny lay on the couch with a blanket tossed on his lap. In his hands was a bowl of cereal. She didn't usually let him eat while on the sofa, but he looked so comfortable. After the night he'd had, Jessie didn't have the heart to encourage him to move to the table.

"You're up." Jack smiled as he walked toward her, greeting her with a cup of coffee. The expression on his face told her he wanted to kiss her, but he glanced over at Danny.

The fact that he was worried about Danny, or at least that's what it appeared to be to Jessie, expressed how very much Jack understood her. "Thank you," she said as she brought the coffee to her lips. He'd even put cream and sugar in the cup.

Thoughtful. Always thoughtful.

"Good morning, Mommy."

Jessie stepped to the couch and placed her cup on the table before touching Danny's forehead. "How are you feeling this morning, buddy?"

His cheeks and nose were still rosy, and his eyes were droopy. But his skin wasn't nearly as hot as it had been the night before.

Danny coughed a couple of times and then said, "Better. I think I could go to the park later on."

Ah, yeah, right. "I don't think that's a good idea today. Maybe by tomorrow." *Or the day after.*

"I checked his temperature when he woke up," Jack told her. "It was 101.2, so I gave him the Motrin like the doctor said to."

Jessie glanced between Jack and Danny before brushing Danny's hair away from his eyes. Danny watched the TV, hardly glancing at her. She stood and walked into the kitchen, where the smell of toast filled the tiny space.

"Thanks for helping Danny out."

"I hope you don't mind."

"Mind? Jack, please, I appreciate it."

He leaned a hip against the counter and sipped his coffee.

"I can't believe I slept in. How long have you guys been up?"

"About an hour. I heard Danny in the bathroom and thought I'd sneak out to check on him and let you sleep."

Jessie stepped around Jack and pulled him out of direct sight of Danny. She leaned up and kissed him. "Thanks," she said before he pulled her down for a more satisfying kiss.

When he let her go, she smiled and felt her cheeks warm. Jessie stared into the warmth of his gaze, unable to pull away. *What is he thinking?* She looked a mess. Hair brushed by her pillow, sleep in her eyes, but still he smiled at her as if she were dressed for the ball.

"You're beautiful," he told her softly.

"I'm a mess," she corrected. But the fact he saw through her messy state first thing in the morning was a huge plus.

He brushed his hand against the side of her face and stared directly into her eyes.

"Marry me."

At first, Jessie thought she'd imagined his words. When Jack kept staring at her, a slight grin on his face, she knew she'd heard him correctly.

"W-what did you say?"

He laughed and wrapped a hand around her waist. "I said, marry me."

No, not this. Not now.

The air in her lungs started to push through with difficulty, and not in a good way. From the expression on Jack's face, she knew her face showed her confusion.

Her smile fell, and her hands began to shake. Jessie's head started to shake. "Jack," she said breathlessly.

"I want this, Jessie. You, me. Danny. I know you have reservations—"

She pushed out of his arms. "No. Don't do this. Please." Dammit. He knew how she felt about dreamers and forever.

Jessie glanced around the corner and saw that Danny had laid his head on a pillow. She grasped Jack's hand and pulled him into her bedroom. There, she shut the door behind them and spoke in a hoarse whisper. "Why are you doing this? You know I can't marry you."

Jack's smile started to fade. The reality that she was turning him down started to sink in. "Because I'm not rich?"

"N-No." She spun away from him, away from the cold that started to penetrate his eyes. "I care for you. Really. Last night was amazing…"

"Then what's the problem?"

"Think about it, Jack. We get married, you move in here. Then the newness wears off and the bills are making us snap at each other. Or you remember how much you love Texas, but then realize you can't afford to move back there. You'll want to run off and I'll be here, holding on." She was rambling. Barely making sense. Why did he have to do this to them? Couldn't they just enjoy a physical relationship? Why make promises he'd want to break later on down the road?

"That's not going to happen." He reached for her arm and she pulled away.

"It will. You need to find someone who can run off with you to make your dreams come true. You don't need me and a kid holding you back." And he'd regret her and Danny before a year was out. Dreamers hated it when reality slapped them in the ass.

"What if I told you I had money?"

"Stop it! Just stop!" She hated this. Hated that she felt her heart breaking after it was so full of life only minutes before. "We're friends, Jack. I don't want to regret last night, because for a moment there I thought maybe we could be 'friends with benefits' or something stupid like that. Obviously that's not the case." She still saw hope in his eyes, and Jessie knew she needed to say something to get him to find his forever with someone else. "It was just sex, Jack."

"That's all it was to you?" he asked harshly. His tone made her want to weep.

Her lip quivered and tears stung her eyes. "Yes." She did her best to sound convincing. When he continued to stare at her, she spun away. "I think you should go."

I'm not going to cry. I'm not going to cry.

"Jessie?"

"Just go." She didn't turn around. She couldn't. If he saw the pain in her eyes, he'd know he meant something to her and keep trying.

Jessie held her breath until she heard him slip from the room. Then she sank to her bed because her legs simply couldn't hold her up any longer. The sound of her apartment door opening and closing prompted the flood of tears she'd been holding back.

Why? Why couldn't he be happy with what they had?

Regret was too small a word for the waterfall of pain that saturated her.

She was right in cutting him loose. He would have grown to hate her for tying him down.

But lord, it hurt.

Like she'd let go of something that only came around once in a lifetime.

Jack held back a strong urge to swipe the Christmas tree in the living room of his suite out the window.

The drink in his hand wasn't numbing him nearly enough. With every hour, his mind vacillated more and more between anger and depression. He blamed himself for blurting out his proposal. If he could have waited, had a ring and done it the right way...

But no. Impulsive Jack jumped right into happily ever after, and now Jessie was out of his reach.

It would be funny if he weren't so miserable. Jessie had denied him marriage because she thought he was a broke loser with nothing to offer.

How friggin' ironic is that?

Considering he'd called the damn car dealer that was working on her broken-down piece of crap and had all but given them a blank check.

He drove away from her apartment thinking he could go back to what they were. Friends.

There was no going back, and moving forward wasn't an option. Damn. He and Jessie couldn't even stand still.

His head fell into his hands.

The phone in his room rang, startling him. When he stood to answer it, the room started to spin.

Jack glanced at the clock on his wall. It was six in the evening, and he still wore the clothes he'd tossed on in the middle of the night to rush Danny to the hospital.

The phone kept ringing.

"I'm coming," he yelled at the phone. Clicking on to the call, Jack nearly dropped the phone before he brought it up to his ear. "What?"

"Well, aren't you just a ray of sunshine?" a female voice purred over the line.

"Katie?"

"Jesus, Jack, it's what…six there? Isn't it early for you to be partying?"

Jack sat before he fell. "You don't hold the rights to self-indulgence." Besides, he'd had a bad day.

"First, I hear you're not coming home for Christmas, now you're wasted in the middle of the day."

"I-It isn't the middle of the day."

"Blurred speech takes some time to achieve, Jacko. What the hell is wrong with you?"

Women! "Nothing. I'm fine." *Drunk, but fine.* As long as he sat perfectly still, the room only swayed when he inhaled…or exhaled.

Katie's uppity voice dropped. "Who is she?"

Damn woman. "I'm hanging up now."

"Jack. Don't you dare. I'll be the—"

He lifted the phone in front of his eyes and hit the End button... twice.

Then, because the bedroom was too far away, Jack sat back and closed his eyes.

———

The next twenty-four hours were a blur for Jessie. Danny's fever rose and fell, but by nightfall, she thought she'd seen the worst of his symptoms. By tomorrow morning, he'd be hard to hold down.

Danny asked about Jack too many times to count.

Where was he?

Was he coming back?

Why did he leave?

Would they be seeing him for Christmas?

With every question, another nail was jammed into the coffin she'd made of her life. Monica was due back that night, and Jessie could hardly wait for her sister to get home so she could cry on her shoulder and hear what a fool she'd been.

Without a doubt, Monica would be calling her all kinds of stupid for saying no.

They would argue. Jessie would put into words why she had to cut Jack loose, and Monica would try to change her mind.

But Jessie was older. She knew better.

Her phone rang. Jessie's heart leapt in her throat. What if it was Jack?

Jessie waited for the answering machine to pick up.

"This call is for Jessica Mann. Ms. Mann, this is Phil Gravis over at Upland Toyota..."

Her car. She scrambled to pick up the phone. "Hello?"

"Ms. Mann?"

"Yes, this is her. Sorry, I was in the other room," she lied. "Didn't hear the phone." Lie number two.

"Not a problem. Ummm, about your car."

Oh, please…no more bad news. She really couldn't take it. "Yes?"

"We had a slight mishap here in the garage."

"Mishap?" That couldn't be good.

"A fire, actually."

Her car. Bad as it was, was only insurance for the other guy. Dammit, the sky was falling and Jessie was standing dead center of the funnel cloud.

"A fire?"

"Yes. A fire mishap. Don't worry, your car is—"

"Fine? My car is fine?"

Mr. Gravis laughed. "Your car is a total loss."

Cue lightning, funnel clouds, and Dorothy's house flying through the air. "That's not funny."

"Well, the car was in need of a lot of work." His voice was flat.

"It's my only transportation." Her voice started to rise, panic started to set in.

"Oh, Ms. Mann, please…it's OK. We here at Toyota are completely responsible and want to invite you over to pick out a replacement vehicle."

"A replacement vehicle?" She was back to parroting his words.

"Let me start over. I can tell you're upset."

Understatement of the year.

"There was a fire, your car is a total loss, but we are offering you a brand-new car in its place. Unless you have some kind of emotional attachment to the early-model Celica, this will turn out to be a good thing for you."

Thank goodness she was sitting, because when his words sunk in, Jessie felt light-headed.

"A new car to replace my broken-down piece of liability?" Her car had probably caused the fire.

"That's right. When would be a good day for you to come in?"

This wasn't happening. She was having a dream and she really needed to wake up.

"Ms. Mann?"

She wasn't waking up. "Yes?"

"Can you come in tomorrow?"

"Tomorrow?" She stared at the wall across the room.

"Yes."

"Yes."

"Yes, you can come in tomorrow?"

Jessie slowly started to nod. "Yes, I can come in tomorrow." The fog started to lift. "Is nine too early?"

"Nine would be great. Just ask for me." He sounded amused.

"This isn't a joke, is it, Mr. Gravis? Because I've had a couple of really shitty days, and I can't take a practical joke right now."

He laughed. "It's not a joke, Ms. Mann. Be thinking about what kind of car you'd like to drive. Four doors, two doors, truck, crossover, or maybe you'd like a hybrid? Your choice."

She thought for a moment about Christmas, Danny, the medical bills that would be coming in. "Can I take the money and pick out a used car?"

"Sorry. I was given specific instructions to offer you any new car we had on the lot."

"Instructions?" The parrot was back.

He hesitated, coughed, and then said, "From my boss."

"Oh, OK. That sounded ungrateful of me. I'm very grateful. Really." She was. It wasn't the new bike Danny wanted, but a new car might make up for it a little. The money she'd save on repairs would help her afford more for her son in the long run. "I'll see you at nine."

They hung up just as the door to the apartment opened.

Monica stepped inside, still bundled in a parka.

The sight of her sister reminded Jessie of Jack.

Monica's eyes caught hers. She opened her mouth to say something, and then her smile fell. "What happened?"

Tears popped up out of nowhere. "I slept with Jack. He asked me to marry him. I said no. He left and hasn't called. I think I may have made a huge mistake."

Monica dropped her bags at the door and walked to Jessie's side. "Oh, Jessie."

Her sister's arms around her brought on a new flood of tears.

Chapter Thirteen

Monica pushed Jessie onto the sofa and let her sob.

"It's OK," Monica cooed. "I'm sure it's not that bad."

No! It was worse.

As her tears started to dry up, the words started tumbling from her mouth. "Danny spiked a fever night before last. I called Jack." Just saying his name brought a physical pain to her chest.

Monica reached over, grabbed a tissue from a box, and handed it to her.

"Thanks."

"Jack gave you a ride to the doctor?"

Jessie nodded. "Yeah. Danny's fever was so high. I got scared."

Monica glanced toward the hall. "Is he OK?"

"The doctor prescribed an antibiotic. He's sleeping now."

Jessie grasped a pillow from the sofa and hugged it as she talked. "Jack insisted on staying the night. In case we needed to go back to the hospital."

"Sounds reasonable. How did the sleeping together fall into place?"

She squeezed her eyes shut. "I caved. I couldn't hold off anymore...ya know?"

Mo smiled and lifted her eyebrows. "I would have given in sooner than you. You guys have been sniffing around this attraction since you met."

Jessie's eyes filled with a new pool of tears. "It was w-wonderful. P-perfect," she stuttered. "Everything I ever wanted." The tears wouldn't stop. Monica handed her fresh tissues and waited for the sobs to calm again.

"Then what happened?"

"Everything was…"

"Perfect, yeah, I get that," Monica said. "When did he ask you to marry him?"

"Out of the blue. The next morning. He helped Danny with breakfast, kissed me, then wham. He asked me to marry him." Even now, the memory shocked her.

"I take it you weren't happy."

"I was shocked. I mean, we'd only just slept together. Who goes from sleeping together to marriage overnight?"

"Jack does…apparently."

"But he knows more than anyone that I wouldn't jump on board the marital train like that. I got scared, Mo."

Monica curled her knee up on the couch. "You told him no?"

"I told him he'd regret marrying me."

"Regret?"

"Yeah, sooner or later he'd realize that marrying a woman with a child would be a burden and he'd hate the fact that we'd hold him back. He has so many ambitions, Mo. Even more than I do." As she said the words again, she felt some of her pride returning.

"So your saying no has less to do with his lack of money and more to do with what you want for him." Monica gave her a half smile.

"Of course. He might think he'd be happy married to me. But he wouldn't. I have a ton of baggage. Becoming an instant dad might sound novel, but it's a job. I can't chance Danny thinking he finally has a father, only to have Jack up and leave." Danny would just have to wait a little longer for a positive male figure to enter his life.

Dammit.

"Jack isn't like our father, Jessie."

"I know that," she said, tapping her head. "In here. But in here," she tapped her chest, "I can't risk it."

Monica took her hand and squeezed. "If you really feel that way, then why are you so upset and torn?"

"Because the thought of never seeing him again hurts. The pain is so deep, and the air is so thick I can't breathe. What if I'm wrong? What if we could work it out? He stormed out of here so fast. I've never seen him so angry." She brushed away a tear and forced the rest back.

"He asked you to marry him and you said no. He's probably hurt, too."

Jessie's lip quivered. "I know."

"Do you love him?" Monica whispered.

Jessie drew in a sharp breath. "I can't, Mo. I can't." But God help her, she did.

"You know what I think?" Monica tapped her hands and smiled. "I think if he really wants you, loves you, he'll be back."

Jessie started to shake her head.

"And if he doesn't love you, he won't be back. And if that's the case, then you made the right decision."

"You're right." Thank God her sister was there to talk reason into her.

"I'm right. But it still hurts."

"It does."

When Monica hugged her again, the last of the day's tears fell.

Jack's eyes fluttered open as lightning attacked his brain. With his tongue stuck to the roof of his mouth and the taste and smell of stale whiskey coating his lips, he thought maybe he had woken in hell.

"So, you decided to wake up?" The unsympathetic voice of his sister forced his gaze across the room.

Katie lounged in a chair opposite him. Her slim legs poked out from under a tight skirt while her high-heeled foot tapped against thin air.

Maybe he was still asleep. Jack closed his eyes and ignored the pain exploding in his head.

"Oh, no you don't, Jacko. I've been watching you sleep for too many hours to let you fall back under again."

Again? How long had she been there? Jack remembered a phone conversation, then a whole lot of nothing.

"What are you doing here?"

"Pulling your sorry butt out of your pity party."

Jack popped one eye open and saw her push out of the chair. Blonde, slim, beautiful, and loaded, Katie looked as if she was made of porcelain and might break if shaken. Jack knew better. Katie Morrison took crap from no one, ever. When the girl had it in her craw that she needed to fix someone or something, there was no stopping her.

Jack decided right then to keep his lips shut about Jessie. He didn't need his sister interfering.

Katie stood over him and handed him a glass. "Here. Drink this."

With his throat dry enough to compete with a desert, Jack drank before he asked what it was. One gulp and Jack sat up, sputtering.

Whiskey.

"What are you trying to do, kill me?"

Katie laughed. "Hair of the pooch."

"Dog. Hair of the dog," he corrected.

"Whatever," she said, sitting down beside him after he'd made room for her on the sofa. "It works when you've been as blitzed as you were."

Jack rubbed a hand over his face and took another gulp for good measure. "How long have you been here?"

She rested a hand on his arm and turned her soft blue eyes on him. "Long enough, big brother."

No, no, no, no…not good. "How long, Katelyn?"

"Oh, I'm Katelyn now. Must mean you're sobering up."

She always was a sassy girl growing up. He could see nothing had changed. Jack finished the contents of the glass in his hands and felt the headache beginning to ease. His clothes were a mess, he smelled bad—even to himself—and if his life depended on it, he wouldn't be able to tell anyone what the date was. The memory of Jessie's refusal added a familiar ache in his chest.

Dammit.

Where is that bottle?

"Come on. Get your ass in the shower and put on some clothes. I'll have a plate of steak and eggs up here by the time you're out. Then we're out of here." Katie stood and pulled on his arm until he was standing beside her. With her heels on, she was nearly his height.

"Where are we going?"

"Home. The plane is waiting." She pushed him toward his room.

"I'm not leaving." *Not without Jessie.*

"Yes you are. Sitting here feeling sorry for yourself isn't going to have you thinking clearly. Not to mention the alcohol factor. You need to jump on Dancer's back and ride the fences. Then maybe you can pull your head out of your ass and figure out what to do. Sitting in this hotel room isn't going to do it."

Dancer...he hadn't thought of his horse back home for months. Riding along the fences of the property was mindless and helped to clear his head. The fact his sister remembered that about him made him smile.

"I think you might be right."

"Hon, I'm always right. Now shower. You stink."

He stumbled into his bathroom and the phone in his pocket rang. He managed to pull it out and recognized Dean's number. "Hello?"

"Well, hell, at least you sound sober this time."

"I take it we talked last night?" Not that Jack remembered.

"You slurred, I listened."

"I'm sure it was very entertaining." He sat on the edge of the counter and pulled off his socks.

"Enlightening, actually. I just wanted to call and make sure you were OK."

His heart was shattered in a zillion pieces. He was anything but OK. "I'm fine."

Dean snorted into the phone. "Right. Listen, while you're sober I thought I might try and give you some advice. You know when you told me that Maggie and I had two different ideas on what life was all about?"

"Yeah." It took Maggie dumping Dean for Jack to tell his friend he was better off without her.

"Well, this girl, Jessie...she's a waitress at Denny's, Jack. Not exactly the kind of woman you've dated before."

Jack's jaw started to throb as his back teeth gritted together. "Dean," he warned.

"I mean, a waitress. C'mon. Did she even finish high school?"

"It's a damn fine thing you're calling on the phone, Dean, or my fist would be through your face." Jack clutched his phone with one hand and pounded on the counter with the other.

"Whoa, OK, Jack. Calm down. Just wanted to point out that these things happen for a reason. You said the same thing to me not too long ago."

Yeah, he had. But this was Jessie they were talking about.

"I'm going to forget we ever had this conversation."

"Just trying to help."

"Well, next time...don't!" Jack hung up and tossed the phone on the counter.

Katelyn watched her brother wobble to the bathroom while talking on his cell phone. She waited until she heard the sound of water before reaching for her phone. She'd learned more of Jack's story than he could possibly remember.

Arriving near midnight, Katie had found Jack sprawled on his sofa, moaning about his life. It took her hours to decipher it, but when she did, she knew she had to help.

Her brother was bonkers over this Jessie he had called out to repeatedly. From what Katie could tell, her brother had decided to find true love by keeping the truth of his wealth from the single mom. Then when the chips fell, the wise woman refused his proposal for fear he'd leave her when he decided to follow his dreams.

He even drove his old beat-up pickup truck he'd had since he was sixteen. No wonder Jessie said no.

"She thinks I'm a w-waiter, here at the hotel," he'd said last night once Katie got him going. "A temporary holiday waiter."

Katie wanted to reason with him, but knew he wouldn't remember much, if any, of their conversation in the morning.

Jack had even showed her a picture he'd taken with his phone of Jessie and her son. The expression on Jessie's face was one of pure devotion. Her son, Danny, had a beaming smile for the camera.

Katie had taken the time to jot down a few phone numbers he'd put in his phone. For later use, she'd told herself, justifying her invasion of his privacy.

But she knew better than to push a man. Her father was just as stubborn as Jack was, or maybe it was the other way around. Still, the two men had one very big thing in common. When they fell in love, they did it all the way. No second time around for either of them. Watching her father pine for her absentee mother for years had made Katie hate her mother more and more.

Katie wouldn't allow her brother similar years of pain.

He was in a tight spot and needed to think.

He needed his little sister to watch his back until he could come up with his own way of fixing the problem.

Sure, Katie could call this Jessie lady up and tell her the truth about her brother, but who knows how that would go? If it went south, Katie and Jack's relationship would be strained more than it was.

She missed her brother. Her own trials in recent life reminded her how much she needed the tiny family she had.

She called room service, ordered a high-protein breakfast for her brother, and then asked the manager of food services to meet her downstairs with the acting manager of the hotel.

She had a few things to cover before she and Jack jumped on the plane.

In the manager's office, Katie asked the two people to sit. "I have a big favor to ask of both of you, a private favor that needs to be between the three of us."

For the first time in months, Katie started to feel good about herself.

Monica stood beside her sister as they walked around the car lot full of shiny new chunks of machinery. Although Danny was feeling better, the cool day had made Jessie ask the neighbor to sit with him long enough for her to pick out a new car.

Something about the whole *We burned your car so come on over and pick out another one* thing bugged the crap out of Monica. If Jessie weren't in such a funk, she'd be questioning the good fortune, too.

Nonetheless, they walked from cars to SUVs to trucks and discussed the merits of all the vehicles.

Mr. Gravis pointed out the attributes. "Navigation is a big thing right now. All the newer cars have hands-free Bluetooth connections for your cell phones, making it safer while on the road."

"Fuel economy is more important than speed," Jessie told the dealer.

"Do you like the hybrid?"

"I live in an apartment. Plugging it in would be a hassle," Jessie told the man.

Monica hadn't thought of that.

"Then a smaller engine with high miles to the gallon. You have a son, right?"

Jessie nodded.

"I think the crossover is perfect," Monica said. "Room for five, plenty of storage in the back. The mileage is better than the bigger SUVs." Monica led her sister over to the cars in question and opened the door of a blue one.

Jessie slid into the seat and placed her hands on the wheel. "It is nice."

"Leather seats with heaters in them on the higher-end models, back-up cameras that display on the navigation system." Mr. Gravis touted the car's statistics while Monica climbed into the passenger seat.

"What do you think, Jessie?"

"I like it…"

"But?"

"The trucks are nice, too."

Monica's smile fell. Jack's truck was old. Even now, Jessie was thinking about him. Monica put her hand over her sister's. "This is *your* car. Jack isn't here."

"I know." Jessie glanced around the interior of the car and shook her head. "I guess this would be a good pick."

"Might I suggest something?" Mr. Gravis asked.

"Go ahead."

"Long trips are made easier with the entertainment package for the kids in the car."

Jessie cocked her head to the side. "The dealer wants me to have a completely loaded crossover?"

Mr. Gravis smiled and nodded.

Jessie glanced at Monica. "What do I have to lose?"

"Take it."

Jessie glanced at the dealer and said, "Show me this car loaded up and I'll take it on a test drive."

"Good choice, Ms. Mann."

Monica stepped out of the car and followed the dealer and her sister around the lot.

When Jessie found the car with all the requirements, Mr. Gravis handed her the keys and let her drive off the lot by herself.

Both Monica and the dealer stepped into the shadow of the building.

"So, Mr. Gravis, do you mind telling me what the real story is here?"

Mr. Gravis glanced her way and the smile on his lips faltered slightly. "It's just as I said. There was a fire, and the dealer—"

"Dealership is responsible. Yeah, I heard that, but I'm having a hard time believing it. Where is Jessie's old car now?"

"We towed it out of here."

Isn't that convenient?

She wasn't buying it.

"Towed it where?"

Mr. Gravis shuffled his feet. "I'm not sure. Junkyard, I guess."

"So if my sister left anything in the glove compartment…"

"Oh, we removed all of her personal items. No worries there."

Yeah, right!

"Sometimes good things happen to good people," Mr. Gravis said. "Your sister seems like a deserving sort. Between you and me, I think my boss is being very generous. Must be the Christmas spirit."

Monica narrowed her eyes. "Christmas spirit?"

"Yeah, 'tis the season and all of that."

She dropped it. She didn't buy his crock of crap for nothing. But she dropped it.

A few minutes later, Jessie drove back into the lot and stepped out of the car. She smiled, but there wasn't any real joy in it. It tore Monica up to see her sister so down.

"I like it. It has everything."

"So shall we fill out the paperwork?"

Jessie nodded.

Two hours later Monica stood beside Jessie as she sat in her new car. "Christmas came early this year," she said, trying to cheer Jessie up.

"I can't believe this. Jack is going to flip…" Her voice trailed off, her eyes fell to her lap.

"Try and think of the good things going on right now. No more broken-down cars or broken heaters. I'll bet you won't even have to roll the windows down on this car to get the air to start working." Her other car was a pile of junk. It was nice to see it go. "Hey, I've got some errands to run. Are you going to be OK if I make it home in a few hours?"

Jessie smiled at her. "I'm a big girl, Mo. I'll be fine."

Monica reached into the car and hugged her sister. "I say we take a road trip the first chance we get."

"Danny is going to be so excited."

"See, that's it. Think of the good things."

Yet as Jessie drove away, Monica knew she was already in tears or near them thinking about Jack.

In her car, Monica drove straight to The Morrison and parked along the street to avoid having to tip the valet. She walked past the marble columns and massive glass doors as if she knew exactly where she was going. Inside, she found the signs pointing toward the lounge. Only a few people were in the bar, none of them Jack. Monica returned to the lobby and found the restaurant. At nearly one o'clock, the lunch crowd was in full swing. The hostess at the desk asked if she wanted to be seated.

"No, I'm sorry. I'm looking for a friend who works here."

"Who are you looking for?"

"His name is Jack Moore."

The hostess had the oddest expression on her face that Monica had ever seen. "Can you wait here?"

"Sure."

Maybe Jack had told the friends he worked with about Jessie and they were watching out for him. Monica thought of what her fellow students might do to help if she were in Jack's shoes.

Monica didn't have to think about it long before an older woman walked up to her, smiling. "Hi, can I help you?"

"Yeah, I'm looking for Jack. It's kind of important or I wouldn't be bothering him at work." Monica realized that her showing up at his place of employment might look bad for him, so she started to explain herself. "He doesn't know I'm coming."

"It's OK. We're not as stuffy as we look. What's your name?"

"Monica. He'll know me as Jessie's sister."

The lady wrote down her name. "Jack isn't working today, I'm afraid. Why don't you give me your number and I'll get him the message."

"Really? I mean, that's nice of you."

"You did say it was important."

"Right. It is. Very important." Monica gave her cell number. "Will Jack be in tomorrow?"

The lady seemed puzzled by the question. "I'm not sure. We allow our employees to switch schedules a lot during the holidays. Honestly, I'm really not supposed to reveal personal schedules."

"Of course. I understand." Monica held her hand out to shake the other woman's. "Thank you."

"My pleasure, Monica. Have a merry Christmas."

"You too."

As Monica left the hotel, she was sure a set of eyes watched her leave. For the second time that day, she thought the Christmas spirit had flown over the people of Ontario and they were all just a little too eager to help.

Chapter Fourteen

Jack pushed his horse into a fast run, enjoying the cool air hitting his face. His head cleared for the first time in days. With that clarity, reason and regret wiggled in.

He'd messed up bad with Jessie. He should have kept his trap shut about marriage and given the girl more time for him to grow on her.

Now he needed to figure out a way to climb back into her life without her running away. More than ever, he needed to know if she loved him. Katie seemed to think she did, and Katie hadn't even met Jessie yet.

"What did she say that made you leave her apartment?" Katie had asked in the plane on the way home to Texas.

"She said it was just sex." Jack had opened up to his sister.

"And you believed her?"

"What was I to think? She turned me down and told me to leave. To find my dreams with someone else. Someone who didn't have a kid that would strap me down."

Katie shook her head and rolled her eyes. "Oh, Jack, you're a fool. Don't you see what she did?"

"I saw it clear enough. She said no."

His kid sister sat forward across the aisle of the Lear and leveled her eyes to his. "When you're riding Dancer, you think long and hard about what you just told me. Long and hard."

Sitting on the back of his horse on his father's Texas ranch gave him plenty of time and silence to think.

Jessie was hurting when she'd told him to leave. Her eyes had glossed over with fear and then her jaw had gone firm with determination. The strong mom gene in her kicked in and she drew her line in the sand. Told him he had pushed too far... too fast.

Yet when she'd given him her reasons for saying no, none of them had to do with the persona he'd presented to her. She didn't say no because he was a transient waiter in a go-nowhere job. No, she'd told him that he would regret asking her one day. So once again, Jessie had to be the adult and say no.

Only she didn't need to say no. And she wasn't the only adult in the relationship.

Jack pushed Dancer to the westernmost part of his father's property and watched the sun move low on the horizon.

He pictured Jessie wearing a sundress and a smile, laughing in the field...a cowboy hat atop her head.

He and Danny could fish on the riverbank. Did Danny like to fish? Chances were the kid hadn't had a chance to do that yet.

Jack's throat started to fill with regret.

He needed to fix this. To make the picture he'd painted in his head come true.

"Is this Monica?" Katie asked when a woman picked up the phone.

"This is. Who's this?"

"Monica, this is Jack's sister, Katelyn. I hope you don't mind, but I hijacked your number and thought I'd give you a call."

Monica hesitated on the line. "I didn't know Jack had a sister."

"A meddling one that he would flip out over if he found out I was calling you."

Monica laughed; the sound was warm and genuine. "Looks like you and I are both in the prying profession. I went to find Jack yesterday, but the people at his work said he wasn't there."

"He needed to clear his head...you know, after."

"After my fool of a sister turned him down."

Katie smiled. "It doesn't sound like my brother was very smooth in his proposal."

"I wasn't there. According to Jessie, it was abrupt. Don't get me wrong, they've been flirting around each other for weeks. It's cute, really. My sister is trying like hell to ignore him, and he's practically flapping his arms to get her to notice."

The thought of her brother acting like a king peacock made Katie giggle. "Oh, that had to be priceless to watch."

"What's sad is how much Jessie wants to disregard him."

Now they were getting to the meat of the conversation. "Why do you think that is?"

"She's scared. It's that simple. Danny is her world. That's my nephew. I'm sure Jack told you about him."

Katie swallowed hard. The smile on her face fell, and her throat tightened. "Yeah. He said something about her son."

"When you have a kid, things aren't as cut and dry. She's always been a worrier. Our mom isn't exactly a stellar example of stability," Monica told her.

"Neither is ours."

"Well, Jessie wants to be nothing like our mom. I think if Jack had taken everything a little slower, things would be different."

Katie liked Monica already. "I can see we are going to get along very well."

"I think so, too. Maybe we can get them both to see reason."

Not with a bunch of lies hiding under the tangled web. "Monica, there are some things about Jack that you should both know, but I'm not going to share those secrets. It's not my place."

"Oh God…please tell me Jack isn't in some kind of trouble. No Texas Mounties or whatever you call them are after him or anything?"

"No! Texas Mounties. That's funny, Monica. No, Jack doesn't have a record or any hidden bad side." Quite the opposite.

"Oh, good."

"Just tell me one thing." Katie waited for Monica to speak.

"What?"

"Does your sister *love* my brother?"

Monica chuckled. "She cries every day and hasn't eaten a whole lot since he left. She tells me she 'can't' love him, but I know love when I see it. Your brother and my sister are made for each other."

Katie felt her heart swell. "Then you keep your sister occupied until I can get my brother's head on straight."

"She has Danny, Christmas, work…and me. She's busy."

"Just remind her that Jack's one of the good guys. He is, by the way."

"Neither of us thought differently. Like I said. She's just scared."

"Yeah, well, I'm more scared of what it's going to look like if they don't make it. Jack was a mess."

"Same with Jessie."

Katie smiled. "So you and I will work together and make this work. Well, as much as we can, anyway."

"Sounds like a plan to me," Monica said before hanging up the phone.

Katie held the phone in her hand. "Now all I have to do is make Jack realize she loves him."

Even with Christmas music playing and Danny tapping on the outside of packages, Jessie's mood circled the drain of life. Even the weather gave its ugly opinion as rain ran down the window of the apartment. It had only been a handful of days since Jack walked out of her life, but it felt like she hadn't smiled in months.

Damn, she missed him.

Danny missed him, too. In fact, when she'd shown Danny the car for the first time, his first reaction was to call Jack.

Even now, Danny talked about Jack and the car. "We should go get Jack and take him for a ride," Danny said from across the room.

"Jack is kind of busy right now." Telling her son they might not ever see him again made her sick to her stomach. She couldn't take any more hits. Danny would mourn the loss of Jack as much as she did. More, probably, because he couldn't understand what had driven him away.

"Is he coming over on Christmas? We should invite him. His family is all the way in Texas, you know."

"He'll probably go home for Christmas, Danny."

"But he can come here. He doesn't even have to buy any presents or anything. He can play with me and my new toys. He said he likes to play with trucks."

Jessie bit her tongue and tried a smile. "I'll play trucks with you."

"I know, but Jack says he used to play with trucks for hours when he was a kid."

Danny reached under the tree and shook another box.

There was underwear in it. Not exactly a toy or a truck, but something to unwrap. She needed to do some more shopping, but Santa...or in her case, Mrs. Claus...was really broke. Jessie had made Monica promise not to buy her a thing and to spend anything she wanted on her son.

"I'm sure he did."

"Did you play with trucks when you were a kid, Mommy?"

Jessie pushed away from the window and moved to her son's side. "Aunt Monica and I played with dolls."

"Dolls?" Danny squished his face into a look of disgust. "Why?"

She sat on the sofa and pulled a pillow into her lap. "Probably because we didn't have a brother to show us how cool trucks were."

Danny liked that answer. "Well, when I get a little sister, I'm going to show her how epic trucks are." *Epic* was the new adjective of choice in his kindergarten class. The first time she'd heard him use it, she doubled over laughing. Not that the word was funny, but such a strong word coming from her small son was strange.

Epic wasn't the word she was stuck on now. "Do you want a little sister?"

Danny returned the underwear gift and started over from gift one to shake and guess. "Yeah...sure. Or a brother. Grown-ups don't like to play as much as kids. And sometimes you're tired. So, yeah...it would be fun having a sister or a brother. That way we can move in together when we're older like you and Auntie Monica."

He'd never told her he wanted a brother or sister. Hearing him talk about a sibling drove home how much she'd messed up with Jack.

"I thought you were going to live with me forever," she teased her son.

He stopped shaking gifts and pondered her words. "But then who is going to live with my brother or sister?"

Oh, the mind of a five-year-old. "Good point," she told him.

Danny switched back to his original topic. "Jack is going to love the car. He can watch *SpongeBob* with me in the backseat. Jack likes cartoons."

"I'm sure he'd love it."

What had she done? Maybe she should call him and see if he would talk to her. Then again, maybe he'd already left, went home

183

to Texas. Regrets, remorse, and what-ifs plagued her every day, every night.

Christmas officially sucked this year.

Jack slid from the saddle and began the process of removing Dancer's tack. The damp smell of hay and horseflesh permeated the walls of the massive barn. Smelled like home. Danny would love it here. The outdoors, the freedom to roam, ride, and explore.

The ranch house had been a great place growing up.

And Jessie...She'd light up like the red and green Christmas lights that twinkled around the edges of the house. The tired eyes she had following a long graveyard shift would drift away in a matter of days if she didn't have to work so hard.

Damn, he wasn't any further along in what he was supposed to do now than he was three hours ago. Jessie had turned him down. Maybe he should walk away. Give her what she wanted.

After brushing Dancer down, he turned him into his paddock and gave him a bucket of oats for his workout. The horse nudged his shoulder as if to say thanks.

As he was walking from the barn, Jack's phone rang. Reception was spotty, so he stood still and took the call.

"This is Jack," he answered, not recognizing the number.

"Mr. Morrison, this is Phil Gravis from Toyota."

The car...He'd nearly forgotten about it.

"Hello, Mr. Gravis."

"I wanted to tell you that everything went smoothly. Ms. Mann picked out a nice crossover that should serve her well for many years."

"Good." At least she wouldn't be walking home from her dates. The thought of her with another man shot fire to his eyes. "No questions from her?"

"No, she seemed a little preoccupied through the entire proc-ess. Her sister seemed to be more suspicious."

"Monica is sharp."

"No argument there. She had to talk Ms. Mann out of taking a truck, which I thought was strange for a lady."

Jack lifted his head, suddenly felt a chill race up his spine. "A truck?"

"Yeah, she kept peeking inside the bigger ones we have on the lot."

"The bigger ones?" *Why would Jessie want a truck?*

"What does a woman like her need with a truck? She lives in an apartment."

"An apartment." Jack's mind went fuzzy. Jessie wouldn't need a truck. But broke Jack had an old, beat-up pickup.

"Are you there, Mr. Morrison?" Mr. Gravis asked.

"Yeah, I'm here."

"She did ask if there was a possibility of switching the car for the truck within a couple of weeks, or five hundred miles. I didn't know what to say to her. You said to let her pick out what she wanted, but I wasn't sure if you wanted to pay the depreciation on one vehicle if she did bring the crossover back."

A slow smile started at one edge of his mouth and spread to the other.

"Mr. Morrison?"

"Sorry, Mr. Gravis. I think Jessie's preoccupied mind is conta-gious. Don't worry about her bringing the car back. I have a feeling she'll be keeping it."

Jessie would give up a new car, something she desperately needed, to put him in a new truck. Or maybe she was thinking *them*…they could use a truck. "Thanks again, Mr. Gravis."

"You're welcome. It was fun. I felt like Santa giving away a car to an unsuspecting woman."

Jack disconnected the call and walked a little faster to the house.

Beth, the housekeeper and cook, scolded him about taking his boots off before he "walked through her clean house." The familiar rant made him smile even more.

"You may have been gone a long time, but the rules around here haven't changed," Beth said, waving her finger at him from the kitchen sink. Part of the reason the Morrison money didn't shoot to Jack's head was because his father employed down-to-earth people like Beth.

A few strong pulls and the boots found their way under a bench in the mudroom. "I see you're just as feisty as ever," he teased.

Beth, somewhere in her late sixties, graced him with a smile of her own. "I see your ride did you good. It's nice to see you smile."

Jack walked over to her and planted a kiss on her forehead.

"What on earth was that for?"

"For everything you do. I don't think I've said thank you enough."

Beth crossed her hands over her chest and narrowed her eyes. "Have you been drinking?"

Jack tossed his head back, laughing. "Not today. Do you know where Katie is?"

"I think she's in the den, fiddling with the Christmas tree."

One more kiss and a wink and Jack went to search for his sister. Sure enough, she was in the process of rearranging the tree ornaments to her liking. Dressed in a big sweater and blue jeans, Katie looked more like the sister he'd grown up with. The flashy-dressing Katie never did sit well with him.

"Jessie picked out a truck," he blurted out, startling his sister. "What?"

"A truck. Well, actually she ended up with a car or crossover, but she looked at trucks."

Katie sat the ornament in her hand down. "Is that supposed to mean something to me? Cuz I have to tell you, it doesn't."

Jack grasped Katie's shoulders. "Why would a woman who lives in an apartment and works as a waitress want to buy a truck?"

"I don't think she would unless her husband pushed it. Seems all you guys need to have your trucks."

"Exactly." Jack pulled his sister close and hugged her hard. "I've got to go."

Katie smiled. "Oh yeah? Where to?"

"You know where I'm going. I'll need to do some shopping first. Can you run interference with Dad? He's going to be ticked when he gets here and I'm gone."

With sure hands, Katie turned him around and pushed him toward the door. "Don't you worry about Dad. Just get back there and fix it. Don't mess it up this time."

Heartbroken didn't describe the pain in her chest nearly enough. Every day was an effort. Jessie scolded herself for the umpteenth time. "I shouldn't have driven him away."

"You're talking to yourself again," Monica called from the living room.

"She's been doing that a lot," Danny said.

Monica and Danny were making handmade cards to send out. Danny drew a picture, and Monica signed the inside with all their names. It was a tradition the three of them had started the first Christmas Danny could scribble on paper.

"I'm not talking to myself."

"Really? Is there someone in the kitchen we can't see from here?" Monica chuckled when she asked.

"You're gonna end up with coal in your stocking, Mo."

Danny laughed.

Jessie stirred the stew simmering on the stove and turned the heat down.

A loud knock on the door brought all six eyes to it. Monica glanced at her watch. "Expecting anyone?"

"Nope."

Jessie walked to the door, wiping her hands on the apron around her waist. Through the peephole, she saw a red box.

"Who is it?"

"Delivery."

Shrugging her shoulders, Jessie opened the door.

In front of her was a set of hands full of beautifully wrapped gifts connected to a pair of jeans and cowboy boots.

Her lips started to tremble.

"Ho, ho, ho." Jack walked into her apartment as if he'd only been gone a few hours instead of nearly a week.

"Jack!" Danny bounced to his feet and ran to Jack's side. He wrapped his arms around Jack's leg and nearly caused him to spill the presents in his hands.

"Howdy, partner."

Monica found her feet and started removing the load from Jack's hands. "Here, let me help you."

"Thanks." Jack hugged Danny with a free hand.

Jessie stood anchored to one spot on the floor, afraid to move.

"Where have you been?" Danny asked. "We missed you."

Jack knelt down at Danny's level after setting the last of the boxes on the table. "I missed you, too."

"Mommy cried." Oh boy, nothing like a five-year-old to blast out the truth.

"She did?" Jack turned his gaze to her and gave a wan smile. "I'm sorry about that. Maybe I can make it up."

"What is all this?" Danny dropped to the floor and started to read the names on the presents. "This one's for me?" Silver paper and a huge green bow adorned the box. Danny shook the thing for dear life.

The sight brought fresh tears to Jessie's eyes.

All eyes were on Danny. "There is one for you, Auntie Monica. And another one for me." He beamed. "Look, Mom, one for you."

Jessie sucked in her lip and bit it. "You didn't have to do this," she said.

Jack stood and ruffled the hair on Danny's head. "I wanted to."

Monica walked to Jessie's side. "Are you OK?"

Jessie nodded. The happiness of seeing Jack shifted to the growing concern of what would happen next. Did he want to go back to being friends? Could she be *only* friends?

"Hey, Danny? How about you and I go to the park and bring candy canes to all your friends?"

Danny glanced between Jack and Monica with uncertainty.

"Are you going to be here when I come back?" he asked Jack.

Jack's eyes leveled with Jessie's. "I'd like to be."

What did that mean?

"Come on, little dude. Let's give Jack and your mom some time to talk." Monica walked over to the closet and removed his coat.

Before they both walked out the door, Monica asked, "Are you sure you're OK?"

Jessie waved her off.

Once the door closed, the room grew silent.

"Danny looks a lot better than the last time I saw him," Jack said, removing his cowboy hat from his head. He looked good. Maybe a little tired, but good.

"He was sick for a few days. Nothing worse than the night in the hospital."

"Good. I'm glad." And nervous, from the way he kept shifting from foot to foot.

"You didn't need to do all this." Jessie waved her hands at the gifts that filled the empty spaces around their Christmas tree.

"I wanted to," he repeated.

Their eyes settled on the tree as painful silence stretched between them.

"Jack."

"Jessie," they both said together, and then laughed.

"Why don't we sit down," she suggested. "Can I get you something to drink?"

He shook his head and waited for her to sit before he took his seat opposite her.

"I've made such a mess of things, Jessie." Jack leaned forward with his elbows on his knees.

"You didn't do it alone."

His eyes traveled to the floor. "Is what Danny said true? Did you cry?"

"Women are emotional creatures."

"I hate the thought of you crying over me."

Jessie sat taller. "I was afraid I'd driven you away forever. We've kinda gotten used to you being around here. Danny hasn't stopped asking where you are."

"Did *you* miss me?"

She swallowed hard and delivered the truth. "More than you would believe."

Jack smiled. "I can believe a lot of things. Like I believe that if I'd waited to ask you to marry me, maybe you'd have said yes. But no, I had to jump in, both feet, and have you turn me down."

"You scared me, Jack."

"Why?"

Why? Good question, one she'd been considering night and day since he left. "I was afraid of loving you. Of what would become of us if I allowed myself to depend on you. I've been doing this alone for a lot of years, and I'd love to share the burden, but I didn't think that was fair to you."

Jack opened his mouth to say something, but she halted him with a hand.

"Wait, I'm not done. Sometimes, when you love someone, you need to do what's best for them. Doing what's best isn't always the easiest thing. I thought you'd have a better shot at all the things you want in your life if you didn't have Danny and me dragging you down."

When Jessie looked, she saw Jack staring at her with his mouth dropped open. "You said no because you love me?"

A tear ran down her cheek. "I said no because Danny and I both love you. Having you walk out of our life one day when you want to pursue your dreams would hurt more than saying good-bye now. At least, that's what I thought last week."

Jack stood, knelt down in front of her, and grasped her hands. "Do you feel the same thing this week?"

"No. This week I was miserable, desperately wishing you wouldn't take my rejection and you'd come back."

Jack lifted his hands to her face and rubbed away the tears with his thumbs. Leaning forward, he brought his lips to hers.

She cried against his lips and crushed him closer. Jack was there, kissing her, mending the pain in her chest that had settled there like a rock.

He leaned her back and covered her with his weight. His lips moved over hers; his hands kneaded her hair. When he pulled away, Jessie's breath was shallow and uneven.

"I came back, Jessie. I'm not going anywhere."

Jessie pulled him down and kissed him hard.

His hands left her hair and ran down her waist. She wanted him, loved him more than she could express. If he were to ask her to marry him all over again, she'd jump at the opportunity of being

Mrs. Jack Moore. There was more to life than money. The caring, thoughtful, and honest man in her arms meant more than any amount of money could.

"Make love to me, Jack," she told him between kisses.

His heated eyes stared down at her. The weight in his jeans spoke of his desire. "What about your sister and Danny?"

Monica wouldn't rush home. "They'll be gone long enough for make-up sex."

"Make-up loving," Jack corrected her.

Jessie laughed for the first time in a week.

Lifting her in his arms, Jack walked her to her bedroom and kicked the door shut. Jessie picked at the buttons of his shirt as he set her down on the bed.

The expanse of his chest was open to her view. Strong, powerful. "You're beautiful," she told him.

"Don't go telling my friends that. Texan cowboys are handsome, rugged, but never beautiful."

Jessie stripped his shirt completely away and tossed it to the floor. Jack was working on her apron and then her jeans. "You're handsome and rugged, too. But so beautiful." She ran her hands down his hips and tugged at the opening of his pants.

When she managed to spring his erection, he said, "You better not call him beautiful."

Running her hand down his shaft and back up again, she was thrilled when Jack hummed his pleasure. "This is rugged and hot."

"Vixen," he said in a hoarse voice.

Jack wiggled out of his clothes and Jessie pulled her sweater from her body. Within seconds, they were both naked and he was crawling back over her body, covering her with his heat. She'd never tire of him holding her down and showering her body with his lips and hands.

Jack nibbled her chin and neck and followed a fiery path of kisses and licks until he rounded over her breast. "This is beautiful," he said before teasing her into a hard pebble and sucking her into the cavern of his mouth. Jack nibbled, the bite playful but hard enough to shoot fire between her legs. He moved to her other breast. "And this is beautiful." He repeated the attention to the second.

Her returned to her mouth and ravished her with his tongue.

She squirmed, wanting him inside her. They rolled over each other, fighting for dominance. Their harsh breathing was the only sound in the room.

Jessie wrapped a leg around him, teasing him at her entrance. He buckled forward, giving her only a taste of him inside her.

"Please," she begged. "Fast now, slow later. I need you."

He rolled them onto their sides and lifted her leg over his hip. Without warning, he entered her and knocked the oxygen from her lungs. "Yes," she hissed.

"Get used to me, Jessie. Us Texans are hard to drive away."

No, instead he drove into her with his body. He slid past her most sensitive spot, the smooth and rough friction of him setting the perfect pace.

Grasping his hips, Jessie helped their canter.

There was nothing slow and melting with their mating. More of a volcano ready to explode. Earthquake quivers and tremors gave a warning until all the feeling and nerves rushed together at the same time.

Finally, her hands clutched his body and her eyes rolled into the back of her head as she trembled and found her toe-curling release. His rode on her heels as the warmth of his orgasm filled her.

Jessie buried her head in his arm, happier than any woman should be.

After, Jack listened as Jessie's breathing eased. He wanted to stay exactly where he was.

Forever.

But he wouldn't make the same mistake twice. He would ask her to marry him once he had a ring and the ability to do it right. She loved him. He heard her say it and, more, he felt it. There had to be a way to tell her the truth about his wealth that wouldn't anger her. For that, he needed a woman's advice. First chance he got, he would call Katie and solicit hers.

Right now Jack wanted to lie in Jessie's arms and forget about all their recent troubles.

The sound of a door opening and Danny's voice calling out ditched his plans.

He stiffened and reached for a blanket and Jessie laughed. "Reality comes crashing in," she said.

Jack kissed her nose and forced his body to slip from hers. It was then he noticed that he hadn't used a condom. He glanced at Jessie to see if she had noticed. If she did, she said nothing.

No matter, I'm marrying this woman if it's the last thing I do. He quickly put his boxers on and tossed Jessie her clothes with a wink.

"Jessie?" Monica called.

"Hold on," Jessie laughed. "I'll, ah, be right out."

Monica laughed.

Sisters.

Chapter Fifteen

They ate the stew she'd made and laughed at Danny shaking the gifts under the tree.

"This one has to be clothes," he scowled as he spoke.

"Why do you say that?" Jack asked.

"Cuz there isn't any sound inside the box and it's not very heavy." Danny tossed the box under the tree and picked up one of the packages Jack had brought.

"Soundless and light, yep, must be clothes," Jack agreed.

"This," he squealed, lifting the beautiful package above his head, "is a toy. It's not heavy, but there are plastic pieces jiggling around in there."

Jessie grasped Jack's hand across the table and smiled at Monica.

"How do you know it's plastic?"

Danny closed his eyes, taking the shaking of the presents to the next level. "I'm five. All my toys are plastic."

Jack squeezed her hand as he spoke to her son. "So, Danny, what do you really, really want for Christmas?"

"I want a bike."

Jessie saw that coming. It was all he'd asked for. The one she had hidden in a box in her bedroom needed some serious assembly for Santa to manage after Danny went to sleep.

"But you know what would be even better than a bike?" he asked.

Oh no. She didn't know there was anything else he wanted. His letter to Santa, the one he wrote the day after Thanksgiving, said a bike. A red bike that was twice the size of the one he had now.

"What's that, buddy?" Jessie queried.

"I want a house where we have a driveway and a place so I can ride my bike. Then Auntie Monica can have her own room so she doesn't need to sleep out here. And Mom can park her new car in a garage." Danny bounced to his feet. "Did you see the new car?" he asked Jack.

"No." Jack slid a smile Jessie's way.

"My goodness, in all the excitement around here I completely forgot to tell you what happened."

Jack's thumb stroked hers as he waited patiently for her explanation.

"After you left, the dealership called. There was some kind of fire in their garage that destroyed my car."

"Really?" Jack asked, his smile never wavering.

"That's what they told me. The dealership gave me my choice of a new car for my loss. Can you believe it?" Jack tilted his head to the side. Something in the way he stared at her made her pause.

Monica stood and cleared a few dishes from the table. "I'm still waiting for the dealer to call and say it was all a big mistake."

"I don't know, Monica. Dealerships hate to be sued," Jack explained as he shifted his gaze to Monica.

"That's what I told her."

"I don't buy it."

"What did you get?" Jack asked, changing the subject.

"Mom got the coolest car ever. It has TVs in the backseat, and there's a lady's voice that gives us directions if we're lost. It's epic." Danny grasped Jack's hand. "C'mon, you need to see it."

Jessie sent a sympathetic look Jack's way as Danny forced him to stand.

"I'd love to see it."

"I'll get the keys." Standing, Jessie found her purse by the door and started to dig in to find her keys.

"Tell you what, why don't we go for ice cream," Jack suggested. "Your mom can give me a ride in her new car."

"Can we, Mom?"

"Sure, why not. You wanna go, Monica?" Jessie turned to her sister, who busied herself cleaning the dishes.

"You guys go. I'll finish cleaning this mess."

Outside, the sun had set and the wind was whipping around the chill in the air. The apartment complex had a carport, but only one designated spot per unit. Until the new car, Monica had parked her car under it.

Jessie used the remote to unlock the car. "I still can't believe it's mine. I kinda feel like I've won the lottery without even playing."

Jack placed his arm around her and rested it on her shoulder as they walked. "Sometimes good things actually come to those who deserve them."

At the car, Danny opened the back door and jumped inside. "Look, Jack. TV."

"It plays DVDs," Jessie told Jack as he ran a hand over the frame of the door Danny had opened.

Jack tickled Danny as he leaned over him to look inside. "Perfect for those long drives."

"That's what the dealer said. I never thought I'd have a car like this."

"Is it safe?" Jack asked.

"The crash rating had a decent score. The gas mileage is great."

Jack rounded the car and popped the hood. "Four cylinder?"

"Again, gas mileage."

From over the hood, Jack said, "I think it's a great pick."

For the first time since she'd driven it home, Jessie felt as if she could enjoy it. Without Jack, everything had seemed a little grayer.

Jack released the hood. "Wanna take me for a spin?"

Danny was already in his seat with the seat belt on.

After ice cream, they drove around looking at Christmas lights until Danny started nodding off in the back.

Jack stared at her as they rounded the street that led to her apartment.

"It's nice to see you with new things," he said. "You smile a little brighter."

Damn, she didn't want him thinking she needed him to provide them for her. Together they'd figure out how to pay the bills and make things work. "It's just a car, Jack. I'm smiling because I'm sharing it with you."

"Danny seemed ready to ask Santa for a garage to park this in."

"Danny doesn't realize what he's asking for when he says he wants a house for Christmas. I think he watched *Miracle on 34th Street.*"

"Kids dream a little bigger than adults do. I think it's part of the innocence."

She agreed. "Adults know that making dreams come true is hard work. Kids think all they have to do is wish on a falling star."

Jessie pulled into her parking space and turned off the engine. "Well, what do you think?" she asked, stroking the steering wheel.

"I think it's perfect." He leaned over then and kissed her. Sweet and short, but so very nice. "I think you need to keep wishing on falling stars," he whispered with a grin.

Jessie watched his gray eyes sparkle and couldn't help but think they looked like stars.

"Come on," he said after pulling away. "Let's tuck Danny into bed. Then I can tuck you into bed."

She wiggled out of the driver's seat. *Now, that sounded like a perfect plan.*

Jack and Jessie spent the night making love. Making up for the time they'd lost. By morning, Jack was prepared to break away for a few hours. He needed a solid plan to execute how to explain his deception to Jessie. He twisted words in his head, trying to phrase things so she wouldn't feel lied to.

The more he pondered his approach, the more he knew she'd be angry. Hell, he would be if he were in her place.

He needed female advice.

Jack needed his kid sister.

Sliding behind Jessie as she assembled the makings for cookies, Jack placed a kiss on the side of her neck. "Sugar cookies?" he asked, holding her around the waist with one hand and dipping his finger into the sticky bowl for a stolen taste. He licked his finger and savored the flavor of the cookie dough.

"The best kind."

"I don't know about that. Chocolate chip cookies always sing to me."

Jessie laughed and slapped his hand when he went in for a second taste. "Cookie cutters don't work with chocolate chips, and you can't frost them."

"Yum, frosted chocolate chip cookies. I think you're on to something."

She giggled and picked up a spoon to stir the batter.

"I hate to say this." Jack swiveled Jessie until they were face-to-face. "But I need to go and run some errands, check in at the hotel."

"Do you have to work today?" She wiped her hands on a towel and set it aside.

"In a way."

"What does that mean?" She smiled when she asked.

"I'll explain later." He avoided lying. Going to the hotel and working were on the agenda, just not exactly in the manner Jessie thought.

"We'll save some of the frosting so you can make your own," Jessie said.

Jack glanced at Danny, who was playing a board game with Monica in the living room, then leaned down to kiss Jessie.

Her lips slid over his in a soft caress. So warm. He couldn't wait to slip a ring on her finger and claim her.

He ended their kiss and squeezed her before moving aside. "I'll be back," he promised.

"You better be," she scolded lightheartedly.

He moved around the counter, waved a hand to the others. "I'll see you later, Danny."

"You're leaving?" His head bounced up.

"Gotta run some errands."

Danny scrambled to his feet and ran to hug him. There was something about a little boy tossing himself into Jack's arms that made everything worthwhile. Jack kissed the top of his head. "Later, partner."

"Later, Uncle Jack," Danny mimicked.

Jack opened the door and shot a glance at Jessie. Her hair was tied back in a ponytail, and her apron hung from her waist with copious amounts of flour on it. She was smiling, even before she looked up and caught him staring at her.

He did not want to mess this up.

Once outside, he turned on his cell phone and noticed a message waiting for him.

"Jack, dammit, where are you?" It was Katie. "Oh, never mind. Listen, Dad came home ticked that he missed you. He and Beth started talking, and between the two of them and my tight lip, they

figured there is a woman involved. One you want to make perma-
nent. I swear I didn't say a thing. He's on his way to you. We're
both coming. I'll try to hold him back until you have things fixed
with Jessie. You are fixing things with Jessie, right? Oh, and he said
something about meeting with your contractor for the new project
while he's there. He's been on the phone for the last hour barking
orders. Anyway, consider yourself warned."

Jack turned off his phone and jumped into his truck. With
a little luck, he'd make it back to the hotel and manage to clean
himself up before his father invaded.

Gaylord Morrison did everything the Texas way.

Big!

Large strides carried Jack through the lobby and to the elevators.
Sam saw him from the reception desk and scrambled to catch up
with him.

"Mr. Morrison…"

"Not now, Sam, I'm in a hurry." Jack summoned the elevator
to the lobby floor.

"Your father is on his way."

"I know." He pressed the button again, frustrated with its
speed.

"The other executive suite in the hotel has a guest. Will your
father be staying with you?"

The elevator light lit up.

Jack slid into the elevator. "I'll take care of it, Sam. Don't
worry."

Housekeeping had erased all evidence of the mess Jack had left
before his short trip to Texas. Jack disrobed as he walked but made
sure all his clothes were shoved into the closet like a good bachelor.
Within twenty minutes, he was shoulder-to-heels Armani, his good

Stetson securely on his head, his polished boots on his feet. Not a huge change from Jack Moore, he decided.

His phone rang as he was placing a watch around his wrist. "Hello?"

"Mr. Morrison, your father and sister have arrived."

Jack drew in a deep breath.

Let the sidestepping begin.

"What meeting room are we using?" he asked.

"The one next to my office," Sam offered.

"I'm on my way down now."

It wasn't that he didn't care for his dad. He loved the man, but he could be intense at times and beyond domineering.

Jack stepped into the lobby and into an array of people and organized chaos. His dad stood in front of Sam, who was talking rapidly and gesturing with his hands. From afar, Gaylord Morrison was a roadblock, someone who demanded your attention. At six-four and two hundred twenty pounds, he could have passed for a retired linebacker. His hair was peppered with gray, but his eyes were sharp and caught everything. Katie stood at his side, wearing one of her ridiculous miniskirts. Probably to piss the man off. She loved getting under his skin and did so on a regular basis.

Gaylord caught sight of Jack and broke off his conversation with the hotel manager.

"Jack," he called as he turned.

Jack extended his hand, which his father took in his firm grip before pulling him into a hug. "What the hell were you thinking running off before I came home?"

"It's good to see you too, Dad." It was, despite the bad timing.

Around them, porters scurried to assist them with their bags, Sam stood ready to accept any task, and a half a dozen men wearing business suits were trailing after the senior Morrison.

"First Thanksgiving, now Christmas," Gaylord bellowed as he pulled away and started to instruct Sam to find a room for his driver and staff.

Katie sauntered to Jack's side and leaned close to his ear so only he could hear. "I swear I didn't say a thing," she whispered.

Jack patted her arm and smiled down at her. "The man's radar has always been superior to any satellite dish."

Katie laughed and tossed her head back.

A couple of flashes went off in the lobby. Jack glanced around and noticed a reporter with a photographer at his side. "What are they doing here?" he asked his sister.

"They're for you." Gaylord returned his attention to his children.

"For me?"

"I heard there's a special lady friend in your life, one who might be joining our family soon." Gaylord's last word was spoken slowly and nearly sounded like a question.

The smile on Jack's face slipped into a scowl. He didn't like the thought of the press invading his personal life to this degree. Besides, he still needed to propose to Jessie...again.

"Isn't it my call to alert the media?" Jack asked his father.

"So there is a future Mrs. Morrison?" The mere thought of Jack getting married obviously pleased the man. It was hard to stay mad at him.

"There is someone," Jack confirmed. "But I'd rather not discuss it out here if you don't mind."

Gaylord puffed his chest out as if he'd just become a father all over again. "Damn good news," he said. "When do we meet her?"

"You're always accusing me of being in the spotlight, Daddy," Katie scolded. "Can we do this in private? I don't think Jack wants to discuss this here."

Jack nodded to the elevators. "I have lunch coming up to my suite before the meeting. Let's talk up there."

Diverting his father took a couple more minutes, but as the man walked toward the elevators, Jack summoned Sam with a crook of his finger. "Lunch for three. Whatever the special is, a bottle of Crown Royal, and a bottle of chardonnay for Miss Morrison."

"What about the meeting? Your father requested—"

"Tell the kitchen to hurry. We'll be down in an hour," Jack interrupted before turning his focus on his family. "Oh boy."

———

Danny swung his feet off the edge of the chair as he placed the little edible silver balls on his cookie. If he took this much time decorating one of the treats, they'd be finished with the batch sometime around Easter.

Monica pushed through the front door with a bundle of clean laundry. The apartment complex had its own washers and dryers, but they were outside and around the carport.

Jessie took the basket from her sister so she could close the door.

"It's getting cold out there," her sister complained.

"Better cold than hot. It doesn't feel like Christmas when it's eighty outside."

Monica motioned toward Danny. "Is Monet creating a master-piece over there or what?"

"He doesn't get that from me. I'd be slapping on frosting and sprinkling those green and red thingies on it and calling it done."

Monica shook her head. "How many has he finished?"

"Two."

"He's going to need these last three days before Christmas to finish the job."

The two of them picked up one piece of laundry at a time and started to fold.

Monica changed the channel to the afternoon news. "Any idea when Jack is coming back?"

"I'm not sure." Jessie set one of Danny's socks aside until its match showed up from the pile. "He said he needed to check in at the hotel."

"Isn't his schedule fixed?"

"I have no idea. Whenever he talks about his job, he acts a little strange."

"Strange? Strange how?"

"I asked him if he had to work today, and he said 'in a way.' What in the heck does that mean? You either have to work or you don't." Jessie shook her head. The next sock she picked up belonged with the other, so she folded them together.

"Maybe he needed to work but was going in to see if they could do without him. So he could spend time here."

"Maybe. Another thing, he's never talked about where he lives." Jessie had thought about this when he disappeared. She had no idea where to look for him outside of his work.

Monica lifted a shirt and tucked it under her chin to fold. "Now that the two of you are a couple, he'll give you all the details. I'm sure you'll be spending some 'alone time' at his place. It can't be terribly relaxing with Danny so close to your room."

Jessie laughed. "Not to mention my kid sister right outside my door."

Monica dropped the shirt into a pile and held up both of her hands. "I didn't hear a thing…all night. Not at two o'clock or at six this morning."

Jessie burst out laughing and knew her cheeks were turning red. She tossed the folded socks at her sister and hit her in the chest. "You're bad."

"I'm not the one who was up *all* night," Monica said, laughing. It felt good to laugh and really mean it.

"Mommy?"

"Yeah, pumpkin."

"Isn't that Uncle Jack?" Danny was pointing to the TV. "He looks funny dressed like that."

Jessie's eyes traveled to the television. The grin on her face held her cheeks so firmly they started to hurt. She expected to see a sexy man in a cowboy hat who "looked like" Jack. What she found stole her breath clean from her lungs.

"Ohmygod." Monica recovered quickly and turned up the volume on the TV.

"…Morrison, billionaire tycoon, and his son, Jack Morrison, arrived in the Inland Empire to celebrate not only the groundbreaking venture of Jack Morrison's chain of 'family affordable' hotels, but rumors have it that an announcement is forthcoming of a wedding in Jack Morrison's future. Sorry, ladies, but it looks like this highly eligible bachelor is about to be taken off the market. Rumors of who the bride is haven't been confirmed or denied."

Jessie dropped the laundry from her hands and felt them start to shake.

Jack stood in the center lobby of The Morrison with a slender blonde woman hanging on his arm. Jessie couldn't see the face of the woman, but whoever she was, Jack was holding on to her arm and smiling down at her with a look that could only be described as loving.

Billionaire?

Jack?

The reporter went on with a list of names, some public, others inconsequential, that the media deemed possible for the future Mrs. Morrison.

Jessie's name wasn't on it.

Her jaw trembled and the blood in her head started a rapid descent to her feet.

"Jessie?"

Jack Moore wasn't even his name. God, how could she have been so blind? How could she have been so bamboozled that she didn't know who Jack really was?

"Jessie?"

The reported cut to a different story, but the imprint of Jack standing in the lobby of *his* hotel, holding on to a different woman, and basking in the spotlight with his billionaire father would forever be stamped in her mind.

He lied to me.

"Mommy, are you OK?"

"Jessie, sit down before you pass out." Monica tugged on her arm, guiding her to sit on the sofa.

"He lied to me," she whispered. Jessie found Monica's eyes and saw her own confusion mirrored in her sister's gaze. "Lied to me, Monica. Why would he do that?"

"I don't know. I'm sure there's an explanation—"

"No. You saw the picture. Who was that woman he was hanging on to?" His intended bride? Jack knew she wouldn't say yes to marriage with a dreamer. Had he planned all along to propose and then remind her that she hadn't accepted? And for what? Did he want to carry on an affair with her after he married someone in his peer circle? The woman at his side was dressed to kill.

"I'm not sure. We've got to be missing something, Jessie."

Jessie took several quick breaths through her nose. The muscles in her chest started to constrict and her head began to ache.

"I've got to go," Jessie said as she stood and searched the apartment for her purse.

Her only thought was to confront Jack. Surprise him as he'd shocked her.

"Jessie, don't be rash. Jack cares about you."

She laughed without humor. "Right!" Jessie found her purse and dug inside for her keys.

"Mommy, what's wrong?" Danny cried.

Jack wasn't hurting only her. Danny had fallen for him, too. "Nothing, buddy. Just stay here with Auntie Monica. I'll be back soon." How dare Jack do this to them!

"Jessie, stop and think about what you're doing."

"Stop and think? Monica, did you just see the same thing I did? Jack lied to us. All of us. From day one." How could she be so stupid? "Stay here with Danny."

Jessie fled the apartment with Monica calling after her, "Maybe he had a reason!"

No reason would be good enough.

Anger in the form of heat raged in her veins. Jessie told herself to calm down so she could drive. She forced her foot off the accelerator and kept her speed to the posted limit.

"Jack Morrison." She wanted to scream and pound her fist into his chest. *Morrison.* He'd played a waiter in the bar to do what, earn her trust? Trust from a woman while he lied to her on a daily basis?

How could he hold her, make love to her...promise tomorrow when he planned on being with someone else? He hadn't repeated his proposal last night. Now Jessie knew why. He didn't plan on her being anything but a diversion. Dipping into the cheap side of town.

"Most eligible bachelor," she mumbled as she found the entrance to the hotel.

Jessie pulled her car up to the valet and jumped out.

The man standing there held his hand out for her keys.

"I'm not staying," she told him as she blew past him.

"You can't park here," he called after her.

Jessie ignored him and walked into the lobby. The lobby Jack *owned*. Her jaw tightened and her nails dug into her skin from fisting her hands.

"Ma'am, you can't leave your car in the turnaround." The valet was running behind her to keep up.

At the reception desk, Jessie pushed her way around the customer standing there. "Where is Jack Morrison?"

"Excuse me," the guest at the desk said.

"If you'll just wait—"

"Where is he?" Jessie raised her voice. "It's urgent." She tried to calm down, but her entire body shook. She now knew what a dragon felt like right before it shot fire from its mouth.

"He's in a meeting, miss. Let me have your name—"

"Where?"

The receptionist glanced over Jessie's shoulder, giving away the general direction of where Jack was holding his *meeting*.

On the far side of the lobby, an archway indicated a conference room.

Jessie pivoted and started marching toward the man she knew as Jack Moore.

The lying bastard.

"You can't go in there!"

Watch me.

Chapter Sixteen

"The market analysis indicated a strong and positive response to the name change, Jack." Eric passed around a copy of the charts Jack had asked for so they could finalize the naming of the hotel chain.

Jack sat at one end of the conference table, and his father sat at the opposite side by the door. In between were employees ranging from marketing, accounting, Dean's second in command from his contracting firm, and a couple of lawyers to ensure the legal department's advice was followed.

"Then it looks like we have everything set for the..." Jack's words trailed off as voices outside the conference door indicated someone wasn't where they were supposed to be.

"You can't go in there," said a frantic woman beyond the door.

Everyone in the room turned.

Gaylord shifted in his chair.

"I'll only be a minute." Jack heard her voice just as the large mahogany door burst open.

Several people in the room gasped.

Jack surged to his feet. "Jessie?"

She locked eyes with him and ground to a halt. The array of emotions that played over her face in the span of two seconds felt like a punch in the gut. *How did she find out?*

"What's the matter, Jack? Can't come up with a lie quick enough to explain this?"

He started walking toward her. "Jessie, I—"

Her hand shot up in front of her, stopping him. "Don't waste your breath. I'm not here for an explanation. I needed to see with my own eyes if what I saw on the news was true."

The news? What the hell is she talking about?

"Obviously the media has a stronger grip on the truth than you do."

"I can explain."

"Let me guess, you made employee of the year and they gave you the hotel."

"Jessie, please."

"Oh, don't even try that with me."

"Jack—" He heard his father's voice but couldn't stop watching Jessie. Her anger was palpable.

"Don't bother, Mr. Morrison. It is Mr. Morrison, isn't it?" Jessie asked his father.

"It is."

Jessie's gaze shot from his father to him. "At least someone in the room knows his own name." She glanced around the room as if noticing it for the first time. "You told me you were a waiter. A waiter? God, I'm so gullible." Her hand shook as she pointed at him. "Stay the hell away from me and my son. You hear me, Jack *Morrison*. Stay away!"

It took him a second to realize that Jessie had turned and was running from the room.

Jack pushed away from the table and started after her.

His father stopped him at the door. "Is that her?" he asked.

Jack shook off his father's hand. "Yes."

Gaylord barked out a laugh. "Ha! I like her already." Jack had explained everything to his father in the hour they'd shared lunch.

Thank God he'd had that hour or this scene would be more difficult to explain. "What are you standing here for, son? Go."

Jack ran from the room but didn't see Jessie in the lobby.

A stunned receptionist stood by sputtering apologies. "I'm so sorry, Mr. Morrison. She just ran in here."

"Where did she go?" he shouted.

The young woman pointed toward the front door.

By the time Jack stepped out into the sun, Jessie was in her new car, tearing out of the parking lot.

Patting his pants, Jack realized his keys were in his briefcase in the conference room and ran to retrieve them.

Bolting into the room, Jack ignored the questions and stares of his team. Once his keys were in his hand, he rushed to his truck and took off after her.

All Jack could see in front of him was the pain in Jessie's eyes. He should have told her the truth, explained who he was and why he kept it a secret from her.

He hit the steering wheel when the light at the intersection to her apartment turned red.

Although Jessie only had a fifteen-minute head start on him, by the time he made it to her apartment, she was gone.

———

Her work said she wouldn't be returning until after Christmas. Jack couldn't let her stay away from him that long. There was no way of knowing where she went. Jack left messages on her cell phone, but she didn't return them. The damn thing was probably sitting in her purse, purposely turned off.

Back at the hotel, Jack learned that his father had finished his meeting and instructed the staff to enjoy their holiday. Luckily, Gaylord wasn't in Jack's suite when he returned. Katie, on the other hand, was.

"Any calls?" he asked, knowing damn well the one he wanted to call wouldn't.

His sister shook her head. "None. Give her some time, Jack. She'll come around."

Katie couldn't know that for certain, but it was nice of her to lend her support. "I should have told her."

"Yes, you should have."

Jack couldn't even muster the energy to be pissed at his sister for siding with Jessie.

"I think I know what tipped Jessie off," Katie said.

Jack threw his keys on the coffee table. "What?"

"The media was in the lobby today and must have overheard something about your personal life. You, big brother, are tonight's entertainment report for the local station. A picture of you and me made it to the headlines."

"What headlines?"

"About an impending wedding announcement between you and a mystery bride."

Jack didn't see the problem. He'd asked Jessie to marry him once and all but promised he'd ask again in the very near future. "Jessie knows how I feel about her."

"Does she? Did you propose again?"

"No, I told you I needed to come clean first."

Katie tilted her head and gave him a wan smile. "Did you tell her you love her? Guys suck with the 'L' word."

"I told her I cared for her more than—"

"Blah. You skipped the 'L' word. Now she thinks you're ready to walk down the aisle with someone else."

"There is no one else."

"She doesn't know that," Katie countered. "She saw a picture of you and me talking; for all we know, she thinks I'm the other woman."

"That's ridiculous," Jack cried. "You're my sister."

"I'm sure you pulled out the ole family album and showed her a picture of me."

No, he hadn't done that. Still, Katie wasn't afraid of the spotlight. Hell, she'd been on more covers of magazines than a lot of top models. Surely Jessie had seen her before. Once Jessie had connected Jack Morrison to Jack Moore, the pieces would fall in line. Jessie would have to know Katie was the woman in the picture.

"Jack, trust me, Jessie is thinking the worst about you right now. A little time will need to pass before she'll give you a minute to talk."

Not the words he wanted to hear. Physical pain settled in his chest when he thought of how Jessie must have painted him.

"I'm going out," Jack said, reaching for the keys he'd placed on the table.

"Where?"

"Anywhere. I can't stand here waiting for her to call." He suspected he'd be waiting for a long time. "I need to find her."

Katie stopped him from leaving the room. "Have dinner," she encouraged. "Regroup so you have an idea where to look."

Food wasn't even on his radar.

Jack placed his hands on his sister's shoulders and moved her out of his way. "If she calls..."

"Yeah, yeah...go. I'll call you."

Jack kissed her cheek and left the penthouse.

Jessie hadn't intended to run home to Mother, but she didn't have anywhere else to go. And although they didn't get along on the day-to-day things, Renee could be counted on in a bind. Besides, when it came to men and the games they played, she could be relied upon to watch Jessie's back.

Something else boded well for Renee, and that was her lack of standing in judgment. Even when Jessie had found herself pregnant as a teenager, Renee never judged her.

She hadn't been happy, but she didn't judge.

Danny fell asleep on the couch, disappointed that they weren't going home.

Jessie sat huddled under a blanket outside on her mother's porch. The cold kept her numb. Numb was a good thing. Feeling nothing would be even better.

How could she be so blind?

What a fool.

Jessie couldn't even take pleasure in the shocked expression that had shot to Jack's face when she'd barged in on his meeting. They'd both been stunned silent. She for seeing him dressed in clothes that would take her a month to purchase. Sitting at the head of the table meant he was the big boss, the leader, the billionaire to whom everyone at the table answered.

If only she could cry, maybe then she'd feel better.

The door to the house opened and Jessie's mother stepped out. "Danny still asleep?"

Renee removed a cigarette from a pack and went through the process of lighting it up. The habit had aged her mother prematurely, Jessie realized. "Like a baby," Renee said.

"Good. It's been a big day for him."

Renee sat beside Jessie on the swing and moved the cigarette to where the smoke wouldn't blow in Jessie's face. Renee was thinner than Jessie would like, her skin weathered for her sixty-two years.

Her mom looked tired.

"It's been a big day for you, too."

Jessie had heard Monica explaining to their mother what had happened before she ran off to stay with a friend. Jessie made her promise not to run to Jack and tell him where she was. Pinky swears and sister pledges went a long way in situations like this. Jessie hoped to hell she'd never be in this exact situation again.

"He lied to me, Mom."

Renee tipped the swing until it rocked back and forth in a gentle motion. "Monica told me, but I kept thinking about something..."

"Thinking about what?"

"About how you would have reacted had you known the truth about his name, his money."

Jessie had thought of that, too. Would she have treated him the same knowing he was loaded to the tens with money? She would have dated him sooner, which was something he'd been after since they met.

"Doesn't account for the fact that there is some other woman in his life I knew nothing about."

Renee took a pull off her cigarette and blew the smoke away. She took her time talking. "Maybe. Or maybe the media got it all wrong. Wouldn't be the first time."

"You didn't see the woman hanging on his arm. I'd be a fool if I thought I could compete with that."

"You stop it right there, young lady. That's my daughter you're talking about. The daughter I know and love doesn't need fancy clothes and makeup to compete. She has everything she needs naturally." Renee pointed a finger in her direction. "This Jack guy could be so lucky to find his forever with you."

Jessie was taken aback by her mother's praise. It had been a long time since her mother had said anything to her like this. "I come with baggage, Mom. I'm not the top pick for the team."

"That's where you're wrong. When Danny's dad ran off, leaving you to raise your beautiful boy all by yourself, I was ready to run after him and force him to stand by you. Then I realized you'd be much better off without him. You'd have a greater chance of falling in love if you didn't have that bum by your side."

"Falling in love is overrated."

"Bite your tongue. Falling in love is what makes this miserable life worthwhile. I should know; I've done it about a hundred times."

Jessie smiled and felt a tiny chuckle rise in her throat.

Renee laughed alongside her. Stubbing the cigarette out under her shoe, Renee patted Jessie's knee. "I know you don't approve of how I live my life—"

"It isn't that I don't approve, Mom. I just want you settled and happy."

"I am settled, little girl. I've been in this house since right after you were born. As for happy…I'm happy most of the time."

"And miserable every time your relationships fall apart." Jessie covered her mother's hand with hers.

"No denying that. I think I've fallen in love with *falling in love*. It's exciting to see your man look at you with diamonds in his eyes, the thrill of a first kiss, the buzz of every touch and taste." Renee gazed off in her memories.

"With all that buzzing and sizzling, I'm surprised you haven't buried your husbands," Jessie joked.

Her mother tossed her head back with laughter. "Life is too short to live it alone."

"Well, it looks like Danny and I'll be alone for a little bit longer." More than a little bit. Jessie wouldn't be jumping into the dating fire any time soon. Her mom might like the buzz, but the dive after wasn't something Jessie wanted to experience again.

"I told you, you could fall in love with a rich man just as easy as a poor man."

As if Jessie could forget those words. "Lotta good that does me."

"Seems to me you fell in love with both."

That's where Jessie disagreed. "I fell in love with Jack Moore. Cowboy waiter who drives an old, beat-up truck."

Renee stood. "You're going to get through this, Jessie. I never did worry about you landing on your feet. Even after you ended up pregnant, I knew you'd be just fine."

A lump formed in the back of Jessie's throat. "Thanks, Mom."

Renee nodded and slipped back inside, leaving Jessie to her own thoughts.

Then the tears finally came.

———

It was Christmas Eve, and Jack had no idea where Jessie was. For the life of him he couldn't remember all the last names Jessie had spouted that belonged to her mother. Driving around Fontana looking for a house with Jessie's new car parked in front of it was a bust.

The hours of sleep he'd had could be counted on one hand, the meals on less than that.

The ring he'd ordered from the jeweler had arrived, and Jack sat on his bed in his room staring at it. It belonged on Jessie's finger. All he had to do was put it there.

The voices of his sister and father carried from the living room. The two of them had actually joined forces in busting Jack's balls for deceiving Jessie as he had. It was nice to see that Jack could bring his overbearing father in sync with his meddlesome daughter.

Between the two of them, you'd think one would have a sure-fire way to find Jessie.

His sister had always butted in uninvited as a kid, so what stopped her now?

Sister.

Jack's thoughts turned to Monica.

Gaylord was riling Katie about the tightness of her jeans when Jack walked into the room.

"I wear 'em to tick you off, Daddy."

"Don't think I don't know it," Gaylord chided.

"There you are," Katie called when Jack walked by them on the way to his computer. "Are you going to eat?"

"Not now, Katie."

"Did you figure out a way to find her?" his father asked.

"Jessie's sister, Monica. I just need to find her cell phone number." Jack sat down at his desk and turned on his computer.

Katie called out a series of numbers, but Jack ignored her.

Then his head popped up and he slowly turned in his seat. "Monica's number?" he asked his sister.

His sassy sister winked at him. "Doubt she'll tell you where Jessie is. I didn't have any luck."

"You talked with Monica?"

At least Katie had the good sense to let the shit-eating grin on her face fall. "Don't look so shocked. Sisters are always looking out for each other."

"You don't have a sister." Jack hoped his sister heard the sternness in his voice.

"I get the divine pleasure of looking out for you."

"When did you talk to Monica?"

"Before we flew back. I've left a message for her since, but she hasn't called me back."

All this time Katie may have held the key to finding Jessie and she had held out on him. Why?

Jack picked up the phone. "What's her number again?"

Katie called out the seven digits and Jack put the number to use. While the phone rang, Jack moved to the patio for some privacy.

He was about to give up when suddenly Monica's voice said, "Well, if it isn't the town snake. How is the grass you're lying in, Jack? Get it, lying in?" There wasn't a drop of humor in Monica's voice.

"I can explain everything."

"Save it. I'm not interested."

Jack knew he'd lose her if he didn't act fast.

"There is no other woman. The picture on TV was of my sister. Sassy woman who talked to you last week."

Monica was breathing into the phone, but not saying a thing.

"I need to talk to Jessie. Please, Monica."

"Next you'll be telling me you're not a millionaire, or is it billionaire?"

The need to apologize for having money held a bit of irony. "I had my reasons. Reasons I need to tell Jessie, not you. Where is she, Monica?"

The cool afternoon wind blew in his face. Jack turned toward it.

"I don't know."

"I can't make this right if I don't talk to Jessie. I can make this right." *Please, dammit, give me an address.*

"The woman in the picture is Katie?"

He was getting somewhere...he knew it. "I swear on my life. She's right here, she'll tell you."

"If you're lying to me—"

"I'm not."

After a long pause, Monica said, "She's at my mom's."

"I need an address."

"I swear if you're bullshitting me, Jack *Morrison*, I'll kick your cowboy ass all the way back to Texas."

"Address, Monica. Please."

"Oh, OK, fine. I'm only telling you this because Jessie's so damn miserable and your sister was sincere when we talked." She rattled off the address while Jack flew into the suite to write it down.

"Thank you." Jack studied the address and committed it to memory.

"Thank me by making my sister happy," she scolded.

"That's my intention."

Jack hung up the phone and noticed his dad and sister staring at him.

"Well?" Gaylord asked.

Across the room was a huge clock hanging on the wall. "I found her." With any luck, he would be able to bring Jessie and Danny back before dinner.

He hoped.

Chapter Seventeen

Jessie's mom had taken Danny for some last-minute Christmas madness known as shopping. At first, Jessie liked the idea of a little solitude so she could think about what she was going to say to Jack when the man showed back up in her life. He would, she knew he would. According to her boss, he'd called her work asking about her schedule. Not to mention the messages he'd left on her cell phone, all of which Jessie had deleted without listening to. Now that the house was empty and there wasn't a single thing to occupy her mind other than Jack, Jessie regretted not leaving with her son and mother.

Gravel kicked up by the wheels of a car sounded outside before Jessie recognized the squeal of brakes. She tossed the magazine in her hands aside and opened the curtains.

Her heart gave a hard kick in her chest when she recognized Jack's truck in the drive.

He sat in the driver's seat with both hands on the steering wheel, staring at her car parked in front of his. Jack moved and Jessie shot back, letting the drapes fall into place.

"Oh God." *Now what?*

Heavy boots climbed the few steps to her mother's porch, and finally Jack knocked on the door.

For a fleeting moment, she thought she could hold still and he would walk away.

"I know you're in there, Jessie. I saw you in the window."

So much for that plan.

"I'm not leaving until you let me explain," he pleaded from the other side of the door.

Jessie moved to the opposite side of the room and sat in a chair. She closed her eyes and gripped the edge of the chair. She'd just as soon get this over with so the healing could begin. As sure as Christmas would come, Jack wouldn't leave until he spoke with her...if only to make himself feel better. "The door's open," she finally said.

The knob on the door made a loud *click* as Jack twisted it. He breached the door quickly and then hesitated before opening it up enough to see her.

His haggard clothing and the growth of stubble on his chin were evidence that he might have had a sleepless night or two. *Good*, she thought. He didn't deserve to sleep after the pain he'd caused her.

Shutting the door slowly, Jack took his time to walk into the room. His eyes drifted around the small mobile home before coming to rest on her. What did he see? Jessie looked around the space and saw memories of her childhood. Some pleasant, others well worth forgetting. For better or for worse, this was home. This was the place she ran to when faced with difficult decisions.

Jack was better and worse and a difficult decision all wrapped up in one package. The dress shirt and slacks she'd seen him in at the hotel were replaced with jeans and a flannel shirt. She couldn't help but wonder if he wore his "Jack Moore" clothes in an effort to look the part. What did he prefer? Business attire or Levi's?

Jessie shook her head, dispelling the questions as fast as she could.

I don't care what you wear. Say your piece and leave so I can get on with my life.

Sounded simple, but she knew getting over Jack was going to take more than words.

"Can I sit down?" he asked, shifting uncomfortably from foot to foot.

"Sit. But don't bother getting comfortable. You're not staying."

A streak of fear slashed over his face.

Jack perched himself on the edge of the sofa and leaned forward on his knees. He opened his mouth, but nothing came out.

"You've had two days to come up with more lies, Jack. What's the matter? Losing your touch?" The harsh words helped stiffen her spine.

"I didn't want to lie to you." As the words left his mouth, Jack sucked in a breath.

"I didn't see anyone with a gun to your head."

His gaze slid to his hands and then back to her. "No."

"Then you must have wanted to lie. Not one little lie, but over again so many times. You must have kept a chart to keep yourself straight. It's quite a talent, when you think about it." Thinking of his massive web of deceit angered her.

"Let me explain."

"You're sitting there, Jack. Weave the best lie ever, but get it over with. I don't want Danny to walk in and have any hopes that his *Uncle Jack* is here to shower him with more attention and gifts." Danny was the innocent one here.

Jack's gaze leveled with hers. "The night we met, after the guys and I returned from Vegas, I walked into your diner and collided with the woman I wanted to share my future with." His words were slow and backed with emotion. "I wasn't expecting you, Jessie. But there you were. All sass and smiles. You blew me away."

Don't fall for it, Jessie, she warned herself.

"Mike, Dean, and Tom are friends I've had for years. True friends that don't hang around because of what I can do for them, of where I can place them on the corporate ladder. Friends who have never and will never use me because of the financial mecca behind my name. I've been feeling like I was missing something for a while. After a weekend with them, I realized what I was missing in my life. I've dated a lot of women. My name has cast a shadow on every relationship I've had."

Jack stood and started to pace. "When you smirked and made that comment about my wallet and my ego, I was both amused and, I'll admit, enchanted."

The memory of that night floated in and out of her head. Her attraction to Jack had been just as instant, although she'd done her best to ignore her feelings.

Jack stood before her mother's fake Christmas tree and ran his finger over an ornament either she or her sister had made when they were about Danny's age. "So I lied to you. Omission of truth, really. I won't deny the overall lie."

A tug in Jessie's neck brought her attention to the fact that she was clenching her jaw. "What else?"

"Excuse me?" He dropped his hand from the ornament and pivoted to face her.

"What else did you lie to me about?"

Jack tilted his head back, as if the answers were written on the ceiling. "There isn't a grand lost and found at the hotel. I bought the dress, shoes…"

"Earrings?"

"I told you I bought those."

That's right. She couldn't fault him for the earrings. Costume jewelry was relatively cheap. "Oh God. The earrings…they're not real. Right?"

Jack's brows lifted and he shrugged one shoulder.

"Holy cow, Jack. What were you thinking? You don't give a woman diamonds and pass them off as cubic zirconium. I could have tossed them on my dresser and lost them." She hadn't, but she could have easily misplaced them like so many pairs of cheap dime-store trinkets.

"I was on duty the night of the Christmas party at the hotel," he continued where he'd left off.

"What?" Jessie was still reeling from the earrings.

"You want me to come clean. I'm telling you that I was serving the guests at the hotel the night of the party. We had a management and waitstaff reversal for the night. Sam, he was the man who was having trouble balancing the tray."

She remembered him and the comments they'd made to each other. None of which clued her in to Jack being anything other than a waiter. "I remember."

"He is the manager of the Ontario Morrison."

"Did you bring me to the party to help me find a date, or was that a complete lie, too?" Even as the question came from her lips, Jessie knew the answer. Jack's half-assed attempts to show her other men in the room had been lame at best.

Jack sat on the arm of the couch and ran a hand through his dark hair. "I'd be lying to myself if I said I wanted you to meet someone who knocked the wind out of you."

He had already done that, she thought.

"I wanted to spend more time with you, get to know you. I wanted to show you that money doesn't buy happiness. All those men at that party might have had money, but none of them would have made you happy. I've had money all my life, but I've never been as happy as I am with you."

"Jack, stop—"

"No, Jessie, I mean what I'm saying. I wanted to come clean with you. The first night we made love, I went to your room to tell you everything. Tell you about me, the hotel, my lack of a job waiting tables."

"Why didn't you?"

He was staring at her now, not letting her eyes waver from his.

"Because you kicked the words out of my mouth when you took off that ridiculous nightshirt and made love with me. Then the next morning I ran away with myself and proposed."

"A proposal you knew I wouldn't accept." It was then Jessie remembered the woman hanging on Jack in the picture snapped by the media photographer. "Besides, wouldn't the other woman at the hotel find fault with a second woman in your life?"

Jack's mouth widened. "What are you talking about? There is no other woman."

"I saw the picture on the news, Jack, heard the headlines about your rumored impending marriage." The photo had cut deep.

Jack started shaking his head. "The only woman in my life is you."

"You forgot the blonde at the hotel already?"

His eyes widened. "Katie? You're talking about my sister. Blonde, wears her skirts too short?"

Jessie seemed to remember seeing a lot of leg and not much of the woman's face. "That was your sister?"

"Yes," he blew out with a half smile. "The rumors about a marriage were all about you."

"I turned you down."

Jack's lips pulled into a full smile. "Do you really think I would have given up after one proposal?"

No, she realized. Jack wasn't the kind of man to give up so easily.

Unfolding from his perch, Jack walked over to her and knelt down. The closer he came her way, the harder it was to detach her heart from the conversation.

He placed one hand on her knee.

Jessie flinched but didn't pull away.

"My father heard about you from my sister. Katie isn't great about butting out of someone else's business."

She sounds like Monica.

"Where my dad goes, so does the media."

Jack grasped one of her hands in both of his. His gray eyes bored into hers, making it difficult for her to remember how angry she was at him for all his deceit. "You are the only woman in my life, Jessie. You are the one I want to introduce to the world as my wife. I lied to you about my wealth for selfish reasons." He took a deep breath and continued. "I needed to know if you could love me for me. Your hang-up about finding a rich husband made me wonder if you could ever separate your feelings for me from my money. If you knew from the beginning I was loaded, how could I truly know if you loved me?"

Her chest started to ache, again. "How do I know if I love Jack Morrison? I don't even know who that man is."

"Yes, you do, Jessie." He stood and pulled her to her feet. Jack let her hands drop and spread his own as wide as his shoulders. "This is me, jeans and boots. I wear suits at the office, but not all the time. On the ranch, you'd have a hard time pointing me out with all the hands that take care of the place."

"The ranch?"

"My father's ranch. I'm comfortable in the boardroom and the barn. Outside of when I'm desperately trying to convince the woman I love that I'm perfect for her, I'm as honest as they get."

Jessie bit her lip and felt some of the ice around her heart drip. "You love me?"

He gasped. "Jesus, Jessie, aren't you listening to me? I love you more than roaches love sticky buns."

She burst out laughing. So much for the poet who'd walked in the door half an hour earlier.

"Not the best way to put that, was it?" he asked with that cocky grin surrounded by dimples.

"It's unique. I doubt I'll ever forget that you compared our love to a cockroach."

Jack placed both hands on her shoulders. "Give me a chance, Jessie. Give *us* a chance."

Suddenly her mouth went dry and her lip started to tremble. "Trust is important to a relationship, Jack. How can I trust that you're telling the truth?"

"Ask me anything. I'll never keep another thing from you."

Now was her time to put every question to the test. "Monica thinks you bought the car for me."

"She's right. I did. I knew you wouldn't accept it if I gave it to you, so I made up the story about a fire."

Little chance she would have accepted a new car from a man who waited tables. Or the rich one in front of her, for that matter.

"Did you sabotage my other car?" The thought had passed through during a dark moment.

"No. I'd never jeopardize you or Danny."

It was silly to think he would do something so low, she realized.

"Clarify rich."

With a dimpled grin, he ran his hands down her arms and up again. "Stupid crazy kinds of money. We have over two hundred hotels under the Morrison name. My father insisted on splitting half the estate when Katie and I came of age. He gave each of us one-quarter of that half. Believe me when I tell you that women with high dreams and fancy needs will do anything to get at what I have."

Jessie lifted a hand to his arm and felt the rest of the ice around her heart melt away. "I get it, Jack. I don't like that you lied to me, but I understand why you did."

"I'll never do it again." He stepped closer, until the heat of his skin met hers. "I love you, Jessie. The last couple days were sheer hell thinking I'd lost you."

A smile breached her lips and a single tear fell from her eye. "You better not ever lie to me again."

Jack scooped her into his arms before bringing his lips to hers. It was a brief kiss, one laced with excitement. "Never again." He leaned in and kissed her again. This time he angled his head for a much more enjoyable meeting of lips. With insides that were jumping high one minute and low the next, it didn't take long for Jessie to feel lightheaded. Then again, Jack's arms were crushing the air out of her lungs.

A small laugh vibrated from her lips to his.

"What?" he asked when he pulled away.

"Can't. Breathe," she managed.

Jack loosened his grip. "Sorry."

"I'm not."

"I'm not either."

Lost in his eyes, Jessie felt his love for her in ways she couldn't describe. Perhaps his test to determine if she loved him would work out for the best in the end. So long as the testing was over.

"I love you," he told her.

"I love you, too. You make me crazy, but I do love you."

Jack pulled away suddenly and glanced around the room. Seeing what he wanted, he led her to a chair.

"What are you doing?"

He smiled. "What I should have done in the first place."

Jack bent down on one knee.

Jessie's heart leapt up into her neck.

Out of his pocket, Jack removed a small black velvety box.

New tears sprang out of both Jessie's eyes, and Jack's face started to blur in front of her.

"Jessica Mann," he started. "Will you do me the honor of becoming my wife?" Jack's eyes didn't waver. He stared hard and held his breath.

Her head started to bob before she could whisper the words. "Yes. I'll marry you, Jack."

Jack grasped the back of her head and sealed his proposal with a soul-shattering kiss. Lips, tongue, and a little bit of teeth, and both of them were laughing as they pulled away.

Jack fiddled with the box and lifted her left hand in his.

He slid a band around her ring finger and sat back staring at her.

Jessie dropped her gaze to her hand. "Shut. Up."

"You like it?"

The air in Jessie's lungs left and the dizzy feeling she had kissing Jack returned, only this time she literally saw stars. Itty-bitty gasps filled her lungs as she started to hyperventilate.

Knowing little about carats and color, Jessie couldn't fathom what the rock on her hand had cost.

A stunning solitaire slightly smaller than her thumbnail sat in a round cluster of diamonds that tapered down both sides, circled her finger. It sat in what Jessie assumed was platinum. It was stunning. "It's gorgeous," she said with a hoarse whisper.

"There's a band that goes with it," he announced.

More? There's more to it?

"I don't know what to say." She lifted her hand and felt the weight of the ring.

"Just say I do, and we're good."

Jessie placed her hand to the side of Jack's face. The stubble on his jaw scratched her hand and she loved the feel of it. "I do. But…"

"But?" Jack grew serious.

A lifetime of teasing him, what could be better than that?

Someone pinch me.

"There is one more person you need to ask." She leaned back.

A bemused expression crossed Jack's face. Then he smiled. "Danny."

"Right."

Jack stood and helped her to her feet. "I have the perfect plan for him."

Bright lights and the sound of Christmas carols playing added to the overall joy in Jessie's heart.

Jack sat on the floor next to Danny in front of the huge Christmas tree. The day had started in Jessie's apartment, where they'd showered Danny with gifts. Now, in Jack's penthouse suite at The Morrison, Jessie and Jack were about to explain some of the changes that were going to take place in Danny's life.

"What's in this box?" Danny lifted the gift-wrapped package and began the obligatory shaking of the box.

Smiling, Jack glanced between Jessie and Danny before saying, "Well, that's a gift for you, your mom, and me."

"You bought yourself a gift, Uncle Jack?"

"Kind of."

"Open it, Danny," Jessie said before moving to sit with the two of them on the floor.

Finding the edge of the paper, Danny ripped through the foil wrap without finesse. Inside a shirt box was a magazine with the title of *Texas* on the cover. Jessie peered closer to see what the publication was about.

"*Homes and Ranches?*" Jessie cocked her head to the side to glance into Jack's eyes.

He winked at her but focused his attention on Danny.

"What is this for?" Danny handed the magazine to Jessie. The magazine featured homes and ranches for sale in the state of Texas.

"Oh, Jack?"

Jack circled his arm around her shoulders and pulled her closer. "I love my father's ranch. He'd be more than happy to share it with us, but I thought this would be better."

"What would be better?" Danny still had no idea what Jack was getting at.

"Our own place," Jack told him. "I want us to pick out our new home together."

Danny's jaw went slack. "You mean a real house with a yard?"

"With a yard big enough for a barn and horses."

"And a puppy? Can I get a puppy?" Danny started to bounce on his behind, grinning ear to ear.

Jack ruffled Danny's hair. "Any animal you can think of."

"Whoohoo!" Danny jumped to his feet and climbed into Jack's lap, nearly knocking him over. "Thanks, Uncle Jack."

A house of our own. Jessie had a hard time picturing it. In the space of one holiday season, her life had completely changed. Grown.

"Danny, about the *Uncle Jack...*"

Danny stopped hugging Jack long enough to look at him. "Yeah?"

"When your mom and I get married, I can't be your uncle Jack anymore."

Danny's smile fell. A cold chill fell on all of them.

"That's because Jack will be your dad," Jessie said quickly.

"My dad?" His little lip started to shake. A confused set of eyes peered up at them.

"I'm new at being a dad, Danny. Do you think you can teach me the ropes?" Jessie grasped Jack's hand as he spoke.

The uncertainty on Danny's face worried her.

"My real dad didn't want me," he said with surprising fear in his voice. "He left us."

Jessie's heart shattered with her little boy's words.

Jack pulled her son close. "I'm never going to leave you, Danny. I love you and your mom more than anything in this whole world."

"Really?"

"Really!"

"Jack wants to adopt you, and then both of us will have a new last name," Jessie told her son. "Would you like that?"

Danny bobbed his head.

The three of them hugged and Jack wiped away Danny's tears.

"Do I get to call you Daddy?"

Jack's smile lit up the room. "I'd love it if you called me Daddy."

"OK." Danny sniffled a couple of times before bouncing out of Jack's lap. He picked up the magazine and thumbed through its pages.

"I think that went well," Jessie told Jack once Danny had moved away from them.

"He had me worried there for a minute," Jack confessed. "He looked so scared when I told him I'd be his dad."

Jessie agreed. "He seldom asked about his real dad. I didn't realize how much it bothered him."

"That's all over with from today on."

Jessie's chest felt full again. "I love you, Jack."

Jack folded her into his arms and kissed her soundly. It seemed he couldn't keep from touching her. Outside of sleeping, Jack was either kissing her, holding her hand, or touching her knee. It was wonderful.

The sound of knocking pounded from the penthouse door.

"Do you want me to answer the door, Daddy?"

Unexpected tears sprang to Jessie's eyes.

"That would be great, Danny." Jessie noticed Jack's eyes well up.

"Who's here?" Jessie asked Jack as he swiped one fallen tear from her cheek.

Jack pulled her to her feet with another cryptic smile. "It's time you meet the members of your new family."

Danny opened the door and ran his gaze up the length of Jack's father's frame. The man was even more massive than Jessie remembered him. Of course, he was sitting in a chair the last time they'd met. In Gaylord's hand was a cowboy hat similar to the one he had on his head...only smaller.

"Well, hello there, little partner. You must be Danny." Gaylord Morrison extended his free hand.

Glancing at it, Danny went ahead and put his tiny palm in the much bigger one.

"You must be my new grandpa?"

Gaylord's jaw dropped. Then his eyes widened. Jessie knew then where Jack had inherited his dimples.

"I think you're right."

"Is that for me?" Danny pointed to the hat.

"Only if it fits."

Danny stepped closer to the big man and ducked his head so Gaylord could secure the Stetson.

Once properly crowned, Danny rolled his eyes up, trying to see the hat. "Does it fit, Grandpa?"

"Now you look like a Morrison," Gaylord boasted before he swept Danny into his arms and tossed him in the air.

Danny giggled as Gaylord sat him back down, then lifted his arms. "Again."

They all laughed.

The elevator outside the suite chimed.

Jessie glanced beyond Gaylord's shoulder to see who was talking in the hall.

Monica filed into the room with a beautiful blonde at her side. The two of them had their heads together, and Monica was laughing about something. Jessie's mom stood beside an older woman Jessie didn't recognize.

Jack pulled her hand and led her to the party of people filing into the suite.

"Jessie, this is my father."

Gaylord set Danny down and pulled Jessie into a bear hug. "You don't know how happy it makes me to see you again."

Overwhelmed by the man's embrace, Jessie remembered her curt words to Jack's father and felt remorseful. "I'm sorry for how we met," Jessie apologized when Gaylord ended the hug and took a moment to stare at her.

"I'm not," Gaylord said. "Jack needs a woman like you to keep him straight."

Jack scowled at his father and continued his introductions. "This is Katie, my sister."

Katie smiled in greeting. "You're just like your sister described."

"My sister? You guys know each other?" Jessie asked Monica.

"Kind of." There was a story buried in Monica's cryptic answer.

"What exactly do you mean, *kind of*?"

Monica sucked in her bottom lip. Bad sign. Jessie knew something was off.

"I called Monica after she searched out Jack here at the hotel," Katie offered.

"You were looking for Jack?" Jessie asked her sister.

The sucking of Monica's lip turned to chewing. "He disappeared. You were miserable."

"I told the managers to call me if anyone came to the hotel asking for Jack Moore," Katie chimed in.

"You did?" Jack glared at his sister with an expression that matched Jessie's feelings.

"Geez, you two, don't look so shocked. We were watching out for both of you." Katie draped her arm around Monica as she spoke. "If you can't depend on your family interfering in your personal life, what can you depend on?"

Jack reached for Jessie's hand and folded it in his. "You have your work cut out for you, darlin'."

"What do you mean?" Jessie asked.

"Planning a wedding with these two is bound to be like a burr buried in a horse's saddle."

Jessie had no idea what a burr in a horse's saddle was like, but it didn't sound good.

"Are you trying to say I'm a pain in the ass?" Katie shoved Jack's shoulder.

"If the shoe fits." They were both laughing.

"You watch that language, young lady," the older woman beside Jessie's mother scolded. "There's a child in the room."

Danny's head was buried in a game he'd set up beside Gaylord and couldn't have heard a thing.

"Yes, ma'am." Katie tugged on Monica's arm. "Come on, sis; let's talk about bridesmaids' gowns and what we absolutely have to veto."

"Turquoise and mauve," Monica said as they walked away.

Jack let Jessie's hand go and embraced the woman who'd given Katie the retort. "You look beautiful as ever, Aunt Bea."

"You're absolutely glowing." The woman patted his face when they pulled away. "Seems as if a family is exactly what you needed."

Jack nodded toward Jessie. "Jessie, this is my aunt Bea."

"It's lovely to meet you."

"A pleasure," Bea said with a warm smile. The sweet southern accent matched her friendly face.

Jessie remembered the pie conversation and Jack's praise. "Jack tells me you make the best pecan pie ever."

Aunt Bea beamed. "It isn't bad."

Jack had met Jessie's mom the day before when she'd returned with Danny. The two of them greeted each other with a friendly smile.

Jessie's mom turned to Jack's aunt. "I never was much of a cook," Renee explained. "Jessie seems at home in the kitchen more than I ever was."

Bea nodded toward Gaylord. "I've always loved the kitchen more than the boardroom. My brother manages the financial end of things. Least I can do is cook."

Renee glanced over her shoulder at Gaylord. "Too bad I didn't have a brother. It would have been nice to have someone figuring out my financial mess."

"He makes it look easy," Bea said as the two women walked deeper into the room, away from Jack and Jessie.

Everyone piled in and scattered around the suite. Gaylord and Danny were already rolling dice on the board game and laughing.

Jessie hung back with Jack for a private word.

"Thank you, Jack."

"What are you thanking me for?"

"For not giving up on me." She glanced at the happy faces in the room. "This is worth more to me than any ring or house. We can celebrate every holiday surrounded by people we love. I know it sounds sappy, but that's the best gift ever."

Jack slid his hands around her waist and stared into her eyes. "I've waited my whole life for you."

His warm kiss spread chills down her neck and spine.

"You're getting better with the poetry," she teased, smiling. "No more roaches and sticky bun analogies?" she asked against his lips.

"How about…I'll play Santa to your Mrs. Claus?" he queried with a wink.

Jessie grasped Jack's hat from his head and popped it on hers. "How about you play cowboy to my cowgirl?"

He lifted his eyes suggestively. "I like the sound of that. We gotta go get you some boots, soon-to-be Mrs. Morrison."

Jessie could get used to that title in a heartbeat. "Why? You'll just want to take them off."

"Exactly."

Jack fiddled with his hat on her head and leaned back with a grin. "I love you."

Jessie stood on her tiptoes and kissed him.

"Oh boy. Guess we're going to need more mistletoe," Monica announced from across the room.

Ignoring her, Jack swiped the hat from Jessie's head and hid their kiss behind it.

Laughing under his lips, Jessie leaned closer, loving Jack with all her heart. A family.

An excerpt from

Not Quite Mine

Book Two
Not Quite Series
Coming Spring 2013

Chapter One

Katelyn Morrison stood at the altar with tears swelling behind her eyes. She forced her attention to the bride and groom and the vows they lovingly gave each other. Her brother Jack reached out to his newly adopted son Danny and took the ring the six-year-old held in his hand. Danny beamed with pride, his smile and sigh catching the attention of everyone in the church.

Katie felt the hair on her arms stand on end when Jack winked at the boy. Her brother deserved the happiness he'd found with his bride and her son. Katie couldn't be more ecstatic in the woman he'd chosen to make a Morrison.

The emotion that clogged her up even more, however, Katie didn't want to name. She had no right to be jealous of her brother. Besides, green wasn't a color she chose to wear.

Squaring her shoulders, Katie witnessed Jessie place a ring on Jack's finger and repeat her vows. When the minister instructed Jack to kiss his bride, dimples spread over his face as he gathered her in his arms. True Texas catcalls and whistles lifted to the eaves of the church when Jack dipped Jessie low and let everyone know she was his. When Danny lifted his hand to shield his eyes from their kiss, the cameras in the church went wild.

Katie let out a laugh and ignored the tears falling from her eyes.

Then she felt him watching, knew the weight of his stare as she slowly lifted her gaze to the best man.

Dean's gaze soaked her in. *Looked through her* would be a better way of putting the expression on his face. An unspoken understanding washed over his face and threatened to release a tidal wave of pain. In that moment, Katie held more regret than she'd ever had in her entire life.

Jack and Jessie turned toward the guests at the ceremony while Monica, Jessie's sister and maid of honor, handed Jessie her bouquet. Katie pulled in her thoughts and memories and moved behind Jessie to fan the train of her dress so she could march down the aisle and not fall on the layers of fabric.

Thank God Jack picked Dean to be his best man, otherwise Katie would be paired with him for the remainder of the evening. Being this close to him was hard enough. Standing side by side all evening would be torture.

Hell, it was still torture.

The photographer ushered the bridal party outside the church while the guests were funneled in another direction. The bride and groom posed in front of the marble columns and ornate doors. Monica stepped beside Katie with Nicole, the other brides-maid, by her side. A buzz overhead brought everyone's attention to the sky.

A helicopter hovered over the church.

"Would have been asking too much for them to wait for a press release," Katie chided.

"I know you said to expect them, but a helicopter?" Monica tilted her head back and shielded the sun from her eyes with her hand.

"With a high-powered lens snapping more pictures than the paid photographer." Having spent the greater part of her life attract-ing the attention of the media, Katie was well rehearsed at ignoring their presence. Every mistake she'd ever made, nearly every kiss or affair she'd partaken in, had ended up on the cover of a magazine.

"Take the damn picture and go already." Dean's voice, even when it was angry, shot up her spine with awareness.

Nearly every affair.

Dean, Tom, and Mike moved closer to the women and shot insults at the hovering chopper.

"Nothing's sacred," Mike said.

"At least Gaylord kept the paparazzi on foot far away."

"Daddy promised them a glimpse from the limo on the way to the reception," Katie informed the wedding party. "Or a trip to jail for trespassing if they stepped one foot on church property."

"A night in jail isn't usually a deterrent."

The three groomsmen had known Jack and Katie for years. Each one came from a family with money and power and knew the media better than their neighbors.

The noise from the chopper elevated, as did the wind it kicked up.

Danny ran up between Monica and Katie with a worried frown on his face. "Auntie Katie, is that helicopter gonna fall on us?"

She knelt down and took Danny's hand in hers. The role of auntie might have been new, but the fierce need to protect her nephew and ease his fears was as automatic as breathing. "They wouldn't dare risk it. Grandpa would tie them up and leave them in the sun to bake if they crashed this party."

Danny's eyes grew big. "Really?"

"Ask Grandpa to tell you about the paparazzi and my sixteenth birthday."

Dean and Tom cleared their throats behind her. She glanced over her shoulder and noticed both of them shaking their heads. A few misguided indiscretions of that day drifted to the surface of her memory. "On second thought, never mind."

Monica leaned in and offered her own advice. "How about we make faces at them, Danny?"

He shot her a big smile before he lifted his head to the chopper and stuck out his tongue. Laughter filled the small group as each one of them wiggled fingers and contorted their faces toward the sky. Danny's giggles kept them all animated. Chances were, the photographer in the chopper wasn't focused on them, but Danny didn't seem at all concerned that the hunk of metal was going to land on them any longer.

Even if their faces did end up on *The Inquisitor*, Katie knew she looked fabulous. The maroon floor-length silk dress hugged her curves like a lover's caress. Lorenzo, the designer, had taken all three of the women in the bridal party into his studio and crafted identical dresses to work perfectly for each of their shapes. How he did it was a mystery. Not that he had to work around anything impossible. Both Monica and Nicole were over five seven and slender. And after a little work, Katie had shown them both the pleasure of designer heels. There was nothing sexier than a shoe that brought a guy's attention to a shapely calf before zinging up a thigh and straight to her ass. The second Katie had slid the three-hundred-dollar pumps onto Monica's feet, she knew she had a partner in crime.

Katie made sure the length of her leg peeked through her dress as she wiggled her fingers by her ears for the paparazzi.

As their laughter ebbed, the photographer waved them all inside the church for more pictures.

Danny took Monica's hand and pulled her with him as the rest of the party followed.

Katie adjusted her dress to make certain the low-cut angle didn't reveal too much.

"You look amazing." Dean's voice was low and heated as he slid up beside her.

She hadn't realized he'd held back, and felt a little trapped in his presence. "You clean up well yourself, Prescott." Boy, did he clean up. He pushed his dusty blond hair that always seemed a little long, but at the same time, perfectly right, out of his eyes. His Texas drawl reminded her of home. She'd worked hard to rid herself of her accent when she was younger, thinking it made her look stupid. Blonde and rich labeled her as dumb, which she fought for some time. It didn't matter if she'd become a doctor or a rocket scientist. The world looked at her as an heiress and treated her differently. Around her sixteenth birthday she'd snapped. Her hormones started to rage and her desire to be noticed ruled her brain. Her skirts rode high, her pants skintight. Those designer heels she loved so well pushed her height past most the boys in school.

But the one she wanted to look didn't.

Katie glanced into Dean's eyes and quickly looked away. Her body tingled knowing he stood so close. The spicy scent of his skin made her want to lean in and take a deep breath. She fought her desire and found the silence between them painful.

She said the only thing she could think of, and then regretted her words instantly. "I'm sorry about Maggie."

Dean's jaw tightened. "It wasn't meant to be." Maggie had broken off her engagement to Dean a week before their planned wedding. According to Jack, there wasn't an explanation as to why. She'd simply disappeared and asked that Dean not contact her.

"It must have been hard for you...watching Jack and Jessie."

Lord knew if she'd been snubbed that close to matrimony she'd never go to another wedding again.

The smile that always played on Dean's lips fell. "It wasn't hard at all."

Katie wanted to tell him he was full of shit. If anyone knew his dreams, it was her. A wife and family had always been in his plans.

"Are you two coming or what?" Tom called from the door to the church.

Dean tilted his head, acknowledging Tom, then spread his fingers low on Katie's back to usher her inside.

Heat spread up her body and licked every nerve ending in her skin. The memory of his hands slipping low on her hips as he explored her lips with his own washed over her. His hand jerked, as if he too shared the memory. He flexed his fingers and guided her forward.

Their time together was in the past, and best forgotten.

Acknowledgments

I absolutely have to take a moment to thank my agent, Jane Dystel, and everyone at Dystel & Goderich Literary Management. Their belief in me and the books I write is unsurpassed by anyone else. If it wasn't for Jane and her nurturing encouragement I'm positive this series wouldn't have found the perfect home.

My second round of kudos is to my editor at Montlake, Kelli Martin. Kelli's attention to detail has made this book shine. Thanks for believing in me.

For the author team at Montlake who worked overtime to turn this book out for the holiday season. I know it wasn't easy, but thank you all just the same.

For my family, who suffers with dirty laundry and warmed-up microwave meals when I'm on a deadline. Thanks!

I'll end my acknowledgments with the person I dedicated this book to: my nana.

I really did think she was spunky enough to outlive all of us. Eventually the body gives out, however, and it was her time to go this year. She truly lived life to the fullest. Changed her name legally at some point to Shamrock and had more husbands than a Hollywood movie star.

Somewhere around my thirteenth birthday she said to me, "Catherine...you can just as easily fall in love with a rich man as you could a poor one. Only date rich men."

For all the husbands she loved, she never did follow her own advice.

I love you, Nana.

Until we see each other again,
Catherine

About the Author

Photograph by Lindsey Meyer, 2012

New York Times bestselling author Catherine Bybee was raised in Washington State, but after graduating high school, she moved to Southern California in hopes of becoming a movie star. After growing bored with waiting tables, she returned to school and became a registered nurse, spending most of her career in urban emergency rooms. She now writes full-time and has penned the novels *Wife by Wednesday* and *Married by Monday*. Bybee lives with her husband and two teenage sons in Southern California.